UNDER-*SKY*
UNDER*GROUND*

The cover artwork and the above illustration incorporate pages from Xu Bing's Tian Shu or 'Book from the Sky'. This work, comprising a limited edition of a four volume, traditionally bound Chinese book in the style of a bibliographic rarity, was first exhibited in Beijing during March 1989 where it caused a sensation. Xu, a printmaker specializing in woodcuts, had carved the printing blocks for the books himself, entirely of 'characters' which are not found in any Chinese dictionary. His characters look as if they should be legible to someone who reads Chinese — they contain familiar strokes and components — but they are not. Neither is this a Chinese Finnegans Wake — although the visual effect of the text is comparable — there are no construable segments of meaningful language. However, the material cultural forms of the Chinese literary and scholarly tradition are strictly, even lovingly, observed: a striking paradox and eloquent contribution to the continuing debate which rages amongst Chinese intellectuals concerning their relationship with their own tradition. Reproduced courtesy of the Trustees of the British Museum (OA 1993.7-9.01).

UNDER-*SKY* UNDER*GROUND*

CHINESE WRITING
TODAY · I

selected *&* edited by
HENRY Y H ZHAO
& JOHN CAYLEY

with a foreword by
JONATHAN D SPENCE

wellsweep

NOTE

This publication is the first biennial selection of works in English translation from the best of the Chinese literary magazine *Jintian (Today)*. *Under-Sky Underground* covers the first six issues of the magazine after it recommenced publication during 1990 in Stockholm. Please note that the actual selection of pieces was undertaken by Henry Y H Zhao in close co-operation with the other editors and regular contributors to *Today*. This book is a selection made by contemporary Chinese writers themselves.

ISSN 0968-4670 (*Chinese Writing* Today, Number 1)

ACKNOWLEDGEMENTS

The cover artwork incorporates material from Xu Bing's 'Tian Shu' ('Book from the Sky'). See the frontispiece and caption for full details.

Bei Dao's 'Prague', 'He opens wide a third eye …', 'Along the Way' and 'At This Moment' were first published in *Old Snow* (Anvil Press Poetry, London, 1992) and are reproduced with kind permission. David Hinton's translations of Bei Dao's new work, including three of the poems here, will shortly be published in the UK by the same press.

A number of Duo Duo's poems in translations by Gregory B Lee have been previously published as follows: 'Crossing the Sea', 'They' and 'In England' in *The Manhattan Review*; 'Residents' in *The Kenyon Review*.

Gu Cheng's 'Smoking' in the translation by John Cayley has appeared in *Eonta* (London). Both this poem and 'We Write Things' are also found, in other translations, in his English *Selected Poems* (Renditions, Hong Kong, 1991).

Yang Lian's '1989' and 'The Book of Exile', in other versions, have appeared in *The Dead in Exile* (Wild Peony, Sydney, 1990). A selection of his poems, *Non-Personal*, translated by Brian Holton, will be published in autumn 1994 by the Wellsweep Press.

Zi An's 'Railway Station' has been published in *Pen International*.

SPECIAL THANKS to Anna Johnston for her help in the preparation of this volume and to the Sino-British Fellowship Trust which funded a portion of her contribution.

Represented & distributed in the UK & Europe by: Password (Books) Ltd
serving independent literary publishers in the United Kingdom
23 New Mount Street, Manchester M4 4DE.

ISBN 0 948454 16 4 paperback

BRITISH LIBRARY CATALOGUING-IN-PUBLICATION DATA
A catalogue record for this book is available from the British Library.

Designed and typeset by *Wellsweep*

FOREWORD

JONATHAN D SPENCE

Which of us would wish to have to prove our significance? But that is the burden fate has placed on Chinese writers today. In the centennial year of the first Sino-Japanese War, these writers are forced to relive their ancestors' predicament: How to decide which elements to draw on from outside, and which internal elements to preserve, as the old internal order crumbles. In 1894, as in 1994, foreign technology jostled with apparently liberating ideologies to attract the attention of a disillusioned generation. In 1894, bereft of faith in the Confucian order, many of China's most ardent minds sought solace in the sheer range of the alternatives offered by the enemy, and found reassurance in the very strength that had laid them low. In 1994, deprived of even lingering residues of faith in communism, many of China's most ardent minds again scan the resources available outside their homeland, at once threatened and reassured.

In many ways, however, the problems for the writers of *Today* are more difficult than they were for those who founded the journal in 1978, and made it such a vibrant part of the movement associated with Democracy Wall. For in 1978 and 1979 the new and forbidden were enough in and of themselves to generate excitement; and when genuine, unmistakable talent burst forth as well, the stage was set — despite repression — for a burst of cultural energy and creativity that carried them through the middle of the 1980s. But now *Today*'s writers are those forced into exile, or those who choose not to return home. Their task is to keep *Today* alive and lively, to make it part of a living present, and yet to do so in a way that reaches Western readers not familiar with China's internal struggles.

The translators and editors of this first English language selection from *Today* face a delicate challenge: how to select and render pieces from Chinese, in which the concepts and diction seem fresh and vigorous, into an English that will preserve that sense of newness. But at the same time, many of the ideas in the original Chinese are purposefully old, conscious borrowings from a vast and complex literary tradition that has never died, a tradition that itself fostered elaborate distinctions between genres and dictions, developed formal metrical patterns of great subtlety and beauty, and explored the strange, the unexpected and the supernatural in a language of the everyday.

The stories, essays and poems gathered here show a restlessness with the past and also a homage to it, a juxtaposition that appears overtly in Nan Fang's story, with the regular invocations of the tenth century collection *Taiping Guangji*, and in the many references in other pieces to serpents, spirits and their transformations that call to mind such seventeenth century fiction masters as Pu Songling. Yet Nan Fang too, like many of the other writers, seems strongly drawn to Borges and Calvino — and the flickering interchanges of mood and time, combined with an apparently meticulous realism, at which both were such consummate masters. So it is, in Nan Fang's self-revelatory words, that his main character performs 'actions so well-worn they might be preserved in a museum' (p. 48); or wears a cap (an evocation of the labelling of the 'bourgeois rightists' in the Cultural Revolution) that is a 'mixture of ancient spirit and modern fervour' (p. 43); or live in the kind of world where 'between present and reality existed that endlessly floating glass wall'. (p. 42)

We need not be surprised that so many of the characters here presented, or the images invoked, are ones of ambiguity, doubt or loss. As with the sad and enigmatic Momo in Ai Yan's story, the photographs they take cut off peoples' arms and faces, and the dog turds are never far away. So with Duo Duo's hitchhiker on the way to Scotland, that quintessential joy of youth, a romp in the hay, can only be shared in a voyeur's way by the narrator — while the two young girls (as he believes) make love next to him, the buckle of one of their belts bites into the narrator's hand. In Du Ma's story 'Into Parting Arms' love cannot be sustained by the narrator any more than his own parents can be taught to love: 'The journey back was just as long as the journey out, and I filled the time by eating endlessly.' (p. 239)

Other images, especially strong in the essays, reminiscences and poems, revolve around language itself, and that is surely as it should be, both from the point of view of tradition and of rebellion against it. For Zhang Langlang in 'The Legend of the Sun Brigade' the point may indeed be that there was no such thing as the Sun Brigade; but what lingers in the mind is the thought of the poems he read as his teeth savoured the tang of a sweet potato bun, two driving hungers expunged at one shared moment of bliss. Just so for Li Tuo, the beat and joy of creativity are expressed in the sudden sound of quick steps on the stairs, where before all had been measured silence, or of a friend taking a train all through the night to read another friend the poem that he has just completed.

It is this pulse, this quick step on the stair, that Today's writers, and we as readers with them, can seek to keep alive. As Bei Dao, who was in on *Today* from the beginning, reminds us:

> streaming word-shoals spawn
> then sleep beside civilization till dawn

(p. 54)

It is a wonderful metaphor for the current intermingling of culture, love, yearning, and history. And that, after all, is what *Today* is about.

CONTENTS

MEMOIRS OF UNDERGROUND LITERATURE

BELLES LETTRES

CRITICISM

FICTION — II

《今天》雙年選集第一集目錄

UNDER-*SKY*
UNDER*GROUND*

O

FICTION — I

FIRST LOVE

Haizi

translated by Steve Balogh

Once there was a man, carrying a snake, seated on a large wooden crate like a raft, floating down an immense river, to seek out the enemy who had killed his father.

He floated down on the current of that huge expanse of river. He had the dry rations he'd brought along with him to eat and every so often he moored by the bank and begged for alms. Apart from this, he'd planted some maize in a little earth on the surface of the crate. Along the whole length of his route, any fisherman who saw him would greet him with a wave of his hand or his hat. He'd been down this river and its many tributaries before, learned a number of the local dialects, and come to understand its ways of love, life, faith and forgetting; but never yet had he found the man who had murdered his own father.

The snake had been resuscitated by his father when he was still alive. His father had taken to feeding it in a little bamboo thicket to the right of the village yard. And the more he fed it the larger it had grown. Day and night it had made a steady recovery, and became intent on repaying the favour. On the evil day his father had fallen into misfortune the snake had crawled out of the thicket for the first time, spitting venom, and in the courtyard of the temple outside the village — writhing along the entire length of its body — had made several circuits of the yard. At the time they merely considered it a bizarre coincidence. Later they made a doleful yarn of the incident. Because of this, he had come to think of the snake as the one remaining connection to his dead father, and so brought it with him aboard his crate when he went to seek out the enemy who'd killed his father.

When, in the ceaseless dreams of his son, the vague, bloodied visage of the father appeared, that snake would retreat to the floor of the crate where it would shrink to form a twitching coil of suffering, because it had a secret love for another snake a thousand miles away. However, the object of this was no flesh and blood snake at all, but a snake that had been woven from bamboo. This kind of a secret love consumed it with ceaseless longing — its thirst, its dream world-suffering, and a hidden joy, little by little, imbued the once lifeless snake with life. At nightfall as the bright moon rose in the south, the bamboo snake would be bathed in supernatural power — around its head there seemed to dance countless haloes and sparks of light. The creature's physique was gradually distilling itself from matter into something more substantial. Slowly but surely a metamorphosis was taking place.

Finally, early one morning, the bamboo snake emerged from its toy box and seizing the opportunity afforded by the landlord's deep sleep, spitting venom round it flame-like tongue, bit him on the stomach. After a short time, the poison's fatal effect took hold, and the landlord died. This landlord was the man whom the son was seeking and who had murdered his father. Besides instilling life and the power to love into its bamboo counterpart, the snake in his crate had also inspired it with its own vendetta.

The snake in the crate wished to depart without taking its leave. In the middle of the night it emerged from the crate. It aimed to make its way — through innumerable torrents, swamps, herds of horses and the stems of flowers, without sleep — to rendezvous with its serpentine, bamboo mate. Its master carried on as before astride the crate tracking his father's deadly enemy. The two lovesick snakes left him to a lifetime drifting on the river, searching — a single flame burning in his heart.

DATURA

JANET TAN

translated by the author

February in Three River Plain was a wet shirt stuck to my back. The dampness soaked into my trousers around the waist and over the front, making me irritable for days, weeks, months. Cold wind gusted the dense rain across the colourless silent plain outside the window. The stench of cow manure and rain-soaked hay was carried into the straw tent by the herdsmen's boots. This sunless, gloomy, filthy season exhausted all the hot water coupons Mother and I had saved for months. I had been waiting and waiting and finally saw the sun come out in the first week of April. Having the sun to warm up the water in the bucket, we could have a slightly warm bath.

Carrying a bucket of water, I slowly approached the bath hut which lay open in the bushes. A sudden wind tore down a sheaf of rotten straw from the sagging hut and added one more hole to the fishnet-like wall. The foul water disgorged thermos covers, sanitary towels, soap and grey suds in a trench, diffusing breath-stopping odours into the open air. I dragged myself into the entrance. People trying to bathe before sundown crowded inside like sparrows huddled in the bushes at sunset. I cut my way through sheaves of bodies, cautiously avoiding touching the wet flesh steaming with sundry odours. Buckets of water waxed them into white steamed buns. Their bodies swelled like plucked chickens. Suddenly touched by a dripping buttock, I skipped a step and almost slipped on the cement ground which had been pasted up by dirty gravy. By the time I reached the corner of the hut, my hand was glued to the bucket's freezing metal handle. Nobody wanted to stand close to this corner which was occupied by two big buckets of urine. A strong female odour burst forth when water splashed onto the dark, bloody napkins on the floor. A trench collected all the body dirt, napkins, and bubbles, channelled them to this corner and washed them out through a hole in the ground. The women who produced this filth were trembling in the cold wind that slipped through the defenceless straw. They ignored their surroundings, using their hands, teeth, and feet to make as much noise as they could. Their breasts, some long, some short, swayed in the cold air. Hurriedly they splashed water on their bodies, smeared the soap without watching, then washed the suds off quickly. When the thick water reached the ground from their bodies they gabbled happily, like ducks coming out of a pond after a good swim.

Fat Aunt started singing, to remind herself that she had once been a famous bass. Rounds of fat shook as she sang. The splashing she made became a little waterfall, making me think of the falls on Bald Head Hill where water gushed from smooth round rocks and fed a clump of rich green grass. But the water from Fat Aunt poured more strongly, forcing several persons to move their buckets. Among those trembling bodies, she was as strong as a cow. No wonder they let her manage the cowsheds. In the mornings when the cows ran wild, everybody panicked, but she had only to stand firm and yell. Even Big Yellow, the wildest bull, would stop suddenly as though thunder had crashed across his horns. Fat Aunt carried so much extra lard around her neck, legs, shoulders, wrists, stomach, and breasts; I wished the camp restaurant could take some fat from her to make up for the cooking oil shortage. But then her huge body might never be able to produce its rumbling organ tones. Since it required so much fat to back up a good bass, I preferred to be a pianist, just like Long Braid Aunt. Long Braid Aunt walked with agility, her two shining black braids swinging on her back. The braids were so thick they tempted me to hang on them and swing. Even though four of Long Braid Aunt's fingers were occupied by her clothes, towel, comb and soapbox, her little finger was gracefully arched. I uncramped my ten carrot-like fingers from the bucket. For three generations, my family had always produced the finest pianist in the country. The glory had no doubt ended with me. But I would rather be nobody than be a bass.

Long Braid Aunt, her body tilted, was wrapping her braid around her head. She threw me a smile. I was a little scared. I had chosen this corner for a better angle to watch her shower. If she had known, she would have stopped smiling at me. She probably thought I liked to watch outside through a hole in the straw. Frogs were hopping up and down out there. At this moment I had already looked her over from top to bottom. She had a pair of breasts as graceful as her little fingers, not swollen like Fat Aunt's, and also not like mother's dried squash figure. Such beautiful breasts stood out in this noisy, filthy place, drawing all of my attention. I smeared soap on my feet. I carefully cleaned the mud from each toenail. She bent down to wet her towel.

Her skin was as smooth as egg whites. The water slipped across her body without touching her. The carrying pole had pressed two bruises on her shoulders. When water slipped over the bruises, her wrist would jerk up abruptly like a young white birch struck by a cow's horns. She hummed as she cleaned her long and beautiful fingers. Those fingers might still play wonderful music if they were put to a keyboard.

It was at this moment that my observations about Long Braid Aunt were interrupted by that snake. He stretched his long, thick neck up to the hole like a traveller attracted to the scene by the singing. His eyes fell on Long Braid Aunt and stopped moving. Once in a while his neck would tilt. I put on my trousers and hurried outside. As I crossed the trench, his tail dragged a bright slash on the grass. His body, though thicker than my arm, glided swimmingly over the plain. Occasionally, he stopped and stretched up his head to look around. His body glowed as bright as a burning pomegranate husk in the purple sunset. My heart suddenly burned. This Three River Plain was replete with poisonous snakes and water snakes. The poisonous snakes would leap up from the deep grass to attack passers-by. The water snakes would only get into your trousers in the river and ponds. Their skinny bodies were not longer than half a foot. They moved around stealthily to avoid the bright sunlight. I had never thought they could be graceful and proud. Fat Aunt often killed them with her bamboo stick, cut off their heads, stripped their skins, and cooked them for the mother cows. It was said that a mother cow would produce more milk after drinking snake soup. But the snake bones could cause damage to a cow's stomach, so Fat Aunt picked out the bones and threw them in a basket outside the kitchen before she fed the cows. Rain washed, sun bleached, the long white spinal bones disconnected at each vertebra. They made such a strange noise when the wind passed that they disturbed my dreams at siesta time.

On tiptoe, I looked around for a trace of the big snake in the sunset. The flat plain was grey and cold like a huge cowhide board. Bald Head Hill humped up on the horizon. I followed the grass flattened down by the snake and walked into the dark. The sound of a thunderstorm ran from the east. I hadn't heard a thunderstorm for the whole winter. Fearful about the coming lightning, I stopped. The wind was getting stronger. Goose bumps rose on my naked chest. Long Braid Aunt was calling me from behind. The wind cut her voice short and sent it in the opposite direction. I returned to her with a handful of dark purple thorn-apple — datura — flowers.

That night I sat cross-legged on Long Braid Aunt's bed and ate a can of pork and soy beans. Wind was shaking the tent. The light bulb swayed with the spider's web above my head. Rain was pouring down. Water dripped through the straw, making a rhythmical sound in the metal plates and porcelain bowls people put on top of their mosquito nets and pillows. I kept sneezing. Several times words came to my lips, wanting to tell the story of the snake, several times I was interrupted by the thunderstorm or lighting. Long Braid Aunt sat cross-legged, tried to make a vase out of a tin can. She stroked my short hair once in a while, and told me what a good, sweet child I was. She stuck her nose to the flowers, while humming some beautiful songs I had never heard before. I watched her through the mirror on top of her suitcase. She was as busy as a bee around a lychee tree. A Chinese herbal medicine book was open on top of her suitcase. I tried to read it with my poor vocabulary, 'Datura, grows all year round, flower purple, core peacock green, leaves stemmed with gold lines, fragrant. Usually grows around a poisonous snake's nest. Flower contains poisonous chemical which can be used to counteract snake poison. I liked the strokes that made up the word 'datura'. They reminded me of the shapes of bushes I ran through every day. The bushes contained so many things: coloured flowers, green leaves, sparrows, cranberries, grasshoppers. Consulting with Long Braid Aunt about the pronunciation, I decided that I liked the sound even better. Its rhythm was as light as a lullaby, and as smooth as Long Braid Aunt's tender face. The word 'datura' slipped out of my lips several times. Long Braid Aunt kissed my forehead every time she heard me mumble. 'Learn how to read. It will help you grow,' she said. When the bugle blew, I suddenly remembered how the snake had set his eyes on Long Braid Aunt. The memory was warm and intimate. I ended up telling her nothing about the snake.

April with her bright face touched Three River Plain. The breeding season came with the warm weather. Mother was assigned to take care of Big Yellow alone because he was chasing every cow that had nipples under its stomach. Big Yellow was the number one breed-bull in the camp. Even farmers from nearby villages tried to sneak their female cows into Big Yellow's line of sight, hoping they could produce Big Yellow's calves. To protect Big Yellow's own health, the camp only allowed him to mate once a day, and the mates were selected by the veterinarian from the most healthy and beautiful female cows in the land.

Long Braid Aunt had made me a blue apron with two pockets. I tied the apron around Big Yellow's neck. If his eyes turned red when cows passed by, I would pull the apron up to cover his eyes. With lunch in one pocket and the medicine book in another, holding a bamboo whip in one hand, I rode on Big Yellow's back to the river bank every morning. Big Yellow's hair was as thick as a metal brush. It pricked my buttocks and irritated my thighs. Once in a while he would run wild as if a bee had stung his tail. I had to lean down across his back and grab the apron around his neck, hoping he wouldn't dump me into one of those filthy muddy ponds. Mother's lips turned white and her breath ran short when she dashed after us. For mother's sake, I stuck on Big Yellow's back like a leech. If he threw me off, I would whip him and beat him to make him know that I was in charge and that he should go wherever I wanted to.

On the river bank, I turned my whip into a fishing pole. Mother took a nap in the shade. The veterinarian and his men handled Big Yellow's breeding matters in the bushes. The water dragged my line far away from the bank. I opened Long Braid Aunt's herbal medicine book, and tried to find a few plants that matched the pictures in the book. But the river bank had only blades of yellow grass that poked out of the white soil and grey rock. The cows were stepping on each other behind the bushes. They disturbed mother's nap. She sat up and hid her face in her arms. I wanted to ask her a word I couldn't understand, but I wasn't sure if she would get angry at me for disturbing her. The air started getting hot. The sun hung in the same position a long time without moving. If only there was a fish jumping out of the water, if only there was a rabbit to run across the grass … but never. The bank had only foolish cows and sneaky snakes, and the restless cows took their time making noises behind the bushes. If the big snake showed up once more … I suddenly missed his curious eyes, his beautiful thick body. If I could ride on him in the river, we could swim together out of this wet, humid, dirty Three River Plain. We could join the Pearl River. We could go to Tiger Bay on the Pacific Ocean.

The vet woke me up. He said I could take my big friend back and feed him clean water and fresh grass. I turned my eyes, Big Yellow was standing behind me. he was dirty and filthy with his stick still hanging beneath his stomach. His eyes were red and he was out of breath. Never could he be my friend! I bit my lips, turned my eyes away, hit his back with my whip.

In late spring, several cowsheds were attacked in the middle of the night by unknown animals. Sometimes people saw fox-shaped little animals, but several times they saw snakes coming out when the cows bellowed and thumped inside the sheds. Fat Aunt led some men to set traps in and around all the sheds. I tried to followed them, to find out how they trapped animals. Fat Aunt turned to me, 'These traps could trap kids as well as animals.' She was half joking. But I never liked her jokes, as mother never liked talking to her. Mother couldn't stand anybody with loud voice. Loud voices made mother tremble. When Fat Aunt's volunteer guard team yelled loudly at night telling every tent to turn off the lights in order to save electricity, mother's face shadowed. Mother didn't like dark either.

Early one morning everybody was awoken by the guards' screams. The frightened cows had broken down a shed and run out under Big Yellow's leadership. People dashed out with bamboo sticks and metal shovels and ran onto the plain. As though joining a parade, I followed the adults into the grass. The wild flowers and bushes lazily half opened their bodies after a night's sleep. The mushrooms were fully awake in the morning dew, but some of them were already smashed by the people's boots. I bent down and picked up a fat white mushroom. It looked plump and fresh and delicious for cooking a soup. I was left behind while collecting more mushrooms. At that moment, the giant snake rose in front of me.

His erect body stood level to my eyes. It was wrapped in a dark green fish-like skin. The flowered pattern of his scales was a blossom in the morning mist. I waited for him to strike. He could catch me with his triangular tongue as though I were a frog in the rice paddy. he could use his long, powerful tail to roll and twist around me. He might even swallow my head in his huge mouth and digest me later. I stood there waiting. A strong foul odour rose up into the morning air, mixed with dew and cow dung. I sucked in the smell slowly, unable to tell if it was fish, fowl, or animal stench. I must have known this odour from somewhere, either the river bank or the cave in Bald Head Hill. I had never explored farther into that cave than the light could reach. It was this smell that scared me back every time. To think that the cave was the home of this giant snake and that the spring water I bathed in so often was also bathed in by this snake made my heart pump.

People's voices were getting closer. The snake was still frozen. His body lay softly on the grass now, unlike those cobras that coil into a plate to support their head while they attack a human being; unlike those Bamboo Greens that bow up their skinny bodies before shooting out at their target. My toes were getting cold from the dew seeping through my sandals. My eyes ached. I said, 'They're coming for you. Why don't you just go?' He tilted his head. I suddenly understood. I said, 'Long Braid Aunt is not here. She won't like them to catch you either.' He lowered his head, stretched his body, and slid away slowly. A few more mushrooms were turned upside down beneath his body. His movement seemed more sluggish than the last time I had seen him. White flesh showed on his tail. his scales had been peeled away by something sharp. After he disappeared into a cranberry bush, I bent down and picked up a mushroom from the spot where he had just lain. Before I could straighten up, a bull's bellow broke like a thunderstorm on top of me. Turning around, I saw big horns and infinite legs. The mushrooms tumbled out of my hands, I fell to the dewy grass and lost consciousness.

I woke up in Long Braid Aunt's arms. Mother was wiping her tears on my sleeve. Fat Aunt immediately sent her voice out over the whole camp, 'She's OK! She's OK!' Big Yellow stood far away, scratching his flank against a rock. His head was facing away, but one of his eyes peeped to this side. I jerked up and yelled, 'You dirty old bull!' They pulled me down. They said Big Yellow had saved my life from a huge boa. I said, 'Liar! Liar!' But they didn't listen. I turned to Long Braid Aunt. She touched my face, touched my forehead. 'You'll be fine. Everything will be fine,' she whispered into my ear. Her whispering calmed me down. I fell like a tree and was carried back to the tent in her arms.

Over the next three months I waited on a big rock outside the bath tent whenever the sun came out. I was supposedly watching my bucket of water there, but my eyes were actually focused on Bald Head Hill. I went to the hill several times because Fat Aunt had said that the hill was the only possible place a boa could hide. That was the first time I knew that they had many names for my giant snake: python, anaconda, boa constrictor, boa, and so on. I dragged enough thorn bushes to block all possible approaches to the cave. I wanted to stop anybody who attempted to go there. The thorns got into my palms making them itchy and painful. Long Braid Aunt asked me how I had got so many little thorns while she patiently picked them out of my hands. I told her I wanted to block a secret cave so that nobody could enter it. She asked if I could make her an exception. I suddenly thought about the way that boa had watched her, and I said yes with a smile.

I didn't see the boa again. He had probably hurt himself in one of the traps. The adults saw blood on a trap. But someone said snakes had no blood. I caught some fish and took them to the cave, but I still didn't see the boa. People continued to guard the cowsheds with sticks and flashlights every night. The summer came with its humidity and heat. Mother started to complain about the way I slept. She insisted on taking away the blanket I always clutched while I lay in bed. Empty-handed, I watched the spider's web on the straw ceiling to pass my nap time. Mother said she would send me back to the city, otherwise I would become a wild girl very soon. She complained about my feet, which had swollen too big to fit into my shoes. She couldn't stand my odour, which consisted of my own sweat, straw from the field, and cow dung from the road. She warned me to beware of the dangers on the hill and in the water. Snakes would feast on me if I didn't watch my step. I wove mother's words as a spider weaves her web. To avoid disturbing the fifteen other women in the tent, I wove my web quietly. When I was getting too tired to continue, I suddenly felt mother's silk dress, her *qipao,* touch my face. She had not worn that dress for so long. I missed her smooth and cold arms in that *qipao*.

The frogs in the rice paddy were getting bigger and fatter. People hungry for meat started hunting frogs at night. The poor frogs had gigantic pop-eyes, but couldn't move an inch under the glare of the flashlights. I had several good frog meals, and even sent two frogs to my boa. But very soon people found clusters of leeches as tiny as a single hair under the legs of the frogs. People's faces changed colour when they talked about frogs again. Under the full moon, people cooked banquets in their memories. They counted the delicious dishes they once had eaten in the city. Almost everybody agreed the most delicious meat was snake meat, and the poisonous snake was the best. Cobra, Golden Wrinkle, Silver Wrinkle, Red Head, Bamboo Green, Crossing Hill Dragon, Hill in Five Feet — all these poisonous snakes were collected by restaurants for banquet dishes. Fat Aunt said that Cobra had a bit of a fishy smell, Crossing Hill Dragon's flesh was not silky enough, Hill in Five Feet had fragile bones, and Red Head sometimes tasted salty. She recommended Golden Wrinkle and Silver Wrinkle. She had once gone to a famous restaurant called 'King Snake Banquet' in Guangzhou. This restaurant was famous for one dish named 'Hundred Snake Festival'. In this dish, they used poisonous snakes together with meaty snakes such as boa. The plate was as big as a table. Whole roasted ducks and chickens swam in white snake meats and green vegetables. A five-foot-long boa was wound on top of these delicacies as alive as a dragon. They called this dish 'The Return of Dragon and Phoenix'.

While I was listening, my nails cut into Long Braid Aunt's hands. Long Braid Aunt covered my ears with her palms. I wanted to listen to the adult talk, but couldn't resist her hands. They were as cold as lotus leaves in a summer pond. I fell asleep on these leaves. When I woke up in the middle of the night, I was in the arms of Long Braid Aunt. Afraid that the sweat of my body would awaken her, I curled myself up like a shrimp. As I sucked in the fragrance from her body, I swore that I would never let her know I was a dirty child trying to watch her shower. When I woke up again, the tent was empty. Outside, the calves mooed for their mothers. I could tell from their voices that the sun was up and the sky was blue.

My summer in that labour camp was cut short. I was stuffed into a cow cart and sent to the station to catch a train back to the city. Mum cried so hard, as if it was I who wanted to leave rather than her forcing me to go. My shoulder bag, which was full of fishhooks and slingshots, pulled my collar to one side. I sat in the cart quietly with my hands covering the *Chinese Herbal Medicine* book on my legs. The old bull shook his yoke impatiently. The hooks and chains hanging on the yoke tinkled like wind chimes. I turned through the book page by page, skipping most of the words I hadn't learned. Long Braid Aunt once said the book held all the secrets I would ever want to know. But Long Braid Aunt was gone and I hadn't found out any secrets in the book. Nobody asked me how this book got into my hands from Long Braid Aunt. Only Fat Aunt said, 'You are a nobody, why are you interested in books?' Her greedy eyes fell on my lap, her tireless thick legs kept circling around the cart. I ignored her.

Nobody wanted to tell me what exactly had happened that night. I woke up as the flashlight beams swept through the mosquito nets like many searchlights across the sky. Grownups were yelling outside. Soon a generator started up, and the light bulbs flickered on and off. The mosquito nets glowed in the dim yellow light, shaped like rows of coffins. Mother ran over from her bed and dragged me out of Long Braid Aunt's mosquito net. Her shaking hands started goose bumps on my skin. We heard people yelling: 'Catch him! Catch him! Don't let him go! Get the cart. Faster! Blanket! Quick! Big Yellow has run away! Catch him!' The sounds came from different directions. The women in the tent stuck their pale faces out of their nets. Finally, we heard, 'Got it! Got it!' The women jumped out of their nets and rushed outside. They yelled, 'Kill him! Kill him!' Mother loosened her grip to cover her face and cried hysterically. I sat on my bed in my underwear with no idea what had just happened.

When the sunlight spotted into the tent, the adults got up with shadows on their faces. Fat Aunt took down Long Braid Aunt's net, and collected some dirty clothes from a bucket. She folded the clothes, piece by piece, and put them into a suitcase. After packing all of the clothes, she stuffed the pillow and blanket into the suitcase. Where the pillow had been lay the stem of a dried flower. Fat Aunt whacked the pillow. The dried flower flew out the window. Dust swam in the beam of sunlight that came in the window. A familiar fragrance rushed into my nose. My urethra suddenly felt tight. I jumped down from the bed and dashed out. Before I reached the bathroom twenty feet from the tent, I lost control of my bladder. I squatted behind the tent. I peed so long that my feet started getting numb. The sun hung high above, and the plain looked flat and infinite. There was not a single cow or a human figure on the plain. Once in a while, the cows yawned in their tent. It made my heart soften.

Somebody was talking inside the tent. The voice was cut off by exclamations. It seemed they were talking about last night. The cowshed was broken. Big Yellow was still missing. Long Braid Aunt was discovered in the grass. She was found half naked on the ground with a black snake wound about her body. 'It wound her so tight! My tongue went stiff the moment I saw it.'

My urine suddenly stopped. I pulled up my pants and walked up the road in a daze. I thought tears were coming down my chin. But I only saw a white body swinging in front of me. On the dry road, rocks were mixed with flesh in the dust. I studied the flesh and scales for a few seconds. Flies hovered over the snakeskin, their wings a blur of motion.

After breakfast, the bell near the well tolled. People carrying sticks and shovels gathered by the bell. The camp committee had just ordered an 'emergency snake termination action'. All the bushes around the cowsheds and tents would be cut down so that no snakes could hide there. Mother ordered me to stay inside. Then she left with the others. I sat cross-legged on the empty spot which once was warmed by Long Braid Aunt's body. The *Chinese Herbal Medicine* was opened on my lap. Searching through the book page by page, I found only a piece of paper inside of the plastic book cover. The paper contained a line of music notes. I recognised it as Long Braid Aunt's hand writing, her light blue ink pen, her little bean sprout notes. But I didn't know how to read the note. 'Music is as important as food to a person,' Long Braid Aunt once said. She had wanted to teach me how to read music. 'Writing is as important as eating to a person,' she had said, and wanted me learn how to write. But it was all too late now. I stared at the ceiling. Even the spiders were gone, leaving a broken web swinging in the air. I only heard the metal tools cutting the bamboo and bushes. I only heard people yelling out the number of snakes they had killed.

The poles that supported the tent shook. Straw and dust fell onto the bed. The foul smell from the trenches was replaced by the fragrance of the soil. Smoke rolled in. People's voices grew distant. I fell into a dark slumber.

When the tent fell into darkness, I slipped down from my bed and moved toward the crowd gathering outside. All the bushes within sight were gone. The wet black soil diffused the smell of fish into the air. A big earthworm twisted its severed body on the ground. The sun was cold and drunk. I made my way into the wall formed by the adults.

Colourful snakes hung twisting on a clothes line. Their scales were glistening and bright. One man took a snake down from the line. He held it by the tail and shook it twice. The snake lost its stiffness immediately, and hung limply in the man's hand like a string. The man had a knife in his other hand. I only saw the knife swing like a light and a piece of gallbladder stood impaled on the tip of the blade. 'Whose turn?' the man asked. He raised the golden green gallbladder. Someone handed him a small cup of wine. He tapped the blade on the cup, and the gallbladder fell into the wine. Then another man moved forward and took the cup. When he finished the wine, he raised his hand and turned the cup upside down. The man with the knife moved to another snake.

Fat Aunt had her turn at drinking the gallbladder wine. her face was as swollen as a cow's placenta, some spots bright, some dark. A few drops of wine clung to the long fine hair above her mouth. She wiped off the wine and yelled out, 'This hundred snake festival would have been more powerful if we had caught that boa. The good thing is that he won't last long. If he didn't burn in the fire, he will be poisoned.' When her voice died down, people rushed forward and took the gallbladderless snakes from the line. They started many camp fires behind the tent and made snake soup.

I ran down the dusty road, tripping in the ruts made by the carts during the rain. The sun was like a snake's gallbladder on the edge of a cup. Its bottom was hesitantly touching the surface of the water. A cloud of cow flies swarmed after me making vague noises. I yelled loud. They divided into several groups, hanging in the air, moving neither backward nor forward. I ran faster. They re-gathered and followed me again. A few bold ones attacked my forehead. I ran. I yelled. I called the boa to leave Bald Head Hill immediately. I knew those cowards were so afraid of my giant snake that they would dare to poison the spring and set traps to kill him.

The sunless Bald Head Hill was like a big grave. The rhythm of the spring water had ceased. They must have spent the whole day moving clay up here. Everywhere I saw the tracks of cartwheels covered by white clay. The white tracks led into the cave along with a set of footprints. The spring that had bubbled out of the cave for four seasons had disappeared, leaving only a damp trace. The dark green grass and cranberry bushes had been cut away and dumped in the water. The formerly clear water was covered by clay, grass and bushes. The thorn bushes I had put around were all burned to ashes.

I bent down and moved into the cave. With one turn, the light disappeared. My legs were shaking. I called to my boa. The echo came back to me. Then the cave sank into silence. I took a deep breath. The familiar fish smell was gone, and the strong smell of clay almost suffocated me. I moved forward, the cave narrowed. After several turns, I had to crouch down. It was at this moment that the breeze from the other end sent a smell of rice paddies and grass and soil into my nostrils. I couldn't move any farther. Lying on the cold rocky ground, I suddenly felt the strength slipping out of me, and tears running down my cheeks.

THE WOMAN IN CRIMSON

HENRY Y H ZHAO

translated by John Minford

The very day the examination results came out, Li went to find a boat to take him home. This was the second time he had failed. He was less desperate this time, less unable to face the world. But there were certain things he needed to know, certain questions demanding an answer.

He was lucky — a boat was just setting out. It punted out into a desolate autumn landscape. 'Uncle' Gu lived in a little *bastide* by the river, not far from town, and the journey took no more than a couple of hours. Heavy clouds, stained purple and gold with the rays of the setting sun, hung over the river, and Li could already make out the dark tiles of the commoners' houses, clustered around the large mansion that rambled up the hillside, layer upon layer folded into the thick shadows of the trees.

He sent his page-boy ahead with a letter, while he tidied his clothes, composed his spirits, then set out along the jetty, into the main street of the village and up to the very end, where it reached into the hills.

'Uncle' Gu was an old family friend. The younger generation referred to him respectfully by his more formal name, as 'Uncle' Zongzhou. When Li had come up to the provincial town for the examination, he had stayed the night in Uncle Gu's house. His grandfather had given him a letter, in which he asked Uncle Gu to take an interest in his grandson's progress. Uncle Gu was a renowned scholar, widely respected both for his personal integrity and for his literary accomplishments. Five years earlier he had resigned from the Academy and had returned to his native district, settling, after consultation with the appropriate diviners, on this particular village. Rumour had it that he had somehow become implicated in a power struggle at court; that he had offended one faction, and fallen in with another which had subsequently been disgraced. Now, at all events, he had shut himself away, and was devoting his days to reading, writing, and the elaboration of his own ideas.

From afar Li saw the gateman standing by the big black-lacquered, brass-bossed door; he went in and discovered his Uncle waiting for him in the inner hall. He was about to launch into an abject recital of his feelings of failure and remorse, when Uncle Gu came forward and took him by the hand, saying, 'A momentary setback in the literary campaign, my boy! The merest trifle. Certainly nothing to be taken to heart!' Li was quite lost for words. His Uncle was a large, impressive man, with a voice like a great bronze bell, and a long beard that trailed onto his chest in wisps, with not a white strand in it. His face inspired a degree of awe in the young. The two of them sat down in the hall, and Uncle Gu asked Li what his plans were for the future. To return home, Li replied, to shut himself away with his books, and to try again the following year. Uncle Gu was loud in his praises, predicting a great future for one who, while still so young, showed such resolution. 'It is my humble opinion that your essay writing is up to scratch: but you need to be even more circumspect, to devote yourself still more to the cultivation of your moral and inner life ...'

Li blushed. He recalled the letter his grandfather had entrusted him with, in which reference had been made to his 'unstable' temperament, his predilection for writing 'pretty nothings', and his general need of discipline. Words of counsel, it had been suggested, would not go amiss. On that occasion, even as he read the letter, Uncle Gu had nodded and had begun holding forth about the poor outlook for those who spent their time writing pretty lyrics like the notorious sentimental poet of the Sung dynasty, Liu Yong, stressing the fact that literary style was built on a foundation of genuine moral integrity.... After this homily, he had handed Li several little hand-written notebooks, explaining that they were part of a journal he was writing, which he had entitled 'Jottings from Chestnut Studio', and suggesting that Li might perhaps benefit by glancing through them.

Uncle Gu was looking more serious this time, almost a little grim. 'Literature in itself is a mere trifle,' he began, 'whereas the advancement of one's career is a matter of the first importance. In answer to your grandfather's request, I feel obliged to offer you whatever counsel and aid I can. Tell me, the last time you came up for the examination, did you read with care the book I gave you?'

'Why, yes sir, I read it right here, in your study.'

'Our provincial town is a cradle of Vanity, a sink of Iniquity, and the young fops who frequent it at examination time are a motley crew. Tell me, were you by any chance led astray?'

Li trembled as he caught sight of Uncle Gu's countenance. 'Absolutely not, sir.'

'It is hard to nurture the inner life that brings true literary distinction — and the easiest thing in the world to do it an injury. The workings of karma and the laws of retribution are quite extraordinary: the slightest deviation from the straight path can be disastrous, the very slightest …' Li began to panic. Uncle Gu seemed to be laying the blame for his failure on some misdemeanour. If Uncle Gu reported anything of the kind to his grandfather, life would be quite unendurable when he returned home. In the heat of the moment he blurted out:

'But haven't you already tested me once, sir?'

Uncle Gu said nothing. He merely laughed.

'No matter, no matter. You must be tired. Why not turn in early this evening? You can sleep in my study again. In the morning I'll see you on your way. And I'd like you to take a letter to your grandfather for me….'

The arrangement was exactly what Li had hoped for. He sent his page-boy back to the boat to say that he would be setting off in the morning, towards noon. And meanwhile one of Uncle Gu's servants led him down the winding walkways of the mansion to the study, where a bed had been made up for him. It had been raining, and the sky had grown dark somewhat early. A dampness in the air had replaced the sultry autumn heat of the day. Uncle Gu's study was spacious and immaculately clean, its bookcases neatly arranged — a place to cheer the young scholar's heart. Li extinguished most of the candles, leaving only one burning, the wick of which he trimmed to make the light still dimmer. A book lay open on the table, which he recognised at a glance as the journal Uncle Gu had lent him on his previous visit. Picking it up idly (it had been kept open with a paper-weight), he looked closer, and, with a twinge of annoyance, found that he knew the passage only too well.

The candle kept spluttering, the light flared, died and flared again. But Uncle Gu's meticulous hand was unmistakable — the large, well-formed ideograms, the punctilious style of the calligraphy. Every stroke of that classic script (done in imitation of the great Tang master Yan Zhenqing) seemed to announce the importance of integrity and truth of character, and the triviality of literature in itself. The autumn wind blew in the courtyard outside, the leaves of the chestnut tree trembled, rustling darkly. Then suddenly a shudder gripped him in the small of the back. He turned, and there she was.

She was just as she had been a month before. She wore a crimson dress. She opened the door silently as she walked in. She bowed solemnly to Li: 'Greetings, my lord.'

Li rose to his feet and stood by the table. 'Have you come to taunt me again?'

She stood in the centre of the room, her breasts drawn up fully, and looked Li in the face. There was not the slightest touch of coyness about her; on the contrary, her eyes seemed to flash a challenge.

'What do you mean, "again"?'

'Wasn't it you last time — when I stayed the night here before?'

The candlelight seemed to revolve in the room. He caught the smile on her glistening face.

'I came tonight because your gift made such a deep impression....'

'And last time?'

'Last time I was just testing you....'

Her frank reply confirmed his suspicions. He felt himself growing angry.

'So when you said you wanted to give yourself to me, you were just play-acting?'

'And you? When you were so prudish and cold — were you play-acting, or was that what you really felt?'

Another of his own doubts. He was touched to the quick again. This woman before him must be some sort of evil spirit, to know every least contour of his mind like that. He grew seriously angry.

'Can an insincere heart ever hope to deceive the gods? It is all your fault that I failed this time....'

The woman in crimson laughed out aloud. She took a few steps forward and Li pushed his chair back and moved away from the table. She began laughing hilariously, showing her brilliant white teeth. He had never seen a grown woman laugh like that before, let herself go in that way. She stopped laughing, and said breathlessly:

'Actually, it's easy to deceive the gods. But it's hard to deceive yourself. If you were already burning with desire, what did you think you could achieve by reciting the words of the *Mantra against Lust* so perfectly — you only have yourself to blame.'

He had never been so humiliated, not even when severely lectured by his own elders — he felt so stupid, so small. He started talking back, almost like a child.

'If you were allowed to pretend that night, wasn't I too?'

She took another step forward, and gripped his hand, her eyes burning into his.

'Today I'm serious: can't you be too?'

Oh the clever, pert, pretty way she said it! The darling! His last question came blurting out:

'Who exactly *are* you here in the Gu household?'

'I've got nothing to do with the Gu household — not any more.'

He was about to ask her what she meant by 'not any more' when his mouth was clamped shut by a pair of burning lips, and a soft warmth enveloped his body. He could hardly breathe. Her own fingers loosened the sash that bound her crimson dress, and it slid to the ground.

Suddenly the sound of a knocking at the door burst in on Li's dream, startling him from his bed. He was still confused in his mind, trying to puzzle out where it was that he had fallen asleep, when he heard Uncle Gu's voice calling him:

'Open the door, dear boy, open the door!'

'Just coming, Uncle!' he cried out hastily, at the same moment remembering that he had a woman by his side and that they were both stark naked. It was too late: the study door was already being pushed open, lanterns were casting their light into the room. He pulled back the bedcovers, flung on his clothes (which lay on the floor), and leapt from the bed, hurrying towards the door.

'What is it?' he asked, his teeth chattering. Uncle Gu was accompanied by several servants, and in the light of their lanterns his face had an air of exceptional severity.

'Why did you not open the door, dear nephew?'

Li prevaricated. He was about to say that he had been sound asleep, when Uncle Gu strode over to the bed. Li froze. Uncle Gu drew apart the silken bed curtains and then stripped back the covers, shining his lantern into the bed. Li closed his eyes and resigned himself to his fate. Suddenly Uncle Gu let out a great guffaw.

Li opened his eyes. Within the bed lay strewn a large number of loose sheets of paper. Uncle Gu had taken up the one that lay nearest the pillow, and now handed it to Li. Li glanced at it. It was surely the very page he had memorised a month earlier!

Rejecting Seduction: The Thirty-sixth Way

My fellow-student Tang Gao was an exceptionally gifted fellow. He was once in the capital for the examinations, and shut himself away with his books. There was a certain young widow who had become a great admirer of his and came to him one night with an eye to seducing him. He promptly recited this Mantra against Lust:

A Breach of Discretion between Man and Woman
  is contrary to the Rites;
Heaven, Earth and the Spirits
  stand in serried ranks.
Be not aroused, be not stirred,
  let not Lust take hold.
Great is the Code,
  and never must be broken!

The widow left in shame. And that year, Tang came Primus on the roll.

'Excellent! Capital!' cried Uncle Gu, rubbing his hands together with glee. 'You have exercised proper restraint, dear boy! You have not disappointed me!'

He paced round the room.

'I came to tell you that I have been into town this very night, to pay a call on Examiner Zhou, and to ask him to look through the examination scripts a second time. He says that the roll has not yet been definitively announced, so he still has a certain flexibility available to him.'

Li was lost for words.

'Your virtuous conduct, my dear boy, your chastity, only deserves this just reward.'

Uncle Gu laughed as he left, saying:

'Stay a little while and wait for the news. I shall write a letter meanwhile for your grandfather. I hardly think he will begrudge the outlay of a few hundred taels of silver....'

All was still again. Lanterns and footsteps disappeared down the passageway. Li sat cross-legged on the edge of his bed. He felt with his hand. No one. No intoxicating warmth. Nothing but a few cold sheets of paper.

He sat there till just before dawn, then dressed and walked outside. He would leave at once, put behind him this whole wretched business, not even bid Uncle Gu farewell. He never wanted to come back. The morning dew was cold in his face, he hurried on his way. He could see the river in the distance, the boat was still moored there, all was quiet, there was not a soul about. The mist drifted on the water. And then suddenly he saw her, on the deck, a woman, in a crimson dress; she seemed to be looking towards him, waiting for him.

He ran headlong down, into the damp, mist-laden breeze the blew up from the river.

MR NANGONG KANSHENG

Nan Fang

translated by Alison Bailey

The person who arrived at the leprosy hospital twenty kilometres from Luoma town in October 1937 was called Nangong Kansheng. It can be deduced from his surname that his paternal ancestors' lineage was exceptionally ancient, while his first name indicated that his maternal relations were village gentry who had prospered by cultivating rice. When he first arrived he wore a cap fashionable in the 1930s and carried a painted suitcase in his right hand. His physique was frail and his light-coloured eyes shaded by the brim of his cap were expressionless and dull, the result of unremittingly and single-mindedly pursuing a particular field of study. Mr Nangong Kansheng was an entomologist specializing in beetles, a field of study the ancient history of which more than adequately rivalled that of his paternal lineage; the *Yellow Emperor Internal Classic* records that a liquid secreted by beetles can remedy the shame of a deflowered virgin and was thus regularly applied by palace ladies selected to make alliances with barbarian tribes in the Western border regions. Mr Nangong Kansheng had an ancestor who had been Court physician and had relied on his unique skills to engage secretly in debauchery at the palace. On discovery, he was able to slip away alone from the capital thanks to a nocturnal warning from one of the emperor's body servants with whom he was on good terms and fled to a small town south of the Yangtze where he changed his name and eked out a living practising medicine. In the early years of the Republic a distant cousin of Nangong Kansheng had joined the army in far-off Guangxi, fleeing not long after to join the Yunnan governor Cai E as a staff officer. During the campaign against Yuan Shikai his extraordinary abilities were recognised by his superiors and he was promoted to general. In 1927 this cousin returned home on sick leave, set the family property in order and resumed his prestigious ancestral surname 'Nangong'. Nangong Kansheng's parents became refugees in the turmoils of 1911, leaving their newly-born child in the care of the old nun Caihuan in Seven Temple Alley. Despite the even greater degree of disorder in 1928 he had already been deeply influenced by his inherited love of tranquillity and reluctance to be involved in mundane affairs. His most common fantasies were contained within a volume spread open on the mahogany table, its yellowing pages gradually fading in dusk's firelight; he often silently recited part of a poem:

> Flaws in white jade tablets can still be ground away,
> Flawed words cannot be mended.

Life's blind will can push someone's life towards a climax, especially when he has not as yet fathomed the true reason for events taking place and is thus involuntarily drawn in. On the 15th of August 1937 Nangong Kansheng received a telegram sent from a certain large city in the south. That evening he sat alone beneath the fragrant Bodhi tree, lustrous moonlight flowing through the gaps in the tree onto the dark brick-paved ground where pied shadows were like symbols of reality and illusion. On the stone table an undisturbed cup of tea had already cooled. A moon cake on a platter had been finely cut into slices of thirty degree angles, making a kind of abstract design. The telegram in his hand had been sent one week previously and consisted of three lines:

> Son, swiftly assume father's tasks,
> Perpetuate the ancestral legacy.
> Father struck down, time is fleeting.

He tried carefully to fathom the telegram's wording, imagining the hidden significance and indistinct associations within the characters' structure and after ten minutes he had linked together the number of characters with the hour-glass with which he had played as a child and at this point he discovered a mistake: the blank space between flowing time and the eternal present should not be filled in by him, but it was now required of him that he should assume this uncomfortable role. So he drafted a nine-character telegram. Once he had sent it off he silently recited the following phrases: 'If parents still live, do not travel afar; if needs must, travel only to a set destination'

That night he did not sleep well. However, he discovered, at the moment he opened his eyes wide in the direction of the far reaches of darkness, that he was in the true realm of dreams; a secret winding road led to a certain place marked in red. Yet, on the map, his route had to traverse several mountain ridges and several dried-up rivers, the beds of which were like flesh-red gums plucked clean of teeth. A month earlier an aircraft carrying ammunition to the northern front line had got into trouble over one of many rivers and to lighten its load had abandoned the ammunition and extra fuel-tanks, destroying an iron bridge below. The next night he dreamt that the train in which he sat plunged headlong into the riverbed at the scene of the accident; on awakening he wept noiselessly and in utter grief. In the morning a telegram was slipped under the door of his room; it said that the father whom he had never met had died.

Nangong Kansheng very swiftly forgot his grief — this was the first time that he had not acted in accordance with his upbringing and training. Before setting off he changed into a clean long black cotton gown and said farewell to the old nun Caihuan. A naturally serious disposition concealed the embarrassing fact that he had already forgotten his deceased parent and the old nun did not discern his feelings, so that Mr Nangong Kansheng's tight heart relaxed somewhat: so much so that he thought that she did not yet realize that his father had died. Yet, after he had said farewell, he clearly heard the old nun saying her rosary behind him, mumbling, 'Amitabha, at the very least wear mourning your parent.'

Nangong Kansheng pretended to have heard nothing and departed swiftly. Later, *en route,* he became intoxicated with the extraordinary beauty of the scenery in the Jiangnan region. At dawn, as the train travelled along the banks of Yangcheng Lake he forced open the window and deeply inhaled the moist lakeside air. Gradually the air became increasingly dense, transforming into a transparent, flowing, light amber-coloured liquid. By this time Nangong Kansheng had already entered the country of dreams. This dream was slightly different from the one before: the train had not plunged into a vast, desolate riverbed, but into the abyss of a bottomless lake. The calamity and the present were sometimes only a foot apart, and the dream built a bridge between the two. When Nangong Kansheng awoke he already could not distinguish between the dream and the present. Later, he almost lost sight of the purpose of this journey and when the train stopped at a little station he leapt off without thinking.

The two hundred and seventy-fourth story in volume six of the *Taiping Guangji,* in the section 'Stories Behind the Poems' records the tale of the young scholar Cui Hu. One day, Cui met with rain on his way to sit the provincial examinations, so he turned aside from the road into a small mountain village. Outside a residence surrounded by a brushwood fence Cui reined in his horse, leapt off and knocked lightly at the gate. After some time, there came the sound of movement within and the almost imperceptible sound of footsteps coming towards him. Cui held his breath, waiting for the brushwood gate to open. Presently a plainly dressed young girl appeared before him and under the reflection of the clusters of peach blossom filling the court-yard Cui felt her whiteness was unreal and, suddenly, as if in a van-ished dream, he was moved to feelings of love. The girl led him into a room and brought him strong tea to dispel the cold. Cui gazed at the girl for a long time until she bashfully slipped into her chamber. The rain stopped and Cui spurred his horse on to the examination halls where, however, he failed. The following spring, Cui once again passed by this place on his way to the examinations and discovered that the building had been left to go wild, as if no-one had looked after it for a long time, making for a desolate scene. He felt hurt, finding it hard to restrain the tears rolling down. Suddenly he caught sight of a branch of peach blossom in full bloom and was moved to write the following poem:

> This day last year within this gate
> A face and peach blossom mirrored each other's red;
> Where the face has gone no-one knows
> The peach alone still smiles at the east wind.

After Mr Nangong Kansheng got off the train he discovered that ev-erything around him was familiar and dear to him, yet he felt as re-mote from the world as if in the early stages of recovery from a lengthy illness. There was but one small thing which made the 'him' of this moment preserve full consciousness: he had come to an unfamiliar place. Between present and reality existed that endlessly floating glass wall, with him sandwiched in the transparent space, yet at the same time he was anxious to break the wall and get out, to see what was re-ally the case. Perhaps by instinct, or through some higher form of reve-lation, without too many twists and turns he found a hidden road through the secretive and curious eyes of the populace of a small town. It was almost dark, the smell of alfalfa floated in the air, the mist was gradually turning thicker, revealing the hidden character of Nature, and the wild, desolate and damp southern plain unfolded features recorded in ancient geographical tomes, mysteriously fusing into the black night. Nangong Kansheng carried his luggage which was very simple: a peeling shellacked leather suitcase within which was a *Chronicle of Events 1911*, a dictionary of Latin medical terms, a dictio-nary of biology, a Song dynasty edition of the *Taiping Guangji* and a pile of newspapers from May 1911 to 1927 with his detailed annota-tions; also two sets of cotton underwear, a student's uniform which he had worn on the 4th of May 1911 which had gone white from washing and had mingled the smells of grass, fresh flowers and the fragrance of a young girl's newly-washed hair; in empty corners were stuffed a towel and toiletry articles in a plastic bag: a silver-plated cup stamped with the date of the Guangxu reign period, an imported English toothbrush and a Western Han dynasty bronze mirror patterned with stars and clouds. The cap that he wore had been given to him by a remote uncle on his eighteenth birthday and was an unsuccessful mixture of ancient spirit and modern fervour, gracing his head — which longed for primitive mysteries — with striking inspiration.

A light wind stirred the wild grass, the entire stretch of the plain swayed gently, the winding, crooked small paths were damp and spongy, as if they were alluvial deposits sunk to the bottom of water. At the moment when he went down the hill he began to notice the path gradually broadening out and changing direction, turning in a Z-shape and stretching up towards the mountain slope to the right. The stars above were unfathomable and very bright, illuminating a limitless vista of infertile rice fields and neglected orchards. Mr Nangong Kansheng, his heart filled with intimate feelings for the pastoral atmosphere, walked within a stretch of almond trees. The thick shading branches criss-crossed, now dim now bright, bringing to mind ancient blood and tenderness, heroic actions and violence. His heart and pulse beat distinctly, quickening vigorously, while his pace increasingly slowed. It was as if all this were not controlled by his will but by another power, as if he now felt a deep, inexplicable amazement as to how he had come to this place.

At midnight he reached the mountain top. Now he stood outside an encircling wall, a surrounding wall with no end, stretching straight up towards the dazzling stars, blending together with the colour of night. The grass was very deep and dew soaked his footwear. He followed the wall round to an archway and after several raps at the door he used the knocker. After a while a faint light appeared in the deep reaches of the courtyard house, bringing with it the slight sound of someone approaching. The light came closer and closer and was increasingly glaring, piercing Nangong Kansheng's eyes unbearably. At this moment he was suddenly aware that before this someone had noiselessly unbolted the door. The approaching person with the light now stood in front of him and Nangong Kansheng dimly perceived that it was a decrepit old man. Saying nothing, the man led him along a brick-paved path. Arriving in front of a huge courtyard house Nangong Kansheng caught a glimpse of a once familiar silhouette disappearing like a flash, but he could not think who it was. He unhurriedly searched his memory as he followed the old man with the light up stone steps and into a large room.

In the room there was no other furniture apart from a pair of Ming style pear-wood chairs and a table. On the north wall hung a very large medical diagram by the legendary physician Bian Que, flanked on either side by finely mounted couplets. The old man motioned to Mr Nangong Kansheng to sit in one of the chairs while he sat opposite and, only after having measured him up for a time, began to speak, 'I am the head and doctor of this hospital. This is a leper hospital. Perhaps, sir, you have got lost and entered my humble home by mistake. I will go and arrange accommodation for you, please wait a brief while. Tomorrow you will be able to find more agreeable lodgings in the town.'

Fate had already mistakenly directed Mr Nangong Kansheng to his destination while his melancholy and unsociable temperament had formed his compliant fatalism, however the solution to these strange events awaited revelation. Mr Nangong Kansheng resolved not to leave this place. So he cast the doctor a steadfast look and laughed silently at the same time: 'Doctor, I am a scholar researching beetles. On a certain point we share similarities, you treat humanity, I classify insects, and our mutually unrelated research could make this collaboration pleasurable.'

'With the exception of the ill I never accept collaborators,' the doctor said in categorical refusal.

Nangong Kansheng once again laughed soundlessly: 'Could it be that you do not consider me to be the best of medical cases? I have already become infected by the leprosy you have devoted yourself to curing, and following my thoroughgoing research, the state of the illness seems increasingly severe.'

In just two days Nangong Kansheng had become accustomed to the new life. In the days and nights that followed during the day he, with a tranquil heart, became familiar with the hospital's environment; at nights he had ample sleep without disturbance from nightmares. Every day when he woke up it was already faint dawn and birds were singing. This tranquil and ascetic existence made him happy to the point of swooning; it was almost as if he could feel that the dark shadow of his youth had been lifted from him, that his inheritance no longer ran in his veins: when young he had been prone to panic and his despairing ancestors, like cornered beasts at an impasse, were forced into fate's cage by a fear it was hard to resist.

In the blink of an eye autumn flew by and midwinter came. Although a very regulated existence had been established which left Mr Nangong's fertile mind even more time for daydreaming, he never once thought of his old home, to the point where he forgot everything in his past. He often browsed through the volumes he had brought with him and which were almost the only link he maintained with the outside world. Many were the abstract shapes he constructed from blurred characters on torn pages: village, river, orchard, wheat field, almond grove, all these were but species of hypothetical memories re-arranged. In a document which textual research proved was about his maternal great-grandfather, there was an anecdote which recorded that the old gentleman had suddenly given up his leadership of the army during an unstable time of war and gone off travelling. This kind of material assisted Nangong Kansheng to make detailed mathematical calculations with a pencil on strawboard paper about the present conflict. The conclusion was very abstract, like a mischievous child naively telling lies. Apart from playing such games he was utterly scrupulous about researching beetles, certainly not with the aid of specimens nor by performing any biological dissections, but by abstractly constructing principles through deep thought. By a certain inference he concluded that intestinal nerve endings linked to cerebral functions at a specific time secreted a damp blue liquid; yet the conclusion of another deduction was completely at odds with the former. Even if this was the case it caused him no vexation. He waited patiently and methodically. Clarity beneath muddle was always a small vague point which moved constantly, and if reasoning at a certain time tallied with its perplexing laws of impulse, a subtle conclusion would emerge.

Today Mr Nangong Kansheng casually opened a book. This book lay quietly in a place which he had unconsciously cultivated as one habitually most close to him, providing a kind of very simple comparison with the disorderly pile of other books. A shaft of light filtering through the skylight fell on the book's cover and Mr Nangong, at this moment when his soul was enshrouded in gloom, stretched out two long, thin and knobbly fingers and thrust them deep within the book to open it up. He slowly touched the damp, cool and rough characters, inhaled the smell of old paper and found that he was reading a poem:

Cut willow branches smell sweetly fragrant,
In regret year after year they are presented at partings.
A leaf in the wind is autumn's sudden herald.
Even if you were to return how could I bear the sundering?

He knew then that he was reading the four hundred and eightieth section of the *Taiping Guangji* in which were the annotations based on his research. These notations, which included triangles, wavy lines and symbols the implications of which only he understood, profoundly disturbed Mr Nangong. He felt as if there were a trap rapaciously revealing its teeth as it awaited him while, ultimately, he had become a component part of the trap. At this point he remembered his father's telegram and pulled it out; it still looked as it had before he put it in his pocket, folded carefully and conscientiously and still retaining its original smell. Mr Nangong re-read the telegram and thereupon, almost without thinking, he discovered that time and space within it had absolutely no significance, being just an emergent unclear state of flowing time, whether it be his unexpected present life of seclusion in this thatched hut or an ancient book which indicates an outcome which will happen now, all of it was without any significance. So he pushed open the wooden gate.

The snow had been falling for a whole week and was now deep enough to block off the walkway. At first all he did was to stand under the thatched eaves inspecting the hazy overcast sky but soon afterwards he began to recall the still, solemn, mysterious and invigorating snowbound southern plain. A tale recorded in a certain old tome exactly accorded with the scene at this moment, but this scene could only appear in another dream. Yet almost all of this was impossible. Mr Nangong's thumb and middle finger stopped in the midst of picking a blade of grass and in his imagination he was calculating the absurdities of probability. He was just striving to eliminate almost heaven-willed probable accuracy from absurdity. At this moment he had still not yet discovered that the piled up snow before him was bit by bit caving in. He had encountered a difficult problem which caused him to prepare to return to his room to consult his Latin dictionary but this decision also caused him to hesitate for a moment because within his trance it was as if he had returned to the past or perhaps the same moment in the future, the same time and place, the same scene, the same weather, with dusk bringing snow in its wake; today he wanted to consult the rhyming dictionary about a certain word in a poem. It was also possible that after a period of dispute with his lonely self, he wanted to find a friend with whom to play chess or drink in honour of the snowy scene; the next day was simply a repetition of the day before. The very last day he could no longer hope to ascertain which year, which month or which day it was, and he felt as if he had achieved liberation; that day during his noontime nap his dream was indeed about browsing through a certain book the text of which changed into the familiar tale of Scholar Cui in the *Taiping Guangji*. Within this very clear dream another indistinct dream was intermingled. Because the familiar words tricked his eyes with illusions, he very quickly lay down over the book and slept, and this time what he dreamed about was his father reading exactly the same story in exactly the same book in the same scene and time. He woke up in perplexity and on awakening he realised that he was in another dream. However, this time he recalled his father's death and his indifference towards it; moreover, from this time on he realised that he was sitting in a train moving towards a destination which was hard to clarify and, closing the pages of the two hundred and seventy-fifth section of the *Taiping Guangji,* he got off the train.

However, the present always harbours hostility towards an individual. It was not long before Nangong Kansheng noticed what was happening in front of him; as before the sky was sombre, the pallid winter afternoon was still, dark and terrible, and apparently there was no living creature to be seen; or perhaps this could be said to be the terror Nature inflicts on someone. The colours of the environment merged into a whole which overstepped the limits his emotions were able to endure, while his aloof calm could rather be said to be a death he had inherited through which he became a link in the chain of the process. The world before his eyes seemed to be caving in. It was not long after that Nangong Kansheng noticed something happen. A crevice slowly appeared in the piled-up snow blocking his path, after which a space like a mountain valley appeared. Following this he saw on another side, the distance of a book away from him, a face emerging: pure, bewildered and pale, with a pair of distracted eyes beneath hair like, like the black traces left by time. She wore a red outfit which had faded not through washing but naturally over a long period of time. It was she who, with her graceful, weak, enervated and despairing form was clearing away the accumulated snow, like the flick of a willow branch in a faint breeze. Even at this moment Nangong Kansheng had not displayed any astonishment — his veins flowed with fatalistic commiseration — his calm was replaced by a harbinger of greater calm. Furthermore, the clues to the harbinger which were emerging little by little were now as if suddenly illuminated by a divine light, and he became profoundly aware of the miracle created by fate within time, or a new image within flowing time. The attitude eventuated was even more calm than the harbingers of calm.

'The evening that I arrived here it was you who opened the main door to me and now I proffer my belated thanks.' It was as if he was hearing a stranger's voice speaking.

The girl shivered listlessly, looking at him with blank eyes almost as if she saw nothing. She clutched a crumpled piece of paper in her hand. In only one glance he knew it was the telegram he had sent off.

'Please guide me to my father's grave,' he said.

Late that night Mr Nangong Kansheng heard in the mists of sleep the faint sound of a door being pushed open. He did not look, knowing what it was, a judgement made only half awake; based on the rustling sounds in the darkness, he knew that the girl was approaching him. Thereupon he moved closer to the edge of the bed to make room, his actions so well-worn they might be preserved in a museum. In the silence the girl lay down next to him with great agility, slipping inside his bedding like a fish into water. At this moment, as chance would have it, Mr Nangong noticed that the moonlight had shifted towards the skylight. A faint sliver of liquid light spilled in, illuminating the girl's blank, wilful and perplexed face, a face which had suffered and been destroyed by several thousand years of expectation.

Mr Nangong Kansheng fell asleep, irreproachable, like a saint.

UNDER-*SKY* UNDER*GROUND*

O

POETRY

BEI DAO

four poems translated by Bonnie S McDougall and
Chen Maiping

PRAGUE

A swarm of country moths attack the city
street lamps, ghostly faces
slender legs supporting the night sky

Where there are ghosts, there's history
underground lodes unmarked on the map
are Prague's stout nerves

Kafka's childhood passed through the square
the dream plays truant, the dream
is the stern father, enthroned above the clouds

Where there's a father, there's a right of succession
a rat strolls through the palace corridors
shadowy attendants cluster round

The calèche that set out from the century's gate
has turned into a tank along the road
truth is choosing its enemies

Where there's truth, there's forgetfulness
swaying like a stamen in the breeze, the drunk
has dropped a dusty curse

Crossing time's bridge over the Vltava
one enters the dazzling daylight
the ancient statues are full of hate

Where there's hate, there's glory
the pedlar mysteriously spreads out a piece of velvet
please buy good weather where pearls join together

'HE OPENS WIDE A THIRD EYE …'

He opens wide a third eye
the star above his head
warm currents from both east and west
have formed an archway
the expressway passes through the setting sun
two mountain peaks have ridden the camel to collapse
its skeleton has been pressed deep down
into a layer of coal

He sits in the narrow cabin under water
calm as ballast
schools of fish around him flash and gleam
freedom, that golden coffin lid
hangs high above the prison
the people queuing behind the giant rock
are waiting to enter the emperor's
memory

The exile of words has begun

ALONG THE WAY

July, an abandoned stone quarry
the slanting wind and fifty paper hawks sweep by
the people kneeling towards the sea
have renounced their thousand year war

I adjust the time
so as to pass through my life

Hailing freedom
the sound of golden sands comes from water
the infant stirring in the belly has tobacco in its mouth
its mother's head is densely wrapped in fog

I adjust the time
so as to pass through my life

The city is migrating
hotels large and small are ranged on the tracks
the tourists' straw hats revolve
someone shoots at them

I adjust the time
so as to pass through my life

The bees in swarms
pursue the itinerants' drifting gardens
the singer and the blind man
agitate the night sky with their twofold glory

I adjust the time
so as to pass through my life

A drop of blood marks the final point
on the map spread over death
conscious stones underneath my feet
forgotten by me

AT THIS MOMENT

The great advance
is checked
by an ingenious gear

The man who gets gunpowder from dreams
also gets salt on his wounds
and gods' voices
the remainder is only farewell
farewell snow
gleams in the night sky

BEI DAO

three poems translated by David Hinton

YEAR'S END

from the year's beginning to its end
I've walked through countless years
time turning back on itself
shoes of those who gave up scattered everywhere
dust of the private
litter of the public

it's been a perfectly normal year
the sledgehammer sits idle, and yet
looking to the light of the future
I glimpse that metric standard in platinum
here on the anvil

MUCH ADO IN AUTUMN

a candle lost in the depths of darkness
hunts fossils in the shale of knowledge
streaming word-shoals spawn
then sleep beside civilization till dawn

inertial wheel, ascetic snowmen
the endgame on chessboard earth's
hung fire for years
a boy escaping regulation
swims across the boundary to deliver a letter
that's the poem, or perhaps an invitation to death

UNTITLED

hawk shadow flickers past
fields of wheat shiver

I'm becoming someone who explicates summer
returning to highways
sporting a thinking cap to train my thoughts

if deep skies never die

DUO DUO

translated by Gregory B Lee

THE RIVERS OF AMSTERDAM

November as the city enters night
there are only the rivers of Amsterdam

suddenly

the mandarins on the tree at home
quiver in the autumn breeze

I shut the window, yet to no avail
the rivers flow backwards, yet to no avail
that sun all inlaid with pearls, has risen

yet to no avail
doves like iron filings scatter and fall
a road devoid of boys suddenly looks vast and empty

after the passing of the autumn rain
that roof crawling with snails
— my motherland

on Amsterdam's rivers, slowly sailing by ...

IN ENGLAND

After the church spires and the city chimneys sink beneath the
horizon
England's sky, is darker than lovers' whispers
Two blind accordion players, heads bowed pass by

There are no farmers, so there are no vespers
There are no tombstones, so there are no declaimers
Two rows of newly planted apple trees, stab my heart

It was my wings that brought me fame, it was England
Made me reach the place where I was lost
Memories, but no longer leaving furrows

Shame, that's my address
The whole of England, does not possess a woman who cannot kiss
The whole of England, cannot contain my pride

From the mud hidden in the cracks of my nails, I
Recognize my homeland — mother
Stuffed into a parcel, and posted faraway

RESIDENTS

When they drink beer in the depths of the sky, then we kiss
When they sing, we turn off the light
When we fall asleep, on silver-plated toenails
They walk into our dream, while we await the dream's end

They have long since formed a river

In timeless sleep
They shave, then we hear the sound of strings
They paddle their oars, then the world stops turning
They don't paddle, they don't paddle

Then we have no chance of awakening

In sleepless time
They wave to us, we wave to the children
When children wave to children
Stars awake from a distant hotel

All who feel pain will awaken

The beer they drank has long since flowed back to the ocean
Those children walking on the surface of the sea
All received their blessing: flowing
Flowing, is but the river's yielding

With secretly shed tears, we formed a river …

WINDMILL

Eternal wheels turning everywhere
yet I do not turn
like a dejected edifice paralysed in the fields
I, yearn for the approach of a fierce wind:

Those aches will be more, even more severe
they are rumbling forth, ruling the crown of my head
thunder and lightning in the sky frantically weaving
the sky is like stone, after breaking apart fantasizing
tails on buttocks flailing about
cattle and sheep, piled together flee
precisely these things, piled into memory
make me once more hold to myself
the roar of darkness …

And, our bad fortune, our master
standing at the head of the field made of flesh
with a terrifying expression, continues clapping for the storm —

CROSSING THE SEA

We cross the sea, and where should that
godforsaken river flow?

we turn around, and behind us
there is no after life at all

is there no life at all
worth repeatedly resurrecting?

people aboard the boat, all stand wooden
relatives, breathe under distant waters

the sound of a bell steadily ringing
the more it rings, the more it lacks faith!

trees on the far shore are like people having sex
standing in for sea shells, sea stars, sea flowers

on the beach are scattered needles, cotton wool
and pubes — we are gazing at the other side

so we turn our heads, like fruits turning their heads
and behind us — a tombstone

stuck into the high school drill ground
only, only beside the sea do women cry over children

grasp how very long this winter will be:
with no dead people, the river can have no end ...

THEY

Fingers stuck into pants pockets jingling coins and genitals
they're playing at another way of growing up

between the striptease artist's elevated buttocks
there is a tiny church, starting to walk on three white horse legs

they use noses to see it
and their fingernails will sprout in the May soil

the yellow earth of May is mound upon mound of flat explosives
imitated by death, and the reason for death is also

in the very last jolt to the soil of the ironware in heat
they will become a part of the sacrificed wilderness

the silence of the long dead dead before dying
makes all they understood immutable

the way they stubbornly thought, they acted
they gave away their childhood

made death preserve intact
their hackneyed use of our experience.

YANG LIAN

translated by Brian Holton

1989

who says the dead can embrace?
like fine horses   manes silver grey
standing outside the window in the freezing moonlight
the dead are buried in the days of the past
in days not long past   madmen were tied onto beds
rigid as iron nails
pinning down the timbers of darkness
the coffin lid each day closing over like this

who says the dead are dead and gone?   the dead
enclosed in the vagrancy of their final days
are the masters of forever
four portraits of themselves on four walls
butchery yet again   blood
is still the only famous landscape
slept into the tomb they were lucky   but they wake again in
a tomorrow the birds fear even more
this is no doubt a perfectly ordinary year

THE BOOK OF EXILE

you are not here   this pen mark
just written is blown away by the gale
is blank as if a dead bird circled above your face
the funeral-following moon a broken hand
turns your days backward
turns to the page where you are absent
as you write   so you are
a connoisseur of your own excision

like the sound of someone else
crushed bones casually spat into a corner
the hollow sound of water clashing on water
casually moving into a breath
into a pear so no-one else is seen
the skulls on the ground are all you
growing old overnight between the words, the lines
your poem has invisibly pierced the world

THE EXTENT OF THE DISASTER

fireglow burns with the swiftness of forgetting
turns to a poison kiss when it touches the skin
the rainstorm stops across the street
waiting until the butchered donkey   washed and scrubbed like new
has been branded all over its backside

the worst news is always shod in a sheet of white paper
so calm   as if it's only the ringing in your ears you hear
in the limbs a space of white untrodden snow
who coughs in the flames
uselessly trying to bind the ashes of the paper into a book?

the street, however, is deserted
the wind so old it doesn't even deserve real pain

CV OF HATE

no twilight stroll ever leads to anyone else
fire   can never be lit once again
like hatred   filling my cup full
making me drink till it hurts
blood sweeter than the sweetness of a fruit tree
a black night dyed blacker by the daylight
limbs slacken   storm shakes violent as a tongue
the eyes left in yesterday's broad sickroom
are a musical instrument that shoots
birds belong to no reality   so their flight is unending
gaze indistinguishable from glass
clearest of water, a blind man still
he who lives in the shark's silent heart, parched, can only split open
seeing the ocean I burn myself up
seeing the coral   scrape my breast clean of surplus flesh
polish death bright like a tiny little ornament
decorate the months and the years after death
— hate me, then   because I'm still thirsty

GU CHENG

SMOKING

none of these flowers
needs the soil
let the soil long for them
let them leave the soil
and grow upwards —
pointed toes of sprouting ginger

none needs the soil
or should long for what is below
let them leave

all evening their skirts have been billowing upwards

WE WRITE THINGS

we write things:
insects   looking for paths in a pine-cone
or moving pieces pawn by pawn
sometimes   all for nothing.
chewing over some gleaned word
malchosen
within it, mould and mildew
so chew another

impossible to drive the cart —
on time — into the pine
seeds fall to an earth
covered over with pine-cones

ZHANG ZHEN

TOO MANY THINGS HAVE ALREADY BEEN FORGOTTEN

Too many things have already been forgotten
yet we still think of doing this or that and going here and there
of becoming big shots or dealers.
We forget what we have done, right or wrong,
we forget the people we used to know, loved or hated,
we forget what happened in the womb,
and we forget the terror of our first period.

We are too anxious to become strangers to ourselves
as if the further we get from where we set out, the better.
We forget too much —
the names of friends, the meanings of words
that people are lying in jail for us,
colourful clothes we wore in childhood,
the feeling as someone kisses your face,
— as if we are living to forget,
as if all we belong to is everything neglected
and denied.

Our futures will also be obliterated,
our diaries and letters will be returned to the dead letter office.
Or perhaps in the midst of the great fire we will be reminded of
                                                    ourselves,
and recall a few remarkable risings or settings of the sun.

STRUGGLING TO RECALL THAT WINTER

My chin resting on a grey wall —
where now has that day gone?
Winter piled on winter,
in the seams, the skirts' shiny red hems.

The sound of ice cracking,
that shock of love which flowed out from me
and became the silk I wore,
the thousandth time I entered this door, passed down this street.

I know you — even burned to ashes,
a well-stuffed face in the sandstorm.
All those places branded with passion
— scarred.

HAIZI

translated by Steve Balogh

FOR THE LAST NIGHT AND THE FIRST DAY

Tonight your black hair is dark night on a lonely crag.
The shepherds' snow-white flocks have invaded the
murky dark all around the aerodrome.

Dark night drop off before I do.
It is the gaping wound of the spirit.
You are my gaping wound.
Flocks of sheep and flower buds, gaping wounds of the crags.

Snow-mountains fill the aerodrome's dark murk
with deep snow; snow-mountain fairies eat wild
game and wear fresh flowers. Tonight ninety-nine snow peaks
tower up to Heaven's Halls
and cause me utter sleeplessness.

MENG LANG

DON'T LET YOUR SORROW LEAVE YOU

Often I wish myself out of this body, breathing far elsewhere
all around me still, my own heart's tremors.
But what really gets the heart thumping: to let yourself rise
without a care or second thought.

A few clothes that couldn't be my own
fill with wind — I'm blown along until I cannot breathe.
People reach out to touch me from all sides
each asking the other: 'What is this miracle?'

In the heart of the void I have abandoned form —
as if I were pure spirit in the faces of the crowd — so close
that distance itself is all but lost.
Everyone shields their breast — don't let your sorrow leave you!

STAGE RIFLES

The measures of this concert are set by rifles.
Mistakes are everywhere.
The over-polite audience is unable to avoid them.

A measure of silence at the concert:
still more people secretly listening —
the strings vibrate —
the players seem to want to flee and hide.

They are false, the ears I brought to this concert, but
they serve as the earphones of happiness
they serve as the earmuffs of happiness
they serve as the earplugs of happiness.

Muffled by this protection, more life-like sounds cease.
Gun fire on all sides.

TIME IS MY SAVIOUR

Time is our saviour!
It races towards us
handing out gold watches
here and there, a prison on our wrists
here and there, a secret rhythm in our hearts.

Have we been awarded with time?
We answer: Yes.
But I do not accept the gold watch
which has fallen to the ground, shattered
like a small dry clod of earth.

The gold watch, walks off ticking.
Its gold is not the time!
We cherish the excitement that has been released
seeing off time with our eyes in the face of a watch.

Have I been awarded with time?
I answer: Yes.
It has swept straight into my heart,
Time and I, we both race off towards liberation.

Time has scattered the gold watches!
You point at me behind my back: that man,
he squanders gold like dust, that man,
he has rejected us.

I answer: Yes I have.
Time is my salvation!

EDUCATIONAL POEM

It's the savage tiger's day of birth:
young animal, you have a precious place
in the heart of my affections because of their transience.

It's the hunter's day of birth:
I did not catch my first glimpse of the world
through cross-hairs.

The first cry of the tiger
was more real than could be imagined;
the first cry of the hunter
was a cry from my own lips:

Young creature, let's grow up together, you and I,
then go our separate ways —

you, tiger, to follow your exquisite animal nature, leaving no more
traces,
hunter — should he be myself —
to be buried in immortality by the savage nature of man.

ZHANG ZAO

THE OPTICIAN

Old summer stuck in the gullet
at the end of the corridor, the seductive footwear of our ancestral
homeland

licking flames, tiger stripes, insomnia
the whole world rolled round in a wind-storm, Arab horsemen
suddenly
spring up, roaring and shouting in a mob, holding high
the negatives, forcing history which has lost its way

into the hands of chance.
Whose falling hair was it that tempted you to fly?

Brewing a nightmare in a dark room filled with unearthly odours
the master optician, reveals the tail of Dante:
close, way-off or spot-on?
What kind of morality might this suggest for our world?

Mutant sunflowers suddenly turn back their heads. The nostrils
of the raw, putrid angels who are shifting the corridor (their finest
feathers clearly distinguishable) drip with grey matter.

CHORUS

a heart-warming chorus aligned on the co-ordinates,
the tongues of freshly scrubbed young girls
like roses plucked out of the air by a magician

who are they for? who are they for?
head, prop up the wafer of my soul
the 'slender white poplar' opens my howling inner warmth

upwards, they all ride you, like a
definition — oh! hard metaphysics
a memo casually thrown away

they drag me off to the edge of the universe
eating dust — god! the pastures of delusion
Wednesday switches its baton

while a fiendish, craven beast of some kind
groans, resounds,
gathers up, with its teeth, May that was about to fall

BAI HUA

THINGS PAST

These innocent messengers
wearing their usual summer dresses
sitting down here, beside me
smiling
giving me a glimpse of their ageing withered dugs

those journeys of such great excitement
and stupefied exhaustion
they come to a halt in this strange moment
this well-meaning, tear-jerking moment

old age, so much bowing and scraping
'received pronunciation' out of town (is it really necessary?)
false teeth — soft, obscene —
the burning throat

already I've pulled myself together, strained to see
the cool breeze of middle age
sweep away the expression in meeting eyes
the sentimentality
the candour and compassion
those dissolute, romantic affairs living purely in the past

ah, these innocent messengers
endlessly bustling about
furtively knocking
bursting with love and respect
visiting our lives which have known too little

HAPPINESS

consider these orphans
sharp but beardless
walking down the street

praising the great spirit, while they
gnaw at their gristle, harshly grinding

deathless determination, pure but impetuous
as if they'd have the whole world swallow back hot tears
or must we all together
join the ranks
of Red Army orphans
sickly, crippled, eyes spilling brightness

ah yes, and they sing
sing for the landscape which listens respectfully
and for silent, modest loveliness,
but who feels any shame?
who dares raise their head
above this halting music of malnutrition?

No. Orphans, how can we
speak of salvation
this is certainly not a matter of fact
they have simply forced themselves to dream it up

there is still the taste of bitterness, still the call
still the spring breeze striking the trees
the orphans are ever more lonely
we feel still more self-effacing desperation

READING THE POET'S LIFE ONE SUMMER

This philosophy makes me uncomfortable.
His expectations were too great.
Twice he thought of giving up.
But, no? Twice he thought of death.
Three endless months were, for him, three months of falling.
My endless suffering followed him
down from Beijing to Chongqing.

Three full months, a little orphan, cloud-wandering
hoping to grow up to be a 'great poet'.
His childhood already at an end,
he'd reached the age of sixteen.
Over and over he repeated,
'Either sacrifice yourself to yourself
or live for others.'
This philosophy makes me uncomfortable.

He expressed himself too hurriedly.
I could not keep up with the sense.
One short summer's day, turning the 89th page —
Look, his neck, alone, becomes inflamed
inflamed with significance, with passion
and he continues downwards.
This philosophy makes me uncomfortable.

Look again, his body,
so sensitive, so ugly
too small, too thin

the corners of his mouth, too plain
but the cunning in his eyes confirms his strength,
albeit the strength of misfortune.
This philosophy makes me uncomfortable.

Besides these, there are some other hopeless details,
one or two details that no one bother to ask about,
one or two details still sleepwalking,
one or two details still raising a finger,
the small detail of suicide over a single word.
That was a small detail of his eighteenth year.
This unique philosophy makes me uncomfortable.

DAXIAN

SONNETS AT THE YEAR'S END — 19

Because we are sun to wine,
the green plum's star
the mint of sleep
the compass of the air,

because our lovers have emptied their hands
and are left holding dust — wind-borne, white —
the sun setting on the mountain side drinks long and low
an exhausted cup, one hundred years of 'shadow and light'.

Because, on that tusk of ivory, we
see Solomon who gently teased a lily,
and because the long-lingering labials of the wine king slip out,
as we breathe within the heavy fragrance of the maenads,

Because bitter herbs have pulled our heart-strings taut,
the west wind chants beneath the city of Beijing.

EATING A CHICKEN

I let the chicken in the oven
relax,
prone (back to the heavens)

'Come on, get your knife out!'
yells the chicken on the dish
(breast upwards now)

I carve off a wing
to reveal an angel from a book I read
when I was young

DEAN LÜ

THE OTHER WINTER

The other winter — he lacked for nothing — there,
he was a shoemaker and nothing more; understood the demands of
his calling
and it wasn't easy to maintain good form; it was a source of pride.
What is a life of freedom? Nothing but a pretty fall of snow,
a pair of shoes with a different smell — he'd found the thoughts he
wanted to express.
He was content. He went home to catch up on his sleep —
There, another fall of snow was about to come down. He had
nothing more to say.

PAIN

It was the impression made by a school, not that it 'made an
impression'
up against the slope; behind where it lay, that small mountain.
When the wind blew, waves of recitation would swell out
but no one cared whether its hopeless roof would last.
We were inside, and learned to keep our distance;
we didn't want to get caught up in it again — no matter what the
weather,
though we all, to this very day, are questions that might be taken
up at any time.

HONG YING

HOW TO BECOME A FISH

Fisherman
passes through   he's shattered the over-cautious protective
barrier — on the waves, it's splintered, ground to powder,
and finally, it's gone.
You follow the fisherman with flattering smiles.
The smell of fish burns into your flesh   you arch off
scales glinting.

Fish swell to bursting   sun dried on the rocks.
What else can you do   the day draws to its end —
the seashore's lined with nets and cooking smoke.
You're no fish   and you never have been.

BRIDGE

The presence of that sculpted head   makes the bridge quiver
think of a crowd of people
gathered there at the bridgehead.

Behind the pine forest, they are
engaged in something unfathomable;
No doubt they will approach
over the pine cones, over the reinforced concrete.

You must remember   amongst them is that sculpted head,
you must understand that, beneath his feet, the bridge
sways
wakes me   brutally   shaken.

DAOZI

SPRING CUTTINGS

Spring: The murderer you've never met.
Spring: Sharp emaciated wolf pack, a mirror dressed in snow.
Spring: One says: Sell!
           Another is driving up the prices.
Spring: Lovers swarm the cliff top. The golden throats ring out.
Spring: Music perseveres. A vigorous old hand writes a careless
           signature. All blood of midnight is black.
Spring: Shame is her storehouse.
Spring: The face has been erased from the prison wall.
           White buttocks, wrenching her sex.
Spring: Spying and overhearing.
Spring: Judas mounting the crucifix, a forgery. A displacement.
           Yet the mask is always the same.
Spring: A market of counterfeits.
Spring: The principles of pygmies.
Spring: Heat and movement. The extravagant aspirations of lilac.
           Light, a metaphysical tiger, descending the mountain to
           drink.
Spring: ————————————————— hostage, ———.
Spring: ———! ————————————————.
Spring: A filthy blade. Anger and shoes.
Spring: From whom will you borrow? —————————
           absent.
Spring: The bud's clue, the secret of the horse's eye. Shadows
           wrestling on the desert. Timidity inscribed on the medical
           history.
Spring: You grind a brick to make a mirror, and see me reflected:
           a man in love with poverty.

Spring: You gather snow as provisions, give aid to these promises
            of promises:

            on the equator of famine
            at the adjudication beneath the apple tree
            during the oath-taking and the weeping
            as blossoms cluster round both nuptial bed and tomb

            Spring.

RAILWAY STATION

Abandoned, given over
to empty spaces, the trailing
breath of far trains still lingers.
From the station — as wheels move off
rust spreads on the rails.

Yet the catastrophe of death is here.
So great, life's overwhelming longings,
that fierce gun battles seem to rage
between one line of carriages and another —

and this is like a time when verbs
set out in linked succession, while the nouns
they disgorge rust in heaps, and adjectives
straggle up like weeds between the rails.

A MAN WHO GETS THROUGH WINTER CUTTING WOOD

A man who gets through winter cutting wood
stirs up its passions more
than the fall of feeble winter sunlight.

A man who gets through winter cutting wood
startles me — the terrifying strength,
the precision of his hands, cutting into things

as deep winter reaches us
a man who gets through winter cutting wood is more profound
than the season at his shoulder and more
concentrated

— the glint of a falling axe head stills
my pen more surely than
revolution.

I lift my head, see him rise to stand in the courtyard
then turn and walk away.
It's not just the winter that he will make it through.

UNDER-*SKY* UNDER*GROUND*

O

MEMOIRS OF UNDERGROUND LITERATURE

THE LEGEND OF THE SUN BRIGADE

ZHANG LANGLANG

translated by Helen Wang

1

Duo Duo and other famous poets of today suddenly remembered a group of not so famous poets of yesterday. In a number of sincere essays they said, yes, there was, there was a 'Sun Brigade'. And, according to them, I was a member of it.

I was taken aback. Was there? Still, Zhang Mingming once called me 'young poet' with much admiration. She was remembering the old days, over twenty years ago.

Guo Lusheng (also known as 'Index Finger') had come looking for me to ask me to take part in the 'Survivors Poetry Festival', and pointing at me with that index finger of his, he said: 'No need to be polite about it, the title of my poem "Believe in the Future" came from you.' I had heard about that famous poem while I was in prison. In the seventies, it had created quite a stir underground. All the lads in Baiyang Lake knew about it, and had read it. It was said, it's like a transmission of fire.

A few words of the title were first spoken by me, but what does that say about anything? The real force of the words lay in his poem, in his sincerity, his sensitivity, his passion. At the time I heard him reading a poem about fish, about fish floating in ice. And today, he is still like he was back then. He is a fish of that particular period.

We were the overture to the emergence of a certain kind of fish.

2

Bei Dao said very matter-of-factly: 'Think back, think back, and write it down.' And what can I remember? A 'Sun Brigade' that had never been an organised body, only a group of poets that had left no poetry behind, merely some hazy images in the background.

The faded sepia photograph that was yesterday was already hazy. That was today in ancient times, that was Western culture winding its way across the Great Wall of Steel, inciting a group of restless young people to commotion.

I just gently open up the source of memory,
and cool clear pictures come floating out ...

3

1958 and, as Mao pronounced, 'Everyone in China is a sage'. Everyone was also a poet, and I was no exception. Everyone had a time limit to hand in his one hundred poems and fifty paintings. I handed over my share as well, never thinking I was dishing out mistakes. At the time, most of the poems were of the kind: 'Dare to let the earth produce more' or 'Only when you have spread muck can you know the fragrance of dung' ... etc., etc. Mine was: 'Like snow breaking away, / flooding down the mountain, / vigorously, forcefully, rapidly, / the great wheel of history rolling. / Who is it? / Us! / Symbols of youth, / pioneers of revolution ...'

The headmaster's face dropped: the poem showed erroneous thinking — it was 'youthism'. It did not mention the party or the Chairman, nor did it mention the 'three red banners' policy.

I cried floods of tears as I threw back my answers: hadn't Lenin approved of Mayakovsky? Loads of his poems hadn't mentioned those things. Mine was hardly an editorial piece.

At the time what we liked to read most of all were old Maya's 'My Love' and 'Clouds in Trousers'. Zhang Jiuxing, Gan Lulin and I used to go walking in the little pine wood every morning, obsessively learning Mayakovsky's poems by heart. We had our heads shaved bald as melons — just like Maya, and wore padded army trousers, tied at the waist with a length of old flex.

I kept it a secret that I wrote poetry, and wrote long and short stanzas that those above wouldn't like. Because it was a secret it was stimulating. We also had secret plans to publish satirical papers to paste up on the walls.

The headmaster, thundered with rage. He said: 'If you were in the final years of secondary school you'd have done enough to be labelled Rightists.' He huffed and snorted as he tore down one of our cartoons: 'Why are you satirizing Communist Youth League members? Why have you drawn dogs fighting? Too noxious and poisonous. You've even written "Wolf, wolf!". Who are you trying to get at?' We all shrivelled up. And only fourteen.

For the first time it was clear: it was a forbidden game.

4

In 1959 I went to the 101 Secondary School. Just like in the army schools we had brass buttons on our uniforms, and wore caps. I put some effort into keeping to the regulations, and didn't dare mention my own poems. In assembly before the whole school I read Mayakovsky's poetry.

When I shouted out another's poetry I was taking the opportunity to vent my own frustrations, and this also took courage. My bravery had its source in the secret love I harboured for a supremely elegant girl — Zhang Meijun. The two of us directed the play, 'New Year's Sacrifice', in commemoration of Lu Xun, and had enjoyed working together. Backstage we would chat with Guo Shiying, who played the lead role, 'the traveller'. I had never been able to stand his father — old revolutionary poet, Guo Moruo. But his son was all right: quite open, easy going, intelligent. Nothing like his rabbit of a father. I had a lot of respect for him, and he also wrote poetry.

Two or three years later, I heard Guo Shiying had been arrested. They had a little literary group, underground of course. In the Cultural Revolution, I heard he took his own life. I couldn't believe it, but he was dead. Just because he wanted to use his brain to think about things. Only later did I hear what really happened: he had been beaten to death.

Humans are truly fragile animals.

5

In 1960 Zhang Wenxing was at the secondary school attached to the Foreign Languages Institute, reading French, playing the guitar, singing, reading poetry, writing poetry, painting.

He was stubborn yet warm-hearted, had a thick brow and large eyes, lips drawn into a line. He was short, but he exercised his body until he had muscles of steel. He had never lost at anything, and he was known as 'Little Napoleon'. His poetry was just like him, it lashed out.

We transferred to the secondary school attached to the Foreign Languages Institute, very near to Liulichang, the secondhand book market. After school we used to linger in the old bookshops. Mayakovsky's poetry could no longer satisfy our hunger. We found

Pushkin, Lermontov ..., and later Longfellow, Whitman ... What excited us most of all was discovering that a girl in our class, Dai Yongxu, was the daughter of a famous poet, Dai Wangshu. We ran over to borrow collections of his poems. But she brought out her father's translations of 'Selected Poems of Lorca'. I flicked it open at the foreword, and one line shook us:

> *The black night made black by the night*

Perhaps it is because I liked to paint, that lines like 'Little black horse, great big moon' made me so happy. I used to read these translated poems, my teeth stuck into a bun made with sweet potato. In times of hardship people look for things to eat. And out of our hunger for art we formed a group. Apart from Zhang Wenxing, there was:

Zhang Xinhua. Crazy about art. Didn't have enough to feed himself but painted in oils. Ready to risk his life for his friends.

Yu Zhixin. Sentimental. Spoke beautiful French. His constant frown was famous. Feet a little off the ground.

Zhang Zhenzhou. A plumpish, tall beauty with a very kind heart. Wrote prose poetry.

Yang Xiaomin. A scholarly type of girl. Wrote prose. Sensitive, seemed slightly nervous.

Dong Shabei. Very dark and very thin, lean and tough. Attached to the College of Fine Art while at secondary school. Painted modernist oil paintings. Interested in religion and mysticism.

Zhang Runfeng. The youngest of us. Quick thinking, very good mimic, outstanding memory.

We often organised poetry evenings, usually at my home, though sometimes at other people's. Gan Lulin and Chen Naiyun who I'd known at secondary school would often join in too.

6

In 1962, there was a group of poetry lovers at the Central College of Applied Arts. Zhang Jiman, the chairman of our Student's Association, and I discussed the two groups coming together to hold a large scale recital.

We were very excited about it, and everyone was busy preparing his weapon. I polished up a long poem 'Burning Heart'. Yang Xiaomin invited another girl along, Jiang Dingyue — the daughter of Jiang Guangding, famous general from the War against Japan. Her eyebrows were straight as swords, truly 'a tiger of a daughter from a general's home'. People said she looked Spanish.

About a hundred and ten people turned up that day, there weren't enough seats, and the back of the room was filled with people standing. We secondary school students were full of valiant spirit, and 'shook' that group of university students. When everyone had left, the university students Huang Wei, Zhang Hongbin and Zhang Mingming (daughter of the celebrated romantic writer, Zhang Henshui) showered us with praise.

My poem's concluding line was:

We — the Sun Brigade!

'Let's start right now!' shouted Shabei, excited. Everyone was talking all at once, volunteering to get on with the printing, and so on, a whole run of plans. Half of us spent the whole night walking up and down the streets, and the other half talked the night away at my house.

At the time, it was no more than our love for poetry, and our love for art. Excitement and feedback. Hadn't given a thought to the threatening shadow of politics. What had that to do with poetry?

7

Dai Qing, who was studying then at the Harbin College of Military Engineering, took us out to the Summer Palace. They had heard that I liked to recite poetry. In the evening, in the long open corridors I started reciting Mayakovsky, then Eluard's 'Freedom' ... and they were all amazed. Dai Qing told me she too loved literature. But it seemed perhaps we were a little too 'modern'. I reckoned she had never even heard of this French poet before.

We were moved by the interest and generosity of these university students. Yet I had not let them hear my strange 'inappropriate-for-the-time' poems. I guessed there'd be trouble if I did.

We had to serve two masters, one was society and the other was our own pleasure.

8

In 1963 I entered the Central College of Fine Art. The College had a poetry society, 'Reed Swords', named for Qu Yuan's life story. The name of this society had been written in the calligraphy of Mr Wen Huaisha. The first leader was Fan Zeng, followed by me and Bai

Rubo. At the poetry readings of the society Fan Zeng chanted Zheng Banqiao's lament:

The old fisherman, a single rod ...

The secretary of the Communist Youth League, believed Fan Zeng was reviving the ancient, and frowned at it. He wanted me to read something modern. All I could offer was old Maya. The secretary frowned even more.

When we came out, I saw Fan Zeng in the corridor; we shook hands and laughed. We were neither of us good children in the eyes of authority.

9

'The Sun Brigade' had really held its first big meeting. That was in the Xiaozhuang Building of the old Beijing Normal University. Taking part were: Zhang Wenxing, Zhang Xinhua, Dong Shabei, Yu Zhixin, Zhang Zhenzhou, Zhang Runfeng and myself. I draft a constitution for the organisation. Its aim was none other than to encourage the national cultures of China to flourish. We planned to hold a salon once a month. We would hang paintings on the walls and read poetry. Only as a formed strong group would we be able to break into society.

At about this time I wrote the one act play 'Dialogue', the film script, 'Turquoise', and a collection of short poems.

However, after only a few days the 'Brigade' disbanded.

Guo Shiying (at the time in the Philosophy Department at Beijing University) and their salon wanted to sneak out to France. They were caught and all of them were arrested — grasses scattered in the piercing winter wind. We immediately ceased all the organisation's activities, and scattered to bide our time.

1 0

During 1964–65 the pressure on the underground salons grew ever greater. The artist Yuan Yunsheng's graduation piece 'Memory of the Water Country' was seen as a product of the Western capitalist artistic view. 'Fine Art' magazine printed the painting. In the schools knives were out and bowstrings taut. This enormous oil painting was removed from the gallery, and placed in the table tennis room, ready for criticism.

The three artists, Yuan Yunsheng, Ding Shaoguang and Zhang Shiyan, were firm friends of ours. By then Yuan Yunsheng had already gone to Jilin, and still didn't realize he was heading for disaster.

Wu Erlu, Yu Zhixin, Jiang Dingyue and I split up to think over how we could save our friend. I had a brainwave: steal the painting! If the target had disappeared there would be nothing to criticise. At the time I really liked that painting.

I decided to do it on my own. During a Youth League meeting, when there was no one in the grounds, I slipped into the gym, and cut the painting out of its frame, rolled it up and sneaked out of the school.

When the painting was laid out on the floor in my sitting room, Wu Erlu came over to enjoy it. I was sweating all over, on the one hand happy for Old Yuan and on the other pleased with myself for this heroic success.

The Public Security came bursting into the College, to sort out the political case. The atmosphere was tense.

My mates all came to look at the painting and do homage to my courage. With true feminine pragmatism Jiang Dingyue warned me that when the authorities found out about this, I'd go to jail.

I couldn't give a toss, not a damn. I believed we were all brothers.

11

The meetings become more and more secret, and the members were changing.

At the time Wu Hong was closest to me. We had both been to 101 Secondary, and were now in the same class. We shared the same interests and ambitions and were both in love with Jiang's daughters; I was wooing Jiang Dingyue, he was courting Jiang Dinghui. Their brother Jiang Zhiqiao wrote classical poetry. Their home hosted the salon during this period.

Another salon was at Zhou Qiyue's. We had been friends since we were little. They had the latest Western records at his house. We began to be fans of modern music.

One day we were having lunch at his house, playing modern German opera. His father came in, looking dreadful. I didn't even notice. I should really have switched to a classical opera when the first side had finished, but I put on the other side. Oh, hell.

I was really letting my friends in for it.

The old couple wanted a word with me, then showed me the yellow card. At the time I thought they were over-cautious. Now when I think back, they had a long, deeply cutting memory of political cruelty.

1 2

Mou Dunbai was the youngest person involved in Guo Shiying's 'French Connection', and was let out first. He came running to find me.

There was a salon at his house too, including: Wang Dongbai, Gan Huili, Guo Dadong, and later I also saw Guo Lusheng. We used to meet quite often, and play secret poetry writing games, and drink wine. We had no money, and could only drink the crudest liquor. Very often we had some pickled or salted vegetables to go with it. There was one time when Dong Shabei brought along a dark beet, and we used a pencil sharpener to peel it, and everyone found it really delicious. Zhang Shiyan was an old friend, and already had a job. Every time he came to see us he would bring a bottle of 'Chinese Red'. Everyone was happy.

1 3

I also tried sending in manuscripts to *People's Literature*, and didn't have any success because the editor in chief lost his position for political reasons.

We decided to publish our own hand-written magazine, which we did on a small scale at my house. My parents also joined in. There was Geng Jun, Wu Feng, Jiang Dingyue, Zhang Dawei, Zhang Liaoliao, and so on. The cover of the issue I edited had an iron bars, behind which you could see two red characters for: Freedom.

Perhaps it was because I didn't feel confident in freedom.

1966. Yuan Yunsheng's painting, 'The Sun Brigade', the secret meetings, the French students here, my political jokes — all kinds of reasons, I was arrested, I fled … In the hurried parting from my friends I wrote on the inside cover of Wang Chenbai's notebook: 'Believe in the future'.

When I escaped to the South, Gan Huili wrote a sad farewell poem 'I don't believe: you have already left' (I'm not sure of the title anymore).

I was arrested again. First in the school, then in the cells of the Public Security Bureau, I was questioned countless times. Again and again I was asked about that 'counter-revolutionary organisation, the 'Sun Brigade'. All of my work was investigated. Maybe to this day it is still in the archives of the Beijing Public Security Bureau, maybe it was cremated long ago.

I am a poet with no works.

14

I've heard that people are already beginning to research the history of the underground literature from this period; that they are actively collecting and editing compilations of the scraps of work that survive from this time.

At the end of the day was there ever an underground literary organisation called the 'Sun Brigade'? That is just hearsay.

UNDERGROUND POETRY IN BEIJING 1970–1978

DUO DUO

translated by John Cayley

I'm often stuck by a thought when I see a packet of 'Hero' cigarettes on a tobaconnist's stall: the heroes of the times we lived through have already been buried in history, while today a bunch of featherweights are in the ascendant. Because of this, I feel I've no choice but to give some account of those times.

The beginning of the winter of 1970 was an early spring for youth in Beijing. Two fashionable books, *Catcher in the Rye* and *The Starred Ticket* blew a breath of fresh air in amongst Beijing's youth. Then there was a 'library' of limited circulation books — intended for the eyes of high officials only — which turned up everywhere in the city: *Zigu and Other Stories*, Ionesco's *The Chair*, Sartre's *Nausea and Other Stories*, etc. And then the first batch of underground books, Bi Ruxie's novel, *The Ninth Wave*, Gan Huili's *When the Lotus Opened Out Once More*, and Guo Lusheng's *Believe in the Future*.

The name of Guo Lusheng is associated with the best poet of Beijing's secondary school students. When I first read his poetry it left me cold. Like any other secondary school student, I didn't like poetry. Only after I became a writer myself did I begin to understand Guo Lusheng's work. Only the passage of many years and meetings with many young poets managed to change its significance for me. As far as I can see, even today there is nobody whose work comes up to the level of purity achieved by Guo's early love poetry. It was the winter of 1974 when I first saw him, by which time he was already in nervous decline, and, as I remember it, Guo Lusheng was a unique example of a poet who went mad, since the suicide of Zhu Xiang in 1931. Guo was the first to fall on the battlefield of New Poetry in the 70s.

Mang Ke, Yue Zhong (who also wrote as Genzi) and I got to know one another in 1964. We were all thirteen, successful entrants to Beijing's Number Three secondary school, class seven. We were all sent down to the countryside in Baiyang Lake in Hebei province at the beginning of 1969. When he entered the first year of secondary school, a piece by Yue Zhong was published in the *Beijing Evening News*. The first line was, 'August, when bright red haw fruit fills the branches ...' In early 1968 Yue Zhong and I wrote a little 'Old Style' classical poetry. I remember that, for the 73rd anniversary of Chairman Mao's birth, he took up his pen and wrote the lines: 'In 1893 / a red sun rose in Yaoshan. / After seventy-four turning years, / light and heat reach all the world.' In the late autumn of 1968, he wrote a traditional lyric for a school-mate, Zhan Weiming, on his being sent down to the countryside: 'Weiming's been sent to Mongolia, / bravely taking the great high road / to the northern borderlands' frost, cold, ice and frozen bones, / the journey's far but his hero's heart is steadfast.' Apart from this sort of stuff, none of us had known anyone to even consider the preposterous idea of writing poetry.

One day in the summer of 1971 turned out to be an important day for me. Mang Ke brought us a poem, and Yue Zhong's reaction took me by surprise. 'The blue flame of the blizzard ...' He repeatedly intoned this line from Mang Ke's poem as if he was savouring some delicacy. Clearly, I had had no previous understanding of Yue Zhong's deep feeling for poetry. My notebook of this period contain extracts from Rommel's *War Diaries* and Garraudi's *Human Perspective*. On the eve of the Spring Festival in 1972, Yue Zhong passed on to me the first great shock of his life, 'March and the Last Days'. I remember sitting on the loo and reading it several times. Not only did I fail to understand it, this poem somehow offended me deeply — I was furious with it! I realized that my saying that I didn't know what poetry was actually concealed an notion concerning my own judgements on poetry: Poetry *must not be* written in this way. Because Yue Zhong's poem was unlike anything else I had ever read before (I'd already read Ai Qing and thought of him as the best poet writing since the vernacular began to be used in poetry in 1917), I came to this conclusion about Yue Zhong's piece: It was not a poem. It was similar to my experience with Guo Lusheng — only the passing of time allowed me more and more to feel my way into Yue Zhong's savage inner world. This poetry is inhuman, unconstrained. Fourteen years later I encapsulated my impression of Yue Zhong: 'Dangling rotting flesh from its beak, bedazzling the sky's brightness'. Following on from 'March and the Last Days', Yue Zhong produced seven more long poems in one single creative flow. Amongst these are 'Baiyang Lake', 'Orange Mist', and 'Bridge over the Abyss'. (At the time I thought this was the best of them and today Yue Zhong still approves of this poem.) What I now regret is only being able to find three of these poems; the rest are lost.

In the summer of 1972 there was a small cultural salon in the residential complex of the State Council with Xu Haoyuan as its main instigator and supporter. She was a graduate of the secondary school attached to the People's University, a favoured radical during the Cultural Revolution and a representative of the old Red Guards. Because her poem 'Whole River Blue' ('Man *jiang qing*') included some insinuations about Jiang Qing, she was put into prison for two years. When she came out she began enthusiastically promoting western culture. Fortunately, as singers, both Yue Zhong and I were able to attend the salon, although the majority attending were artists and poets. The musical Yue Zhong immediately became a central figure in the salon — he was soon to be selected as a bass singer for the Central Musical Ensemble (and is still of the company). I am tenor who will never be able to reach the high notes. Together we sang, went to exhibitions, exchanged books, celebrated birthdays, went on outings … At that time no one knew that Yue Zhong was a poet. One name rang out louder than the others as following in the wake of Guo Lusheng: that was Yi Qun.

Yi Qun was a graduate of the Beijing Fifth secondary school. He was not only a poet but wrote scripts for films. He caused a sensation with *Centenary Memoirs of the Paris Commune*, *The Avenue of Everlasting Peace*, *Hello Sorrow* (published in *Today*). Even the early work of Yi Qun is formally quite distinct from that of Guo Lusheng; it is heavily laced with symbolism. Guo Lusheng's mentor was He Jingzhi and his work paid careful attention to ornate diction. By contrast, Yi Qun's poetry concentrates on image; its influences came from Europe and its language searched for concision. Yi Qun may be considered the first formal revolutionary.

Yue Zhong's poetry was quickly introduced into the salon. Xu Haoyuan immediately gave her verdict: 'Yue Zhong is the Overlord of Poetry. No one can match him in writing verse.' During the second half of 1972, the salon was confined within Yue Zhong's gilded cage and Yi Qun's influence gradually declined. The artists Peng Gang, Tan Xiaochun, Lu Yansheng, Lu Shuangjin were also part of the salon and they all wrote poetry. A line from Tan Xiaochun runs, '… your red head scarf stiffens on the edge of the sky …' Peng Gang was one of the first modernist painters, after Dong Shabei and Zhou Manyou. At the time he was just seventeen and his untamed power rocked the salon. He was something of a genius. Later he was accepted into the Department of Chemistry at Beijing University, and now lives in America.

Yue Zhong was also a natural talent. His father was a script writer at the Beijing Film Studio, and had a library of over four thousand books. Before he was fifteen, he read such limited circulation books as Erenberg's P*eople, Time, Life*. These were the kind of things that made him wiser than his years. He was nineteen when he wrote 'March and the Last Days' and the seven other long poems; then nothing for fifteen years. His history was miraculous: in secondary school he re-sat the examination in mathematics; he played the flute as soon as he picked it up; his caricatures made even their victims laugh; and he could master a talent without a teacher — on the pier in Baiyang Lake he just sang out a few notes and got into the Central Musical Ensemble. When we were younger, we were inseparable. If it hadn't been for Yue Zhong's poetry (or you might say, if it hadn't been for my hatred of his poetry) I would never have been able to write verse.

On the nineteenth of June 1972, while seeing off a friend at Beijing rail station, a line of verse came to me: 'The windows open like eyelids.' It was at this point that I started writing and by the end of the year I had produced my first volume of poetry. Xu Haoyuan heard about it before I had finished, she said to me, 'I've heard you've been 'stringing some lines together'. Let's have a look at them.' She wasn't the only one to be suspicious, since I was interested in serious thinking. Peng Gang had this reaction: 'You write better than you talk — When you talk you're too 'correct'!' Yi Qun's response was about the same as Yue Zhong's, dubious, unconvinced. Yet my arrogant heroic heart was clearly infectious. He wanted me to write with greater simplicity, more emotional sincerity, and at the same time to show concern for the fate of Chinese culture. This provides some explanation why Yi Qun himself finally gave up writing poetry.

As the summer of 1973 was coming in, Yue Zhong's luck took a turn for the worse. A poem of his that had been much copied and widely circulated was sent to the Public Security Bureau. Only after it had been vetted by the Institute of Chinese Literature and found to be of no great harm, was the matter settled. Yue Zhong put down his pen. When, towards the end of 1973, my first volume of poetry won praise from a good many young poets, Yue Zhong gave me a piece of advice: Never again look for fame by carrying your poems about all over the place! The salon was dissolved due to political pressures, but the circle in which hand-written copies of poems circulated had broadened. My poetic friendship with Mang Ke dates from this time. We agreed, at the end of every year, as if exchanging pistol shots in a duel, to exchange collections of poetry.

It was also in this year that I noted down the first lines from Mang Ke:

'Suddenly, hope turns to tears falling on the ground,
and how can we know if tomorrow may be without sadness?'
'You, great earth, you arouse my passion.'

Mang Ke was a natural poet. When we were sixteen we rode the same horse-drawn cart on the journey to Baiyang Lake. Baiyang Lake was a place full of undiscovered genius, with a long-standing reputation for producing valiant inhabitants. I lived there for six years, Yue Zhong for three, and Mang Ke for seven years. I never imagined it would be turn out to be a sort of cradle. At that time there were quite a few people in Baiyang Lake writing poetry, such as Song Haiquan and Fang Han. Later Bei Dao, Jiang He and Gan Tiesheng all came to have a look. Mang Ke really took to the life of mother nature's son: playing ball, fighting, fooling around. The 'I' of his poetry is always naked, sensual, wild. What he wanted to express was perplexity not conclusiveness. The effect of perplexity endures most strongly, clear argument only begins to take control outside the realm of art. The force of life in Mang Ke is what we most admire; never reading books, but reading newspapers; singing by and from the heart. Yet we shouldn't consider it strange if, in Mang Ke's more recent poetry, we find 'thought' — he was a top pupil in mathematics at our secondary school.

There were more poets after 1973: Shi Baojia, Ma Jia, Yang Hua, Lu Yansheng, Peng Gang, Lu Shuangjin, Yan Li, and so on. Amongst them I also see an older generation including Mou Dunbai. He was the same generation as Gan Huili and Zhang Langlang, who had begun their artistic activities in the sixties. And there were the painters, Zhou Manyou, Dong Shabei, etc. My contacts with this generation were limited. They had truly been born at the wrong time, caught up in the Cultural Revolution during their most creative years. After these ten years, they gave up writing.

In 1973 I read Shi Baojia's 'Old Style' classical poetry, and was impressed by his talent. Unfortunately, I didn't record any of it. Today I have only a few fragments from other writers to hand.

Ma Jia:

• Only if
            you can learn
                        to accept permission
from a young girl's lips
will you
            walk with love
                        over all this earth ...

• My poetry has no flag
It emits a ray
                        of sunlight
                                    more naked than
                                                a girl's breasts

• I am as heavy
as the wild fruits of autumn,
I am filled with all of October, everything ...

• Apart from wine
there's always wine.
Before I was twenty
every day was a party.

Lu Shengjin (female):

• It's not that life is vile
but we are not innocent, not for a minute, faced with the past.

• My life is like a field that's been ploughed.
Take what you want. Leave. There's nothing I can say about it ...

Lu Yansheng:

• Everything
            is so banal
            so reasonable
            so intolerable to me.

• Following a road I cannot see
I keep on walking, walking.
Indistinctly
    I sense
        the quiet, the pleasant sadness

Peng Gang:

• Whenever I see the sun
    my heart melts
        comfort and ease
            spreading out all over the earth.

• Oh!
    Father
        Mother
I'm like a little child.
    Walking, walking
        I have given up everything that was mine …

Yang Hua:

• The pluck of the English and the cut of their trousers —
I am a handsome and elegant young man.
My songs rang out from behind the fence …

At the end 1974 I brought out my third collection of poems, and Mang Ke swapped it for one of his own right on time. Mang Ke and Peng Gang had formed the very first 'Avant-garde' school, and dragged me into it. In total there were only the two of them in the group and it survived for two months. Beijing had no other salons or literary organizations apart from a few small, scattered circles. I had met Bei Dao and Jiang He early on in the winter of 1970. I was introduced to Bei Dao at this time as a fellow tenor. Later he became very close to Mang Ke, and made a special trip to meet him in Baiyang Lake. I didn't see Bei Dao again after that until 1978. So the first poem of his which I recall is 'Golden Trumpet'. Later I was part of a social circle with Jiang He and Gong Jisui, often talking through the night with them. After 1973, you might as well say that poetic activity on any significant scale amongst Beijing youth had ceased. As far as the disparate manifestations of poetry during the years 1970–78 are concerned, I've only touched on a very small part of the whole, and have proved a rather unsatisfactory witness to its poets. But we were one generation. I can't conceive of closer, blood-like, relationships than those between myself, Mang Ke and Yue Zhong. Since we were all thirteen, nearly twenty-five years have passed. The friendship between us, our disputes and confrontations, have pulled us even closer together amongst the teeming poetic constellations. With some satisfaction I see that Mang Ke has recently achieved the pinnacle of poetic maturity, and I believe that Yue Zhong may also rise at any time.

In 1978, *Today* confronted the world.

YESTERDAY'S TODAY OR TODAY'S YESTERDAY

A CHENG

translated by Frances Wood*

It was when I hit twenty that I began to reminisce about the past. People say that only the old dwell on the past. I agree. At a time like this, when everyone is afraid of growing old, it's not easy to be frank.

Lots of people pride themselves on their memory for detail, but I'm not like that; I can only recall atmosphere. At the beginning of his memoirs, Shostakovich quotes Meyerhold who apparently told a story about a Professor of Law. When he was lecturing on the reliability of witnesses, he was suddenly interrupted by a hooligan who burst into the lecture theatre, causing complete mayhem and finally becoming violent. After he'd been taken away by the police, the Professor asked his students to describe the event. Each student said what he or she thought had happened and what the hooligan had looked like, some even insisted that there were several of them. The Professor finally put an end to it by explaining that the whole incident had been set up to demonstrate the limited value of eye-witness testimony.

And why can't I avoid the use of reported speech and quotation in this memoir? Well, that's my style.

THE FIRST POET

In the 1980s, Guo Lusheng used to come to my home near the Desheng Gate, to talk. Often, as we chatted, I told him how much I'd enjoyed his poetry, twenty years before, in the late 1960s. His poems were widely circulated as hand-copied samizdat. 'Widely circulated' is how I'd put it — emotionally, subjectively — not that I have access to statistics on manuscript circulation. It's just that I think his poems deserved wide circulation. Like everyone else, I obtained copies of his po-

---

* With much help from Wang Tao.

ems and then I lent my notebooks to other friends to copy. At the time, I couldn't even spell the characters of his name.

Once I opened my notebook to look at a poem which I'd copied back then, the *Shoal of Fish* trilogy. When I'd copied it, I could only find two parts of the trilogy and because I still hoped to find the third part, I'd left two blank pages: a fisherman waiting patiently for a bite.

I remember that in 1969, I was sent to work in the countryside in the Arong Banner in Inner Mongolia. I was assigned to a village called Dongxingfa. In winter the wind whistled outside so that when I got hold of a copy of Guo Lusheng's poem, 'Wine', I copied it using the heated brick bed as a table.

After the Campaign against Spiritual Pollution, Guo Lusheng was being treated in the Anding Mental Hospital. He was one of their 'model patients'. Whenever he felt a bit off, he'd get on a number 14 bus and go to the hospital. If it was serious, he'd stay a while and then get on a number 14 and go back home. The number 14 passed by Desheng Gate, and sometimes, on his way in or out of hospital, Guo Lusheng would get off the bus at the stop near my home and call in. If I say he came quite often, it isn't that he was often ill, it's just that he came quite often. I also used to visit his home near the Fucheng Gate. He lived with his parents in a typical 1950s Soviet-style block of flats. We ate dumplings which often burst as they were boiled. The stuffing was no great shakes but there was plenty of it.

In winter, Guo Lusheng used to wear a cotton 'pig's ear' hat, a Russian-style hat with ear flaps that can be lowered or tied on the top or just left sticking out like a pig's ears. Hats like that had virtually disappeared in the 1960s but Guo Lusheng still looked fine in his. Some people look good in fashionable clothes; some, like Guo Lusheng, have style, even when dressed unfashionably. When he knocked at the door, I saw him through the window. He would look up at the sky, his hands tucked into his sleeves, quietly waiting for the door to be opened. He looked like a small figure in an ancient painting, knocking at an old door on a snowy night.

He'd often say, 'I've just written a poem, have a listen and see what you think.' Then he'd throw his head back, pause for a moment and begin the recital. His voice was low; perhaps I shouldn't call it a recitation, the sounds rose and fell, almost like Russian.

Listening to him, I often thought of his poems of the 1960s but whenever I asked about them, he became embarrassed and said they were all poor, childish stuff. When he talked like that, I thought that perhaps it was because of my youth that I'd enjoyed them. But then I thought of the text I'd learnt in the last year of primary school: 'Autumn has come, / the geese fly south, / now in a wing shape, / now in a line', which is something you can appreciate whatever your age.

Once, Guo Lusheng spoke of a poem he was about to write. He'd visited an old General and planned to compose an epic about Mao Zedong and the Civil War period. This seemed, to say the least, a bit out of step, since this was just the moment when grave doubts were being raised about the events and people involved, although it's true that that fashionable word 'culture' hadn't come into it yet.

I listened attentively. I'm pretty slow by nature and often give people the wrong impression. Guo Lusheng paused and waited for my reaction. When I'm struggling to express myself, I often resort to polite formulae, rather like when someone knocks at the door and you are struggling to get your trousers on, calling out, 'I'm coming, please wait a moment, I'm coming,' instead of just swearing at them.

It struck me that this was the second time he was doing something out of step, the first being the *Shoal of Fish* trilogy. I can't remember if I told him so or not — it's a constant problem with me, thinking I've told people what I think when in fact I haven't. It's the result of years of education at the hands of poor and lower-middle peasants. When you are forever on your own, working hard in the mountains, thoughts run through your head and create the illusion of conversation. I remember once in Mongolia listening to someone singing loudly. When I asked him what it was he was singing, he asked me, 'Was I singing?'

Guo Lusheng was in high spirits and we arranged to meet at someone's house a few days later. I think I gave him a definite opinion: that there were plenty of eulogies and laments about the Revolutionary Struggle and Mao Zedong but that poetry was lacking and he, Guo, was a poet.

A few days later, I followed Guo Lusheng to a house in a military compound outside the Fuxing Gate. It was the first time I'd ever been there; a telephone call had to be made by the sentry at the gate who only let me in after confirmation and we made our way to one of the many courtyard houses off the main square. I saw a young cripple in a wheelchair and, though he explained in a low voice how he'd been injured, seeing him so full of life, I forgot the reason. Guo Lusheng explained that he'd been talking about the past with the cripple's father. The young man looked rather uncomfortable with this and changed the subject to the current economic reforms. Some others came in, all full of confidence, including several tall, extremely good-looking young ladies in fashionable clothes, what the Book of Songs would have called 'merciless beauties'. Guo Lusheng recited a poem and everyone listened politely, and then began to talk about politics. Guo Lusheng seemed drab in their company, sickly, smiling modestly yet maintaining a sense of his own worth. His parents must also have been part of this 'ruling class'. His name Lusheng, 'Born on the March' must mean that he was born while they were on a military campaign. The room was centrally heated and very hot. Outside the window, the branches of a willow swayed back and forth and a dry autumn leaf fell pattering like rain against the glass.

I suddenly realised that what Guo Lusheng was about to write was something that came out of his own emotions and experiences. In the room there was an overpowering feeling that 'this country belongs to us'. You could dismiss everyone present as the 'sons and daughters of high officials' but I like people with confidence, no matter who they are. Mao Zedong said to young people, 'The world is yours, it is also ours, but in the final analysis, it is yours,' and it was evident that all these confident and privileged young people were indeed their parents' children. Twenty years before, in the Cultural Revolution, many young people had been angry, feeling that Mao had deceived them. But they'd been wrong. You dream — a thigh-tremblingly pretty girl smiles up at you but before you come, 'suddenly you turn your head and she's there in shadows, hidden from the light'. You have to learn to tell where their eyes are really focused.

I must have been very immature at the time. It wasn't until I was in the first year of secondary school that I realised I definitely wasn't 'one of the Future Masters of the New China' or even a 'Scion of the Motherland'. I know a monk who told me that when he entered the monastery and practised meditation, he always kept his eyes open. When the novice master noticed, he gave my friend a slap on the face, shouting, 'There's nothing here for you to look at!' And my friend was instantly enlightened.

I found the spectacle of these people talking about politics immensely pleasurable. I couldn't decide whether they were ambitious or just arrogant, especially with the tall, healthy girls sitting in their midst. Their fashionable clothes were skimpy and slightly out of place; but they did seem properly looked-after. Their high-heeled boots bore a resemblance to pig's trotters and were so high you felt there should be spurs on them to perfect the charming ensemble they composed with the girls' long legs and broad hips.

But I must keep this poetic. Guo Lusheng wrote poems; he was poetic, and I don't give a damn about his ideology.

THE SECOND POET
(PROVISIONALLY WITHDRAWN)

THE THIRD POET
(PROVISIONALLY WITHDRAWN)

THE FOURTH POET

Not long ago, I heard that Sanwu was dead. The person who told me definitely said 'dead' and not that he'd 'passed away' or 'gone to a better place' or any such thing.

Sanwu's surname was Ye and I don't know what his given name ('Three Noons') referred to. His family lived in a courtyard house at Dong Si, opposite the headquarters of the Writers' Union. I got to know him very late, in 1981, or was it 1982? The way I met him was very simple. I considered myself a music lover and a friend invited me to meet another music lover. It was evening and the street door of the Ye's courtyard was shut. When we knocked, there was no response for a long time. I said there was nobody in, but my friend said he'd phoned. Finally we heard the sound of footsteps and the door opened, whereupon we heard the footsteps receding. The dim light revealed an unusual courtyard house. In old Beijing, officials and merchants lived in the east of the city while intellectuals, lived to the west, like Lu Xun, who lived near the Fucheng Gate. The old houses in the eastern part of the city were still larger than those in the west. Though the Ye's courtyard was filled with rubbish, there was a light in the west wing. It was very dark — I felt that there was a fox spirit hiding there somewhere. People were densely packed in Beijing and when the foxes realised how cramped the city was and how polluting people were, they all moved out, together with the other ghosts and spirits. Things were no longer the same as when I was a child and adults talked of ghosts. Now all you heard about was 'bad elements' while in the 1960s and '70s it had been 'class enemies'.

We entered the west wing. Bedclothes were scattered about in confusion and in the middle of the room was an upright piano. A white arm supported a lolling head lying on the sofa. I was introduced and the white arm was extended. I shook an insubstantial hand; the inclined head, with its watery eyes, nodded. He motioned me to sit down. I hesitated, regretting that I'd come out at the wrong time, to the wrong place, to meet the wrong person, and planned leaving as soon as we'd made our musical introductions. He asked what I'd been listening to recently and I answered, 'Beijing Drum-beat Narrative' The white-armed, drooping head said after a long while, 'I've been listening to Mahler'.

This was Sanwu.

Then we talked about Pavarotti and the atmosphere changed. Sanwu said he had a tape. He got up, found the tape and put it into the tape recorder. When he went to stand, I realised that Sanwu was bent double by rheumatism and couldn't straighten up. His back hurt him and his stomach gave him pain so that his hands were often pressed to his belly. When he coughed, he'd suddenly cringe with pain.

The wonderful voice of Pavarotti filled the room, the strong notes striking the roof and piercing the walls, reaching the spaces formerly occupied by foxes and ghosts. I asked if we shouldn't turn it down but Sanwu said that the courtyard was being repaired and no-one in his family was there. In the front court were strangers who had moved in during the Cultural Revolution and there hadn't been anyway to force them out so — it didn't matter — we just enjoyed the music. Sanwu only had a small portable tape-recorder and the sound was pretty intolerable at that volume but Sanwu listened happily. I realised that he was a music lover, not a hi-fi enthusiast. I've got a friend who is, however. When he invites friends to listen to music it's on a system with a range from 16 hertz bass to 15,000 hertz treble. He's so professional that in the inner circle of hi-fi enthusiasts he's nicknamed 'Balanced Frequency', rather like a modern version of the nicknames assigned to the outlaws in *The Water Margin*.

Night fell on the western wing. Because I had nowhere to live at the time, I often had to scrounge somewhere to sleep and was happy to be offered a camp bed. First we went for a pee. The Ye family had a proper Western toilet which was new to me; I pulled the chain twice just to watch the water running out. Before we went to sleep, Sanwu said he'd read me one of his most recent poems. It was then that I realised that Ye Sanwu was one of the older generation of Beijing poets. When he recited, his voice shook, and when he'd finished, he always said, 'But there's another verse,' or 'Let's hear another,' turning the pages of several notebooks until he found one. 'I wrote this twenty years ago; listen ...'

At dawn, I went out onto the veranda. It was a lovely courtyard though it was a pity that the great tower of the Writers' Union blocked out the sun. I felt jealous. I asked Sanwu what great and virtuous things he'd done to deserve such a fine place. Doubled-up, with his head on one side, Sanwu looked over the scattered building materials and said, 'Fuck it, Ye Shengtao is my grandfather.' Ye Shengtao, writer, educationalist, and political hard-liner was one of the survivors of the vernacular literature movement early in the century. His 'Fuck it' was resonant, and I understood the significance of that surname.

Ye Sanwu kindly suggested that I might meet his grandfather but I never took up the invitation because there are some people I'd rather observe from a distance. Sometimes, when I was sitting in the west wing, the old man would stroll up and down on the veranda, his grey shadow moving back and forth against the frosted glass while I silently repeated the title of a story of his that was in every secondary school textbook, 'We're thirty-five pecks over, we're thirty-five pecks over ...'

Of all the poets I knew in Beijing, Sanwu was unique in that politics never entered into his verse, and he never used poetry to discuss politics in metaphor. I don't know if it was the influence of his family but poems are private things and I think that's just how Sanwu thought of them. Perhaps not, I don't know.

Sanwu had two daughters. The younger one was learning the piano. She was very bright: playing Mozart in a singlet and shorts. She would suddenly interrupt any accompanying conversation to argue with her father. Sanwu's voice was hard and harsh. She'd shake her head, her hands keeping up with the melody all the time. Sanwu knew the composer Shi Wanchun and said he hoped his daughter would study composition with him because being a pianist was too competitive.

Sanwu had his own poetical contacts. Whenever I talked about poets I admired, Sanwu was most content and would say warmly, 'Ah, when Bei Dao first came here I taught him how to write and now he's famous ... Mang Ke, Duo Duo, I taught them all. But Duo Duo has a bad temper.'

I didn't want to check out his references like a personnel officer, not the kinds of things someone says when they're happily carried away and especially not if it's someone in constant pain.

Sanwu's stomach pains didn't affect his appetite. If anyone invited him for a meal, he immediately became serious and rather pathetic, combing his hair well in advance and shouting at his daughters if they were slow getting ready. Once autumn arrived, Mongolian hotpot was served in Beijing and Sanwu would respond to every invitation to eat it. He always rode his old bike, even in the cold winter wind. Thinking of him bent double on his bike in the cold, some people could hardly bear to invite him out but if he discovered such an omission, he'd get so angry that both his back *and* his stomach would hurt. He could only ride a slow-moving ladies' bike because he couldn't swing his leg over a crossbar and he'd fix his walking stick to the back carrier. When he arrived at a restaurant, he'd park his bike, pay his two cent parking fee, take up his walking stick and make his way in. He had to be careful at the door because Sanwu could only see if someone was out at the same time if he twisted his lowered head sideways. Once inside, he'd spot the table and the other diners instantly. He sat down, his eyes moist and expectant, for good food of all sorts was to be cherished. 'Cracking fire and dry wood' is a phrase usually used to describe sexual attraction between a man and a woman but it is hardly adequate to describe Sanwu's approach to food. He was the best eater I've ever seen. The Han dynasty rhapsodic rhyme prose, *Drinking Wine,* sings the joy of drinking in a poetic manner. Since Sanwu's death, eating as a poetic theme has, alas, disappeared.

His enthusiasm for food didn't prevent Sanwu from noticing women. He could swallow at great speed at the same time as twisting his head to follow a girl with his eyes and murmur his approval. In Zhang Zongzi's *Dream Memory of Tao'an* he describes someone and goes on to say that a man without any flaw can never be a true friend since he has no real essence. Whenever it was a question of food or women, Sanwu didn't seem like a sick man. I loved to see him at these times. He was a hedonist and so what? If a nation of 1.2 billion people perishes, it will probably be because they didn't have any flaws.

Sanwu often talked of the women he'd had affairs with in the past. I don't know any of them so I can't comment. The private affairs of men and women are not like food and drink. Careless talk can cost you your relationships.

Sanwu must have had quite a bad reputation for it was not uncommon for people to disparage him. When he talked about people, he, too, was frequently disdainful. He had an awful lot of acquaintances but they gradually drifted away so I often saw new faces in his rooms. 'Hmm, so-and-so wants to go to such-and-such a country,' he'd say, prodding his stomach, 'I'll give him a hand'. He often asked me, with great seriousness, whether I wanted to go abroad and said he could help. I didn't know what to answer and wouldn't commit myself, but I quite enjoyed listening to his boasts. But now when I think of him, 'stuck' in Beijing until he died, I believe that he was a true hedonist and worthy of our admiration.

He didn't write traditional poetry, at least he may have written some, but he never recited any of it. He wrote in a foreign style. Once when, as usual, he had been lying on the sofa for a long time, he said, 'A poem came to me yesterday,' and his voice began to tremble, 'When your daughter's wedding day comes round, / you'll reach for the bottle as midnight strikes …'

1985

LI TUO

translated by Anne Wedell-Wedellsborg

Such was 1985: although various exciting events occurred, people did not think that this year had any special significance. Nor did they realize that in the future they would often look back at 1985 (or, to use a more popular and vivid Beijing expression: look back after each step). However, as time goes by, the uniqueness of 1985 and the profound significance of the changes that quietly took place that year, as well as their omnipresent influence on China, have become increasingly evident and exciting to consider. These days, the year 1985 has become a topic that can make the eyes of many mainland intellectuals shine with excitement. People ceaselessly ask and discuss the question: what was going on during that year? Why should so many changes all have happened then? How should we evaluate these changes?

However, I do not intend to answer or discuss these questions with a straight face right now as I write what will follow under the title '1985'. That would be too serious. I only want to talk about 1985, and randomly at that, but I do want to mix it with some memories to draw out the talk or rather, play it down. Certainly, no matter how randomly I do it, I know that it is hard for me to escape the fate of making a myth out of 1985. Yet I do not want to escape this fate. How can I escape it? Once a person realizes that whatever they say actually has nothing to do with what is signified in their speech or writing, that this is a game of power, they should relax and play the game rather than look around in hesitation.

In discussing the year 1985, I believe that it is best to start with what led up to it. However, this requires a lot of writing and research. Furthermore, it calls for a serious academic attitude. I do not want to do it this way, not only because that will run counter to the purpose of this paper, but also because I cannot bear it — my heart just cannot. Why must exact facts, cold analysis or ruthless 'internal logic' kill an extremely vivid, though obscure, bit of the past? Let it live. Therefore, although I know clearly that most of the events of 1985 germinated at the end of 1983 or the beginning of 1984, and that we need to go there to create a plausible explanation for 1985, I still just want to talk about my own experience. I do not mind that its fragmentary nature will cause my version to lack the necessary authority.

I remember on one night either at the end of 1983 or the beginning of 1984 (I do not recall the exact date) some friends, including Chen Jiangong, Zheng Wanlong and A Cheng came to my home to eat Mongolian hotpot. The room was small and so was the table. We could only sit tightly around the table, our hands and feet knocking against each other. It was not very convenient. What was exciting was the glittering and steaming copper hotpot in the centre of the table. The mixture of smells of mutton and charcoal was so tantalising that the crowding at that moment became a kind of comfort. As usual, A Cheng told stories. At that time he was already well known among friends for his ability to tell stories. He once told me that during the years he spent labouring in the countryside he used to make a living telling stories. Many of the 'educated youth' who had been sent to work there would save their scarce supply of meat, cigarettes and wine to reward A Cheng when he made the rounds of their residential area to tell stories.

Interestingly enough, among the 'long stories' that he was good at telling was *Anna Karenina*. To suit the taste of his listeners he had to delete the character 'na' at the end and so it became, in Chinese, simply 'Anna Kalieni'. He was so famous that some writers would treat him to wine just to seek out his stories. Although we urged him time and again to tell stories, he still refused to be hurried and concentrated on his food and drink. To muffle our anxiety, he chewed loudly with relish and said occasionally 'Eat. Eat first.' He did not raise his sweaty head until after he had eaten like this for nearly an hour. Then he produced the big pipe that he always had with him, slowly packed it, ignited it and inhaled a couple of times. After that he said unhurriedly, 'OK. Today I'm going to tell a story about playing chess.' Then he stopped and continued to smoke one drag after another. Knowing that he was trying to keep us in suspense, we had to beg him again and again: 'Go on! Go on!' 'There's no hurry', A Cheng answered with a smile, and only after all this did he calmly tell us the story of 'The King of Chess', all the while drawing on his pipe and spewing clouds of smoke. Of course the story was still quite different from the novella he wrote later. For example, the character who was to become Wang Yisheng was then simply called the King of Chess. However, the basic structure was already there. The climax of the story, for instance, was the episode where several opponents took turns playing with him. Many details were identical to those in the novella. To this day I still remember how our friends trembled with fear as they listened with bated breath to this episode, as if everybody was walking a tightrope with A Cheng in the sky. The originally brightly-lit room was suddenly a lot darker. Now that I think about it, due to the lack of tones, gesticulations and facial expressions, the novella *The King of Chess* is, in many aspects, far inferior to A Cheng's storytelling version. The former is not as rich as the latter. Friends who are familiar with him might ask him to tell the story once more, but I am afraid that he would decline to do so. At that time, however, the situation was just the opposite. After listening to the story, Chen Jiangong, Zheng Wanlong and I all urged A Cheng to write it down. In our eyes, A Cheng was principally a painter, an important member of the 'Stars Art Exhibition', a guy with a wide range of knowledge, gifted in many ways and uncannily clever. Yet nobody was sure whether he had what it takes to be a good writer. (Actually, among the friends at the table, I seemed to be the only one who knew of his interest in writing, because he showed me several stories he had written, probably when he was working in the countryside in Yunnan Province. He did not pay much attention to writing, nor did he think that he should work hard at it.) But why did that matter? Everyone tried to get a word in to give him some advice. It was chaos, especially when A Cheng calmly tossed a question at us, his glasses glistening: 'Is it going to work? Can this be written into a novella?' Advising turned to scolding, even bullying, the copper pot steaming all the while; it could not have been more chaotic around the dining table.

Perhaps I have written too much about my recollections, but I am seeking to convey the atmosphere then and there, which permeated the entire literary arena. The expression 'the new takes the place of the old' became popular at that time in the media. Our hearts were filled with an indescribable joy whenever we read the expression or used it ourselves. I think that such an atmosphere in the literary arena was also a product of a situation where the new really was taking the place of the old in all areas of life: many writers had started to have doubts about the values implied by the concept of 'collectivism'. However, old habits were still more powerful. The writers always unknowingly took writing as some kind of collective undertaking. At the mention of 'the literary cause', even the most idiosyncratic and naughty writers would get serious. Thus, with the inspiration of a strong sense of mission, writers, poets and critics of different backgrounds, different inclinations and different dispositions formed countless 'small circles', small coteries, small centres. I dare say that from 1983 to 1984, such literary circles could be found all over mainland China. They were ubiquitous, like hot winds whipping around, stimulating each other and making an unprecedented literary storm.

A couple of days ago Zhang Zao, a poet, told me that things like this often happened among a group of young poets in the Chengdu area: after finishing a poem, one would spend a whole night travelling by train to a friend's home. They would then read and analyse the poem and unwittingly spend an entire day in heated disputes and discussions. I was very much moved by this. I can understand this kind of passion. Behind or within the frantic, or even morbid, passion is a kind of pain one experiences when one has to live with a gradual spiritual suicide. In mainland China, every clear-headed and reasonably self-reflexive intellectual experiences this kind of pain: bit by bit you have to commit suicide, to kill the self that contains all your past pursuits and the values for which you lived. From this point of view, Bei Dao's poem, 'The Answer', can be viewed as a proclamation of spiritual suicide, and that is why it created a huge sensation. Of course not everybody could go through the painful and tormenting process of spiritual suicide. Some people lacked courage and others made it clear that they were merely putting on an act.

I believe that all the changes that occurred in 1985 were closely related to this collective spiritual suicide among the intellectuals, especially if we look upon spiritual suicide not only as a real occurrence, but also as a metaphor that has broader implications. To a certain extent, this kind of spiritual suicide provided the motive power for the formation and existence of the innumerable small circles in literary, artistic and scholarly arenas, as well as the cementing power to hold these small organisations together. Maybe it is funny, a comedy: why should a group of people gather together if they were going to commit suicide? Why should it be so lively and noisy? I admit that this question embarrasses me. I can only say that the Chinese cultural tradition lacks a lifestyle which permits a single person to live alone, interrogating his heart and developing his thoughts. Ever since the Spring and Autumn Period (722–481 BC), the habit of thinking of Chinese intellectuals has been collective: The Confucian *Analects* is a prime example. It cannot be merely a coincidence that later books such as the *Analects of Zhu Xi* and *Records of Transmitted Learnings* consist mostly of questions, answers, and correspondences between the thinkers and their disciples.

When this tradition transformed itself in the 1980s into so many small organisations and circles that were doing some frantic thinking, I believe that the new historical circumstances gave it a new nature. If we consider how Deng Xiaoping's reforms caused the market economy to develop vigorously, even feverishly, forming countless cracks and crevices in the fixed structure of socialist China, these small organisations and circles became the embryonic form of some kind of 'public sphere'. Over the decade they would gradually acquire more stable forms and play a more important role in China's development. However, in the early eighties when they were being formed, no one considered, and it would not be possible to consider, these prospects. People gathered together to work on some very urgent problems. After the two earthquakes of the Cultural Revolution and the 'Reforms' (the latter still ongoing), what was not in ruins?

The July issue of *Shanghai Literature* published A Cheng's *The King of Chess,* which led to many repercussions. But this time the repercussions were a bit extraordinary, making the readers as well as the critics feel strange, as they were already accustomed to the kind of interrelationship between the 'Wound Literature' — dealing with abuses during the Cultural Revolution — and society whereby the two stimulated and echoed each other. As far as its function was concerned, the literature of the time really played a similar role to journalism. It was considered natural that the line between literature and journalism was a blurry one. Perhaps this was the most important characteristic of mainland Chinese literature between 1976 and 1984, and warrants further exploration. However, it was very hard for *The King of Chess* to be involved in this type of interrelationship. It was not right either for A Cheng's writing career or for the responses of the readers. Thus, praises for the novella could be heard everywhere, but there were very few articles that offered criticism. This formed a sharp contrast with the 'Wound Literature', which had created a sensation. The same indifference had greeted works by the veteran writer Wang Zengqi, who published the story *Monastic Ordination* as early as October 1980. At that time no one realized that such an uneventful story would have any revolutionary significance. On the contrary, it became popular because of its 'harmlessness', which was like a refreshing breeze in air permeated with a strong smell of gunpowder. The critics, thinking that his story was 'harmless' and that it would run its course, politely yielded some space to his writing, probably in order to manifest the special magnanimity of the 'literature of the new period'. What is interesting, however, is that in the meantime, the 'Misty' (*menglong*) poetry school came under attack and was in a difficult situation. The critic Xie Mian came to its defence and was instantly caught up in the cross-fire. He fought on his own most of the time. This should be considered as the point where literature in mainland China got lucky: during those several years, Wang Zengqi's writing was never suppressed. I am not evaluating Wang's writing, or thinking that he is superior to other contemporary writers. I am in no hurry to do it, as it will surely be done in the future. What I mean by the word 'lucky' is that without Wang's stories, Chinese literature in the eighties would have lost a very important thread, which would lead to the 'Root-seeking Literature' of 1985. To my mind, it was 'Root-seeking Literature' that enabled literature in mainland China to bid farewell to the period of the 'worker-peasant-soldier literature and art' created by Mao Zedong, and to enter a completely new era. However, between 1980 and 1985, this thread was quite insignificant. He Liwei, a young, unknown writer from Hunan Province, whose short story *The Small Town Has No Stories* was published in the September 1983 issue of *People's Literature*, may have been the only one whose writing echoed Wang Zengqi's. It was a year later that another story of He's, *The White Bird* — which had the terseness of a classical quatrain — received more attention. With the active support of Wang Meng, it received 'China's Best Short Story Award', adding another strand to the hidden thread that we talked about. Therefore, the appearance of *The King of Chess* was timely. A Cheng's writing was obviously related to that of Wang and He. Some sensitive people were already aware that their writing was fundamentally different from what had come before. However, the significance of the new writing to contemporary Chinese literature would only be manifested in the 'Root-seeking Literature' which suddenly erupted in 1985.

In January 1985, *Tibetan Literature* and *Shanghai Literature* respectively published Zhaxi Dawa's novella *Jizai Pishenshang de Hun* and Zheng Wanlong's short story *Laobangzi Public House*. After that, almost every month novellas and short stories that can now be classified as 'Root-seeking Literature' would be published in magazines. For the readers who were interested in literature, as well as the critics, that was a happy festival. Moreover, during this year, Liu Suola published *You Have No Alternative*, Ma Yuan published *The Seduction of Gandisi*, Zhu Xiaoping published *The Chronicle of Shangshuping*, Can Xue published *Mountain Cabin*, Zhang Xinxin and Shang Ye published *Beijing Voices*, and Liu Xinwu published *The Telephoto Lens on May 19*. These authors and their writings demonstrated some creative tendencies that were completely different from those of the 'Root-seeking Literature'. The literary scene looked as gorgeous as a riot of autumn colours. It was really an exciting year.

However, not everyone understood what happened: that the era of 'worker-peasant-soldier literature and art' had finally come to an end. 'Worker-peasant-soldier literature and art' lasted for a few decades and was a cultural construct closely tied up with the name Mao Zedong and his vivid imagination. I believe that future historiographers, cultural historians and literary critics will write many books to review the history of those years, and will realize more and more deeply what kind of profound impact it has had on China. For several years, criticism of 'worker-peasant-soldier literature and art' never ceased, but the critics often neglected the fact that Mao successfully achieved his goal, which was to create a kind of completely new mass pop culture congruent with the revolution under his leadership. Those who are interested in it may pay attention to the 'new *yangge*' movement which became popular after the publication of *Talks at the Yan'an Forum on Literature and Art*. This was Mao's first opportunity to practise revolutionary pop culture after he put forward the 'worker-peasant-soldier' direction. If we look at the achievement of revolutionary art and literature in the next decades, including representative works in poetry, fiction, theatre and music, I believe that it is easy to conclude that they were merely the continuation and expansion of the *yangge* movement. What the literary critics failed to understand for all those years was that, if what they were faced with was a kind of pop culture, they should have treated it as such, no matter how new or how creative it was. However, to take a step back, it was impossible for the critics to sober up before the eighties, because at the heart of the ideology established by Mao was the pop quality of literature, art, and culture.

The literary metalanguage developed from the Yan'an Forum had two functions. On the one hand, it encouraged popular literary discourse to spread unchecked. On the other hand, it strictly monitored any literary efforts to deviate from the popular level, because no matter how weak these efforts were, they might constitute a betrayal and opposition to the value system whose slogan was to 'serve the workers, peasants and soldiers', or in other words, to 'serve the people'. Such betrayal and opposition, of course, were never permissible. Mao himself was highly vigilant. Although there were various political and economic considerations, the fundamental reason that he started one political movement after another in the cultural arena (including the Cultural Revolution) was that he wanted to firmly defend the purity and consistency of this value system. I cannot offer any incisive criticism on revolutionary pop culture in this paper, nor do I intend to do so. I mentioned it just to explain the literary and social environment of 1985 when 'Root-seeking Literature' thrived. According to popular critical opinion, the 'Wound Literature' that emerged in the seventies and the 'Reform Literature' that emerged in the early eighties had innovative significance, and even started a new literary period. This opinion is not without its reasons, as the 'Wound Literature' and the 'Reform Literature' indeed brought some new dimensions to the literary scene. As literary discourse, not only were they different from the 'Model Operas' staged during the Cultural Revolution, but they were different from the literary and artistic works produced during the previous seventeen years, between 1949 and 1966. Therefore there was a subtle and complex oppositional relationship among the literatures of these three periods. Nevertheless, 'Wound Literature' and 'Reform Literature' did not change the power structure underlying the discourse of 'worker-peasant-soldier literature and art'. On the contrary, the opposition and union of these three literatures formed a kind of strategy which suppressed the emergence of a new literary discourse.

An example of such suppression would be the criticism and disputes which followed the publication in the early 1980s of several novels by Wang Meng, such a *The Voice of Spring* and *The Dream of the Sea*. These novels had a very unique literary form because he employed a narrative style in imitation of the 'stream of consciousness' technique (or rather, a parody of it). Some readers, however, immediately wrote to the newspapers, complaining that the novels were unintelligible, and literary critics actively echoed these complaints. A dispute ensued. The focus of the dispute was whether the writers would forfeit their revolutionary responsibility if they wrote unintelligible works. To tell the truth, the dispute would have been an idle one under different historical circumstances. However, because Wang Meng's style ran counter to the orientation towards 'the masses' prescribed by revolutionary pop culture, the dispute not only gave rise to an extremely heated response in wider society, but the participants also believed that they were defending their unbending principles concerning the direction of literature. What is noteworthy is that the dispute did not lead to political suppression, as the political environment had greatly changed. It was the attempted suppression of one discourse by another. Wang Meng's style certainly deviated from the literary norm established by the 'Model Operas', 'Wound Literature' and the literature of the 'seventeen years'. Therefore its legitimacy would certainly be doubted. It made Wang Meng's novels look like visitors of unknown identity, constantly under the host's surveillance, though not evicted yet.

The dispute about Wang Meng's novels was merely the beginning of the conflict between old and new discourses in the eighties, and the many conflicts in its wake were similar to it. In view of this fact, I believe that when reviewing literary developments in the past decade, the critics have to look squarely at this fact: disregarding their popularized artistic style or the values contained in the works, 'Wound Literature' and 'Reform Literature' not only had no fundamental difference from 'worker-peasant-soldier literature and art', but were a new stage (and probably also the last stage) of the latter. Therefore we may say that the 'worker-peasant-soldier literature and art' were not shaken up until 1985, and that they continued to monitor the production of literary discourse according to the standards of revolutionary popular literature set up by Mao Zedong. However, along with the emergence of 'Root-seeking Literature' in 1985, I believe that the history of 'worker-peasant-soldier literature and art' finally came to an end. This is not to say that examples of 'worker-peasant-soldier literature and art' would never appear again. Rather, it was no longer dominant as a cultural form, and the 'worker-peasant-soldier literature' at its centre was no longer the sole narrative discourse in literary narratives. Over the years there have been many attempts to create another literary discourse outside of the domain of 'worker-peasant-soldier literature and art'. However, they were either suppressed and forbidden as a discursive taboo, or they could not express themselves at all (they did not qualify as a discourse). The enchanting scene where 'a hundred schools of thought contend' remained illusory. Therefore, people were very happy, indeed wild with joy, at the changes in the literary scene during the year 1985. Now that we think about it, there might be a better reason: instead of having just one voice, millions of people could now have dialogues with each other. It is self-evident how important that was for those who were enduring the torture of drawn out spiritual suicide.

True, 'Root-seeking Literature' played an instrumental role in the 'sudden change' during 1985, yet I do not think that we should exaggerate its role. I do not believe that a simple cause and effect relationship existed between the emergence of 'Root-seeking Literature' and the end of the era of 'worker-peasant-soldier literature and art'. It would not be true to say that the former caused the latter to come to an end. As a cultural phenomenon and a complicated historical process, the rise and fall of 'worker-peasant-soldier literature and art' had to do with many factors, and was definitely not shaped merely by the works of a group of writers. Moreover, the flourishing of 'Root-seeking Literature' lasted only a bit more than a year. In 1987 very few works had this inclination. Wang Zengqi, a lonely old fellow, was the only one left who still carried on calmly. Therefore, the main function of 'Root-seeking Literature' during the 'sudden change' in 1985 was its opposition to 'Wound Literature' and 'Reform Literature'. These oppositional forces were not balanced, because in comparison, 'Root-seeking Literature' was really weak. Fortunately, however, in the world of literature there were many other 'streams' that converged with 'Root-seeking Literature' and built up a great momentum. Besides, what is more important is that such a sudden change not only happened in cultural arenas such as fiction, poetry, painting, films, music, theatre and literary criticism, but they happened everywhere. It could be said that 'every place that had a well had a change'.

It was also in 1985 that some younger and more radical poets were shouting the slogan 'Down with Bei Dao!' In their view, Bei Dao, Duo Duo, Jiang He and Yang Lian were old fellows who should have died already. The 'Great Poetry Show' put on by *Shenzhen Youth Gazette* suddenly enabled quite a few forbidden voices to cry out. The voices were so varied and loud that they proclaimed the arrival of a new era of poetry. However, I believe that in the field of painting the changes were more radical than in the field of poetry. As early as 1983 there was an art exhibition featuring works by Huang Yongbeng and four other people. (Several years later it transformed into a school called 'Xiamen Dada'.) Huang Yongbeng wrote: 'On a certain spiritual level, it can be said that Zen is Dada. Dada is Zen.' In 1985, not only were there various schools in the field of painting, but a succession of exhibitions featuring modern art were held all over the country. In Hangzhou, for instance, there was an exhibition of works by graduates of Zhejiang College of Fine Arts as well as a '1985 New Space Exhibition', which later became the cause of a serious dispute. There was 'The First Exhibition of Hunan "O" Art Circle' in Changsha, 'The November Art Show' in Beijing, 'The Exhibition of New Paintings from Yunnan and Shanghai' in Shanghai, 'The Jiangsu Youth Art Week — the Grand Art Exhibition' in Nanjing, 'Shengsheng Exhibition' in Xi'an, 'The Modern Art Show' in Chongqing, put on by the 'Artistic Circle of the Anonymous', and so forth. I did not have the chance to see most of these shows, but I always kept track of them from *The Chinese Art Gazette* and other art magazines. I remember to this day the surprise and shock I experienced when I first saw works by such painters as Gu Wenda and Wang Guangyi.

We cannot but talk about films when discussing the year 1985. I am probably more familiar with films than with painting. I have a great deal to say, but I only want to mention one thing. In the spring of '84, I was writing a script in the guest house of the Xi'an Film Studio. The production unit of the film *Yellow Earth* also stayed there for a few days. My room faced the stairs and so I could clearly hear the steps of the passers-by. The steps were very slow, as if the guest house were a nursing home, but after Chen Kaige, the director, took his people there, the steps outside my door started to sound more lively. As soon as someone called 'Let's go! Let's go!' I would hear some quick steps and it would be noisy on the stairs for a few minutes. Then, the laughter and teasing sounds fading away with the steps, the guest house would fall back into a deadly silence. At such moments, I used to be indescribably moved by the quick steps. Several days later, the production unit left for Shangbei to shoot on location. Some acquaintances and friends got together in the guest house to see them off. It was not until then that I had an opportunity to see the people of the production unit for the first time. I was really amazed: most of them were so young that they looked like kids. I was already used to the prejudice in film circles (in all other circles, for that matter) that people in their twenties were good-for-nothing, only fit for work as assistants or running errands. It was not until they had endured this for about a dozen years that they could do something more important in the production unit. However, in front of me was this group of young men and women — all of them in their twenties or early thirties. Male or female, they all wore jeans and sun hats with wide brims. Laughing and joking, in spite of the serious look on the face of Chen Kaige, they boarded the bus fully loaded with equipment. I was moved again. I still remember how I tried to hold back my tears, saying to myself, 'Wait and see. There will surely be a big change.'

The big change took place much earlier than I expected. It happened in 1985, although at that time no one could recognize the deep impact it brought to the country. *Yellow Earth* was completed at the end of 1984. The rolling yellow earth on the screen became one of the most exciting events in 1985.

After the end of the seventies, 'modernization' increasingly became a word that could mobilize the imaginative power of the Chinese people, who were already used to connecting all current events with 'modernization'. *Yellow Earth*, however, had nothing to do with 'modernization'. The screen was filled with magnificent yellow earth, whereas in comparison, the people in the film always seemed negligible. Such a relationship between nature and human beings reminded one of the artistic conception in the scenery paintings of the Song and Yuan dynasties, of the ancient thought that 'the humans are modelled after the earth, the earth after the heaven, the heaven after the Way, and the Way after nature'. But in what aspect is this idea related to 'modernization'? Of course, the text is always at the mercy of the readers. Our elaborations on the yellow earth could always be related to 'modernisation' in one way or another and some film critics did exactly that. However, the distance between *Yellow Earth* and 'modernization' was not an isolated phenomenon. In film, there were *The Horse Thief* and *The Sacrifice of Youth*; in music there were Tan Dun and Qu Xiaosong; in painting, there was a big group of artists of the 'New Wave of 1985'. Moreover, there was fiction: *Dad Dad Dad* by Han Shaogong, *The Transparent Red Turnip* by Mo Yan, *The King of Trees* by A Cheng, *Life on a String* by Shi Tiesheng, *The Mud Hut* by Zhang Chengzhi, *You Have No Alternative* by Liu Suola, *The Seduction of Gandisi* by Ma Yuan, *Strange Stories from a Strange Land* by Zheng Wanlong, and many more. Though varied in subject matter and writing style, these works were similar to *Yellow Earth* on one account: none of them had anything to do with the magic word 'modernization', no matter whether one judges from the images used in the works, or from the hermeneutic possibility of the texts. Why did the enthusiastic illusions and the hard thinking of so many writers and artists no longer orient towards the big and exciting theme of 'modernization'? Why? It seems that this question was never raised before 1985.

As a matter of fact, from the early eighties to 1985, writers, poets, painters and other artists were always inspired by the goal of 'modernization', just like other people. I believe that everyone tried to do his or her bit for the process of Chinese modernization. The ways by which they made their contribution were very different: some writers directly reflected and praised the historical process of modernization in their works, under the rubric of 'Reform Literature'. Some other writers believed that 'modernization' in the literary arena meant that literature itself needed to be modernized. A necessary precondition for this was the *introduction* and the study of modern Western literature (as in the expression 'the *introduction* of Western advanced technology'). Those who held this view were generally called the 'modernists' over the next few years. I do not want to elaborate on the different treatment received by the two kinds of writers, who were both highly enthusiastic about 'modernization'. All those who have experienced or studied those events know about them and so it is unnecessary to mention them again. What I am now ready to recall is just how naive I and my friends were at that time.

In the summer of 1980, the Writers' Association invited some writers to stay at Beidaihe Beach. It was there that I was first exposed to modernist literature. My teacher was Gao Xingjian. The class was held every evening, from dusk to midnight. I was surprised and happy to be introduced to a new way of thinking. When Gao Xingjian mentioned that Breton's 'surrealism' advocated 'automatic writing', several students and I were surprised: how could one write like that? When Gao said that as a matter of fact in the modernist movement some poets, writers and directors, such as Mayakovsky, Aragon, and Eisenstein, were left wing revolutionaries, we felt really happy. We had known about them all along, but how come we never knew that they were also modernists.? I believe that some readers will find it strange: how could the writers in mainland China be so ignorant? Anyway it was a fact. For many years, due to such ignorance, a great number of young writers and readers were fascinated by modernist literature and seriously believed that the only way out for Chinese literature lay in the study of Western modernism. (Some people still believe so today.)

I do not have the slightest intention of rejecting or refusing to study Western modernism. On the contrary, the confusion and puzzlement of those several years was quite worthwhile. Without the strong influence of Western modernism (and postmodernism, to a certain extent), mainland Chinese literature would not have experienced those changes later, nor would there have been the 'sudden change' in 1985. Prior to the emergence of 'Root-seeking Literature', the writers who sincerely hoped for changes could only 'borrow' Western modernist discourse, using it to oppose 'worker-peasant-soldier literature and art' and thereby gain some space for their own writings. However, it was only after the ravenous and often careless study of Western modernism that Chinese writers were finally able to stick their heads out of the well and look at the world of the twentieth century. The importance of such studies cannot be overvalued, because they provided the most basic condition for Chinese literature to carry on a dialogue with all kinds of world literature, past, present and future.

However, after this positive evaluation, I would like to criticize the superstitious worship of Western modernism from 1980 to 1985. A sharp question should be raised: if 'Westernization', or the superstitions about modernism, caused a serious disaster in Chinese literature after the May Fourth Movement, why then should we repeat history today? To raise such a question causes some inconvenience, since it entails a complete re-evaluation of Chinese literature since the May Fourth Movement, which will bring forth many problems. But it also has some advantages, because it links with criticism of the May Fourth Movement and redirects it towards the basic goal of the May Fourth Movement, i.e., that China needed to realize a Western-style modernization. The many upheavals that China experienced since the May Fourth Movement made the goal of 'modernization' now obscure, now clear, but it has never lost its appeal.

At present, an increasing number of Chinese intellectuals are even more superstitious about that goal. An example of this would be the 'Forum on the Methodology of Literary Criticism' held in Xiamen, Fujian Province in March 1983. During the meeting, many people advocated a mixture of the scientific methods used in the natural sciences, such as cybernetics, information science, with aesthetics and art theories. They believed that literary theory could be modernized in this way. Whether these ideas were correct or feasible was unknown, and yet it was not difficult to see how unconditionally enthusiastic many people were about 'modernization' and how superstitious they were about Western theories of discourse. Let me cite another example. In recent years, there are people on both sides of the Taiwan Straits who insist that modernist literature exists in Taiwan and mainland China. They write articles to comment on the similarities and differences between Chinese and Western modernism. Some of them emphasize that the essence of Chinese modernism is the continuation of Western modernism and that Chinese modernism is a part of the world-wide modernist literary movement. These commentaries and critiques often vary in opinion, but they all share the idea that Chinese literature is after all modernized, while the standard of the modernization is, of course, Western.

This criticism of mine will surely be sharply criticized: the emergence of modernism cannot be decided by the subjective will of certain people; if it is a world-wide trend, it is useless to shut one's eyes and to refuse to acknowledge it. However, this is precisely the crux of the problem: is Western-style (There is something wrong with this expression; what and who is the West? But I will just make do with it) modernization (which includes an ideology and other spiritual productions congruent with it) really an irresistible trend? Do we have an alternative? Besides, we should not forget that all Western discourses on 'modernization' and 'modernity' are after all discourses, which represent some kind of will to power. Can we treat them as truth and law?

These are some big questions that go far beyond the scope of literature. The reason that I have to mention them is that they constituted the general background for the transformations of 1985. The significance of the literature of 1985 can be seen more clearly if placed against this background. The writers who were active in that literary transformation did not (as far as I know) intentionally evaluate their works against this background. What was surprising then, and even more so today, is that they spontaneously took the same attitude toward writing. Objectively speaking, they not only rejected the superstitious worship of Western modernist literature that was prevalent during those years but, more importantly, unconsciously questioned the idea of 'modernization'. Such questioning was virtually unnoticed and the critics did not refine it or make a theory out of it. However, the impact of the year 1985 was obvious, which was evidenced by the works of a generation of even younger writers (Yu Hua, Su Tong, Ye Zhaoyan, Ge Fei, Liu Heng, Li Rui, and so forth). These newcomers have surpassed the old-timers who were active in 1985.

At the end of 1984, *Shanghai Literature* and the Zhejiang Art Publishing House organized a forum on literature in Hangzhou. The participants included writers as well as critics. This conference was intense, both extremely exhausting and extremely exciting. It seemed to have resulted in some considerable influence on the literary transformations of 1985. Some people even believe that the intention to 'look for roots' in 'Root-seeking Literature' was basically put forward during that conference. I clearly remember that Huang Ziping told a story during his talk at the meeting: 'A young monk asked an old monk what Buddha was. The old monk did not speak and only raised a finger. A few days later, the old monk asked the young one what Buddha was. The young monk did not speak either and then raised a finger. Unexpectedly, the old monk produced a knife and cut off the younger one's hand'. I have completely forgotten the reason he told the story or its context. Besides, he did not make it clear where the story came from (probably from the *Wudeng Hui Yuan*, a collection of Chan — Zen — classics, but retold by Huang). I only recall that, his face flushed, he used his hand as the knife, whizzed it at his other hand, and then said nothing. After so many years, I still remember the little story and see it as Ziping's own creation. It frequently jumps into my mind and makes me think that probably someone had to cut off all ten fingers.

INTERMEDIATE ZONE

Zhong Ming

translated by Steve Balogh and John Cayley

To understand Haizi's suicide, or his life, requires a sense of his crossing back and forth between two different milieux. On the one hand, the tedium of small-town monotony, a tedium arising when the joys of collective life degenerate into whispering campaigns about private or family matters and personal idiosyncrasies of no wider significance. Haizi was weighed down by the drudgery, vacuity, literalism, obscurantism, ponderousness of it all. You felt that he was endlessly sinking.

By contrast, up at the capital, and at Beijing University, where he took a law degree, he made a wide circle of intimate friends — nor did he lack opportunities when it came to developing and cultivating his vitality at that centre of cultural abundance. The city, a hotbed of architectural absurdities and conflicts, seethed with political fantasies, intricate and complex family lineages, celebrities whose shrewdness paraded as *politesse*. In the temperate mainland climate, where feminine beauty degenerates, caught between sand-blown aridity and overwhelming monsoon, the city was filled with busy and exhausted faces — successful tax dodgers, the ambiguous middle classes, plummy conservatives sounding off, newcomers with awkward manners and motives, endless socialising, banqueting, ceremonies, glory-seeking, pipedreams, frivolity, impetuosity ...

Haizi had to present a separate persona in each of these two milieux. In one place he seemed to have a keen nose — even after long disuse — for sniffing out whatever the town found acceptable and, indeed, whatever it rejected. The cosmopolitan city offered him the ancient portals of the vanished state of Yan alongside Hilton-style modern edifices, but it somehow lacked the ability to bring them together. Here, he could find scenes from Paris, New York, London, a hybrid of Salem and Borobudur, or the sacred Shinto mysteries of Japan — a bizarre miscellany. It was both radical and conservative, arrogant but lacking in self-confidence, bossy and short-sighted, loudly promoting the ideals of justice and equality, but keeping strictly to the official line. At the same time, in the other place, Haizi could set that over-burdened nose of his to perplexedly sniffing out the particular charms of unbearable small-town isolation. Every Chinese city has several satellite towns of this kind — dormitory suburbs, servants at the beck and call of their geographical location. In the case of Beijing they are a sort of sacrifice to rationality; and as for how these satellites dotted everywhere see the capital — they look up to it as something high and mighty and frivolous.

Haizi never lingered long in either haunt; both conferred on him a kind of residential status with particular responsibilities and points of view — each of them was, in turn, where he set out from and where he'd end up next. Thus, if ever it came to court proceedings, Haizi, a protagonist for both sides, could face searching, confrontational inter-rogation from either — seeking out weak points with which to put down the other, or any oversights with which to catch the them out. You can imagine that soon he found himself an unwelcome stranger in both places. Haizi was like a village postman who through personally, constantly, exploring the features, habits and behaviour of his localities, through observing how the people passed their time, picked up every little detail or scrap that fell to the ground, and so became a thorn in the flesh of both places. He made use of both varieties of local patois to visit them with weekly ridicule. When he did this kind of thing both sides found themselves abashed, speechless, and it was easy to abandon or disown him as it suited them, for the sake of a quiet life in whichever place. His nonconformity was eventually a threat to such brazen hypocrisy and bullying. Only if he was absolutely in the right and could make these two openly conniving parties see that he was also some use to them or, further, could convey something tacitly — during times when it was nearly all bad news — in a form that was understood by everyone. Otherwise he was ostracized by both parties. This kind of situation naturally lent itself to writing — of course that meant the ordinary man's idea of writing. It had nothing to do with the city's decorated columns, arched doorways and pergolas. However, in Haizi's hands, writing became a quite different matter. He would throw himself into a moral conflict, beyond his competence, with a sort of simultaneous physical and literary bi-directional exertion. Writing enabled him to peel off the shell of the material world and investigate the inner beauty of essences; it helped him transcend common convention, relying on his acute sense of the eccentric. When writing rapidly, he resembled a large bird adorned with bronze pendants, hanging high in the air, surveying the wide world's mutual violence, and municipal rivalries. The more impartial he was, the more he isolated himself; his judgements and concerns preventing the least shred of compromise. His emotions were always split: one half weeping, one half laughing; one half condemning, one half respectful; one part bestride the cyclone, one part plumbing the depths of hell.

He fervently wished to throw off this condition, so much at variance with his physical and mental state, wished to raise still higher the exertion that would enable him to reconcile and unite the two areas of his existence. This yearning to occupy a position of vantage intensified his conscious urge toward an intermediate zone whence he would be able to view a hitherto untrammelled expanse. His life's dual compartmentalization, or rather, his two types of life-style, was like a twilit countryside, gathered among bloodstains. This kind of thing he found shocking and he would suddenly feel that he had not captured the need for trust between the two sides: the many-splendoured worlds were debased and polluted as they flowed together, when all he had sought was a kind of spiritual harmony, to draw people towards some less joyless political set-up in the municipality. Now what he sought was the height and neutrality which his soul achieved after a small amount of effort, a new kind of viewpoint, a pitiable bodily abandonment, but something useful to him. Of course that perch had to be somewhere he selected, it had to be an intermediate zone at the level of, but beyond, the two areas in which he had made his life, and at no distance away. There would be an oblivion to extinguish all differences, a prospect of imaginative beauty, encompassing moon, sea, lemons, trees, traditions, cherished memories of living and departed men and women, the muddled atmosphere of medieval emotions.

Where he took leave of the flesh, he could hear the sound of the sea. A stretch of railway — when you think about it, it's laughable — the dumb, cold rail crossed here, between the two worlds that made up the fabric of his existence. This stretch of the line had taken him to the scenes of his conflicts, but now completed his abandonment of them, smashing all his instruments as well, it was a pivot on which his body regained a necessary balance, and it was the heavenly terminus towards which he walked. Climbing up a slope, the train approached very slowly. Haizi selected the middle portion of the train, exactly between two of the wheels, at a point of separation that left vanishingly little time, adequate but not long enough for fear or suffering. After his death on the tracks, others merely busied themselves with the identification of the body, the post-mortem report and inquiry, mourning, bringing out the 'Posthumous Works', collecting donations. There was no one, however, who dwelt on the implications of the lengths to which Haizi had gone in order to divide himself so precisely in two. Nor was anyone struck by the orange he had on him at the end — was it according to or at variance with the rules of a game he played with death — sliced clean in two, without spraying blood around or leaving behind any great untidiness ...

UNDER-*SKY*
UNDER*GROUND*

O

BELLES LETTRES

PRISON LETTER

SONG LIN

translated by Beth McKillop and John Cayley

Loss of liberty is a human disaster and to have liberty taken away is to be caught up in a process which, completed, encompasses the beginnings and ends of human life. When Camus claimed that all existence could be reduced to the absurd, this theory of existential predetermination implied that the myth of Sysiphus contains reason enough for living. Sysiphus' defiance — in repeatedly pushing his rock up the mountain — kept him from suicide, the termination of life in the body. He transformed the pain of bondage into a form of pleasure. Whoever wishes to escape the 'bitter sea' of life must surely see eternal happiness as of absolute value. There, paradise or elysium is the fountainhead of joy. Twentieth-century literary thought progressed from the theory of the anti-hero, proposed by Kafka, through existentialism, to the total dehumanization of the Nouveau Roman. I would summarize these changes in zeitgeist as a progress from 'insignificant man', through 'outsider', to 'man as object'.

The dream of being supernaturally saved from disaster can produce a wound in paradise as the individual gradually loses vitality. In reality, you remain always in the human world. And since paradise is a utopia you have conjured up, it can turn you into a figure of cardboard. Utopians (I mean those afflicted people who will not reclaim their souls from god) are helped by 'scripture' to strangle themselves, even though they'd be happy to extend their corporal lives. This paradox is still unresolved today. Take the case of artists. Nietzche's hero-worship cannot reverse the roles of man and god. You are determined by a particular set of affinities and circumstances, and you must be ready to perish in the midst of those same affinities and circumstances. To wipe out the circumstances which condition you is to wipe out the self, because the only possible way forward is to 'co-exist' with them. The 'wounded image of the world' which is posited by Camus' philosophy (or aesthetics) of the absurd is etched in the memories of people whom I know so well and who have set out to sacrifice themselves. It opened my eyes to the unholy alliance concluded surreptitiously in Oriental and Western thought between 'co-existence' and 'nirvana', two concepts which are seemingly incompatible. As early as the composition of his *Divine Comedy*, Dante heard God's warning, 'Human kind, be content with your lot.' Dante praised Paradise and railed against Hell, depicting in all manner of ways the eternal sufferings and futile struggles which result from the quest to transcend what has been determined.

The ever deepening awareness of lost liberty distances the people of today from the numinous and bends them to rule of this world. To flee is just an misguided attempt to escape from rudderless fate. Everywhere poets and artists have been revealed — ribs as darkly defined as lines of charcoal — the soul has lost its resting place. A harsh reality with its origins in the self has been neglected — memory causes ill-defined and false impressions to become the object of deliberate, drawn-out praise. All those poets, drifting in the space-time of annihilation, are blind, flying off to Homer or places still more distant. They remain motionless, like monks sitting in meditation, casting their minds back to recall ever more clearly the time before they were born. And in the direction of the future, the one real thing they have dreamed about is death. Most people speak of death as if they were describing a dream; they prefer to believe it to be unreal, or to have occurred already. But death, rather than being a thing of the past or of the future, exists in the present. Once we have thought of death then we have died. The characterization, 'sick unto death', is a product of the romantic's narcissistic grief. They postpone what has been pre-ordained, awaiting what may be an advantageous time, but are mesmerised by it as if lost in contemplation of a rose. This death is no ending of the self; it is the self.

However, true loss of liberty is not the prelude to disaster (like an imitation of death), it is the real, painful separation of spirit and flesh. Because of this, the true fugitive is unable to find final comfort in religion. Nothing in the order of human society (the universal principles of philosophy, religion, aesthetics, or sociology) can bring lasting salvation to the fugitive. Taking flight means cutting oneself off from salvation; it achieves the full significance of the word 'cruelty' through self-annihilation. 'The Woman Who Rode Away' (as in D H Lawrence's story) did so to present her skull to an Indian tribe, not as a sacrifice to the tribal gods; her singular altar ritual was preparation for a descent into hell. This descent is the only action which requires no spiritual transcendence or advance warning. 'I am damned to hell what / alarmclock is ringing ...' (Ginsberg). 'I'll have a two-sided coffin so that I'll be able to pop my head into the other world.' (Nicanor Parra). Here, death evokes neither fear nor pain. It is an entirely commonplace event, in no way different from any other experience. And it is precisely here that poetry transcends the human, by saying, in a new voice, 'Let's go to hell; let's forget paradise!' The spirit of poetry is not the spirit of Olympus or the spirit of the Indians; poetry establishes its unparalleled value in the splendour of mythologies created by the pure individual.

Poets and artists are the archetypal fugitives. If they decide on real, complete self-sacrifice then they are soon overtaken by another worldly calamity on the highway of language — the cruel fantasies of the 'dystopians' become their solace before death (here, the aesthetics of brutality are closer to the nature of the relationship between circumstance, object, manifestation and reception than the aesthetics of the absurd). For poets, language is a maze, not a way forward. Language can be created only by talking to oneself, groaning, raving, crying and even keeping silence. But whatever the form or structure of language, it conveys meaning only when it is fully possessed of creativity, and, moreover, its the meaning remains always original. The linguistic orientation of poetry is essentially that of genesis. It emerges once and once only.

Thus I regard the language of art as a third type of language, to distinguish it from the 'informative' and the 'mythological'. The latter two types of language may differ functionally as do statement and metaphor, but both derive from the human order, while the language of art springs from the breaking of this order. It first deconstructs and then constructs anew. The language of art does not exist because of the need to communicate. It is something buried in the forms of life, but separated out from ordinary experience by artists so that it becomes the product of transcendence, beyond the ability of most people to grasp. It is this for which poets spend their entire lives searching. On the pathway of language, the poet creates a personal hell in which the self is finally annihilated within language itself.

ABSTRACT TASTE

Yan Li

translated by Deborah Mills

A painter who relies on selling his paintings to make a living always has a couple of incidents from his marketing experience which are more memorable than the others. I have had over ten years experience of making my living by selling my paintings, and so of course I have a number of such stories to tell. Many people will have heard of the business of someone buying his or her own paintings, and I myself know more than one example. One of them happened like this: there was a painter who, at an exhibition of his work, in order to show that his paintings were not only capable of forming an exhibition on their own but also sold well, got one of his brothers to pretend to be a buyer and go, negotiate with the gallery, and have 'reserved stickers' stuck below some of the paintings he fancied. After the exhibition was over there was of course a phone call telling the gallery that he had changed his mind. I've also heard of a gallery which, hoping to get some business, selected a couple of highly unsaleable paintings from an exhibition that they had organised and stuck sold signs on them. All in all, the market place is a battleground. In every move you can see something out of Sun Zi's *Art of War*. The instance I came across is not in the least exceptional, as you will see from what I am about to relate.

In China, the custom of giving away paintings is quite firmly entrenched. If a friend asks me for a painting, it shows how good a friend he is, and I will happily give him a painting. But in America, in fact in the West generally, this custom is much less current. According to the Western view, all labour should be paid for. A painting is the product of labour, and so it should not be given away, or at least should not be given away lightly. During the third year I spent in New York I met an American called Tom. We became friends, and within a year we had become extremely close. He ran an import-export business dealing with China, but due to bad luck and various other circumstances he wasn't really making any money. So he occasionally helped me with the sale of my paintings, and we came to an agreement that he would receive a ten per cent commission on any painting that he helped me to sell. He was not a particularly good salesman: in over a year he had helped me to sell only one and a half paintings. The half-painting was one that was sold to an uncle of his who only paid half the money at the time, and later decided not to buy it. This was because shortly after buying the painting the uncle got divorced, because he'd fallen in love with a young girl and, since he wanted to get his divorce as quickly as possible, he'd distributed most of his belongings amongst his wife and children. In the circumstances, he wasn't inclined to pay the other half of the money. So he brought the painting back to exchange it for any painting that I considered to be worth half as much, and I ended up choosing another painting to give to Tom's uncle. This is not one of those selling experiences which I consider to be particularly memorable.

One day Tom rang to say that a friend of his had seen an exhibition of mine and was very impressed. He'd just bought himself a new house, and was preparing to acquire one or two paintings to hang in it. He was thinking of having a look at my paintings, as he felt that the tone of my work would go very well with the character of his house. Actually, it's true that my abstract paintings have a lot in common with modern buildings. I always put my signature, which risks being distinctly meaningful in some way, on the back of the painting, so that the language of the painting comes over as completely and utterly abstract. On the day we had arranged for him to view the paintings I suddenly had a call from a friend of mine who was in hospital, so I told Tom to take the pictures that I had prepared for sale over to his friend's place. In the meantime I rushed off to the hospital to visit my sick friend, who was on the point of leaving this world as a result of sudden illness. Perhaps it was AIDS, or maybe alcoholic poisoning; if not, it would be an unsuccessful suicide attempt.

This friend of Tom's was called Burns. He chose one painting and Tom brought the rest of them back. I gave Tom one tenth of the asking price and also treated him to a Greek meal, because Greek food was his favourite (he was half Greek), and also because Tom had doubled the price of my painting, I asked him if Burns had a lot of money. Tom said that, during the past year, Burns had been amazingly percipient about the stock exchange, and had made a lot of money in some big deals.

Two weeks later Tom told me that Burns had asked us both over to his house. The decoration of the new house was already finished. Tom and I arrived at the duly appointed time. Burns led me humorously into his study to look at my painting. As soon as I saw it I knew that he'd hung it the wrong way — not upside down, but on its side. Out of politeness, I didn't say anything just then, and anyway my paintings are abstract colour paintings which can be hung any way up, as long as the owner feels comfortable with it. Burns had also invited a few other friends, among them one man who knew that I had painted the picture, and began to chat to me there in the study. The others went into the lounge and the bedrooms to get a taste of Burns' sumptuous house. The man who was chatting to me was called David. He asked me about the position of Chinese painters in New York, and began to express an opinion on the painting on the wall. He tilted his head to one side to look at it and said that it seemed to him as though the painting would look better hung vertically. At that stage, I still wasn't inclined to reveal that the painting was originally meant to be hung vertically, so I just said that abstract paintings could be looked at any way up, whereas figurative pictures could only be looked at one way. Thus, in certain respects, abstract paintings allowed artists more freedom. At this moment Burns came in, and David immediately began to tell him that if the painting were hung vertically it might give it a different feel, and asked Burns if he had tried it that way. He replied cunningly that the way he had hung it accorded best with his understanding of material structure, and added that a bank note was still money whichever way you looked at it. We all laughed.

As well as being a humorous man, Burns was also careful. After a few minutes, he quietly drew me aside and asked me which way up the picture should really be hung, or in other words, which way up had I painted it. Following his train of thought I said that I had painted it *my* way up, but that if someone else hung it *his* way up, there would be no contradiction. Laughing, he said he would like to know which way up my world was. I felt obliged to tell him that I had painted it vertically. When I had finished speaking I noticed that, contrary to my expectations, he seemed a bit unhappy. However, he soon became even more jolly and humorous. He grabbed Tom who was standing drinking nearby, and told him that I had done some divination for him and reckoned that his eyes were different from other people's, and that, as a result, he'd have much better luck in business than an ordinary man. Tom looked at me completely baffled, but I began laughing, in a knowing way, along with Burns. Burns abruptly changed the subject and said he must thank Tom because the picture he had recommended particularly suited his tastes.

It wasn't long before Burns again called me to one side and asked me wasn't the signature on the back of the painting and if so, which way up was it signed? I said I had signed it in the vertical position. He then dragged me back into the study (the other people at this point were all in the lounge listening to music and drinking coffee), shut the study door, took the picture down, and asked me to sign it horizontally as well, which I did. Before he re-opened the study door he suddenly thought of something else, plucked the picture back off the wall and asked me to sign it in the other two directions. That way there'd be a signature in all four directions.

Before we left that day Burns gave Tom an envelope to pass on to me. I opened it in front of Tom and inside was a hundred dollar bill, and on the envelope was Burns' signature, signed in all four directions. Tom was bewildered and asked me what it was all about, so I told him what had happened, and also pulled out a ten dollar bill and gave it to him, in line with our agreement. Tom didn't want to take it so I forcibly stuffed it into his pocket, saying that money was also abstract, depending on how you used it. The sale of the painting was thus concluded. To begin with Burns had paid $1,500, added to that this $100 made $1,600 altogether. Perhaps Burns saw it as having bought four paintings. This is not most people's idea of humour, or perhaps Burns has his own and different form of logic; I'm really not too sure.

THE WAY OF HEAVEN
BEGINNING OF AUTUMN

ZHANG CHENGZHI

translated by Helen Wang

Beginning of Autumn 1990 was a very mysterious day.

Year after year, at the end of spring the people of Beijing have come to wait in terror for the onslaught of summer — stewing every single day, until this year when they stewed every single moment. The cruel, incessant Beijing summer had quite simply reached its extreme.

Time dragged hour upon hour — impossible to read, impossible to sit at a table. Not only in the broad daylight; the nights were also indescribably stifling. Burning in the pitch blackness was truly fearsome.

Sometimes I would sit by myself in this black heat, like a cinder in a stove not long since put out. Burning in my heart, a red red spark, constantly irritating me. Only as if everything depended upon it could one even begin to contend with this enormous dark heat. Sitting for ages in confrontation with it, sweat streaming down my back, conscious of the cold smile on my face.

In the few hours after dawn the world sinks once again into the brutal fry-roast. Rain is useless: running along the road your eyes see the rain drops as hot water hitting the ground. Under a raincoat, sweat seeps through your shirt, God knows why people still wear raincoats.

Could anyone ever fully understand our cruel summers?

Foreigners on the street, faces full of ignorance, covered in perspiration.

The taste of getting through the summer, Chinese people cannot describe it.

Later, even hotter, even more scorching, bit by bit I lose hope. If the heat persists even I will begin to doubt the Way of Heaven.

But that day was Beginning of Autumn. In the morning I walked imperviously into the fry-roast, my mind filled memories of sunny days in summer. On the wide steppes of Inner Mongolia the ultra-violet rays of summer were like paint, in one afternoon they could stain your

145

cheeks red. One year when we were out on the grass, a student had returned from Beijing, everyone had laughed; his little white face among a crowd of round red faces. The next day his face was red too. From then on I understood how the ultra-violet could burn.

But the ultra-violet rays that burn skin are nothing like the summer days in Beijing. The summer heat in Beijing is repulsive, irritating, shameful, fills you with hate, though you don't know what for. I was thinking about this as I walked into the dazzling sunlight, my mind a little shut off, weakened a little by the tiresome heat. So, as the moment drew closer I wasn't paying very much attention. I hadn't held much store by the calendrical divisions for some time, and couldn't believe that Beginning of Autumn would ever come at the end of this Beijing summer. I was determined to hold out against this noxious day. There is an ancient poem: 'Until the end of time I will stay with you.' I could really appreciate its poetry now. I should have written that moment down as it happened, but there was not the slightest need to record anything. It was printed on every calendar hanging in every home: August 8th 1990, 'Beginning of Autumn'. But I hadn't any idea it was coming. I wasn't awaiting it in any way, hadn't imagined the pleasure it would bring. In the long age of the fry-stew, foresight and intelligence, even imagination, had all wilted.

The morning of fire had passed.

Even at midday I had no notion of it. Just madly doing what I like doing best. It's the only way of getting through life: to grasp firmly in the depths and testify with all one's might. In the horrific sweltering heat everything assumed a ruthlessness, and a beauty which is hard to describe. This act was a religious ritual for me, body and soul were cleansed, transparent, it even felt as if life was exhausted.

As I walked into the afternoon sunlight I saw people's shadows bending. I felt the sense of victory sweep over my face. Life has triumphed again, I thought to myself, here where one lives as a warrior.

The afternoon sunlight began to blaze with colour, so beautiful one forgot the ruthlessness; there was almost the illusion of a thread of gentleness. As if a railway signalman in the middle of the Gobi desert suddenly heard behind him a soft, gentle sound like the beckoning voice of woman. Even if it was like that … at that moment I was not aware of it.

Suddenly, the moment I felt the 'cool freshness' I stopped dead. The soft, gentle call seeped slowly, gently out, and in an instant — unimaginable — the unending stream of sweat pouring down my back dried. I looked around in surprise, and found that the people on the street — the people of Beijing were all looking around too. Then, although there was no wind, the leaves of the lush trees quivered high up in the sky, a message passing between the crossing branches. I could have shouted out loud, everything was being taken by surprise, and in that one second the fresh air filled heaven, earth and the human world.

I all but wept. The cruel, age-long grilling really could come to an end, Beginning of Autumn was a reality. I was still for a moment, then the freshness in the sky began to move, swiftly. Like an enormous, formless hand pressing down a formless Way-of-Heaven-switch, sending down compassion and fairness, together with the cool freshness, into this cruel hard world. The blue sky suddenly lost that dazzling brightness, and was pure blue now; and the wind rose higher. Even the leaves on the tips of the branches were deep in contemplation, but the gushing cool freshness came filling the sky and land, and in this one moment all the cruel heat was wiped out.

I stood in the middle of the road, so moved.

I shouted aloud in silence. I am a witness, I testify to the reality of the Way of Heaven. The freshness is melting me, caressing me. It is a witness, it testifies that I have held out till today.

Beginning of Autumn … China's terse conclusion, right. Suddenly I understood what the ancients meant: their bitter experiences, their patience, their feelings and judgements, found their way into their distinctions and conclusions. Beginning of Autumn, these three words, divide heat from coolness; they show a regular pattern, year after year they tell us stupid descendants — there is order in the Way of Heaven, everything is in the embrace of something much larger.

From that Beginning of Autumn — I should say after that Beginning of Autumn moment — the people of Beijing and I began to enjoy the pleasures of the cool freshness. Everyone was calmer and friendlier, waiting for the next even happier calendrical division. Northerners and Southerners alike could share in this pleasure. The rule of Beginning of Autumn had been upheld throughout China. I once heard of a foreigner who said in excitement, You Chinese people, your calendrical divisions are spot on! I think this is perhaps the last thing you can teach to a foreigner.

I thought back over the many years but couldn't remember. Every year Beginning of Autumn had come, but I had no feelings that I could remember. Maybe there'd never been such a ruthlessly cruel summer like this one past. Maybe I'd never learnt enough about the Way of Heaven.

For a long time I was moved by the great, gentle, cleansing infusion of the cool freshness. From that Beginning of Autumn moment to this day I am reminded, every instance of every day, of Beginning of Autumn's power. I will no longer react slowly, I will no longer mistake it, I will use body and soul to savour it, drop by drop, and make a record of it. I want to testify — the Way of Heaven does exist — although I already perceive the difficulty of bearing witness.

For China has long since concluded its testimony, in language so terse that only three words were used.

HUTONG
THE LANE

GU XIAOYANG

translated by Duncan Hewitt

Nowadays, 'hutong' is no longer just a word to me; it is even further removed from the physical object that I saw, touched, walked along, every day for thirty years.... It has come to signify a period of history, a nostalgic longing, an incurable sickness of the heart. I may be in Tokyo, Paris, New York, but I've never quite shaken the habit of asking: 'Which hutong should I take?' The result, of course, is that I tend to get lost rather frequently.

The hutong where I lived was in the east of Beijing, inside the Jianguo Gate. It was a poverty-stricken, decrepit place, full of rough, crude people. I shall never forget how, on dark stormy nights, the men and young lads of the lane would come charging out of their houses with a great shout, grabbing door-poles, choppers, bricks, ready to wage war against anyone — men and lads from other lanes, the police, it made no difference — who might have the temerity to attack us. The fighting was often over nothing more than a dove, a marble or some casual obscenity.... One big tough, who had a blue dragon tattooed on his upper arm, used to stand guard, bare-chested, at the entrance to the lane, like the protective idol in a temple doorway. He wasn't frightened of the police — on the contrary, they were terrified of him and did their best to keep out of his way. Whenever they arrested him they used to have to surround his house with twenty or thirty men, then call out: Shange'r! Come out you bastard, or we'll clap your mum in handcuffs and take her away!' And so, for the sake of his beloved mother and the three strands of white hair on her head, Shange'r would come out, spitting at the ground as he held his hands out for the policemen to put the cuffs on him.

Amidst the clusters of low, dingy, communal courtyard houses, long fallen into disrepair, a few elegant dwellings remained.... Like the luxurious mansion which had been the home of the famous painter Xu

Beihong. Once, during the Cultural Revolution, we crouched at the foot of its tall grey-brick walls, listening, while inside the Red Guards interrogated and beat his widow Liao Jingwen. After each round of whipping and cursing, she would reply: 'Long live Chairman Mao!' When it was all over, the 'Xu family fool', her backward son who used to play chess with us, went shuffling off to the local junk shop and sold off the family's treasured collection of antique bronzes.... So now you know that my childhood education contained these two lessons at least: violence and contempt for culture.

The *hutong* and its inhabitants were prey to all the whims of fortune. In 1966, when Beijing was building its Underground, the lane was cut in two by a huge ditch forty metres deep and forty metres across. The people on either side could do little but gaze at each other from afar; social contact, long-standing feuds and friendships, all were abruptly broken off. A prefabricated wooden building was put up in the middle of the lane, and a squad of army construction troops with strange accents swarmed in, like a plague of locusts, shattering the lane's age-old tranquillity. A few years later, they vanished without trace, leaving behind a gleaming white roadway and a handful of illegitimate children. The prefabricated building still stood arrogantly halfway along the lane. Now though, it had become concrete, stretching out towards the ancient walls of our houses and up towards the shrunken sky. It had also acquired an imposing gateway, with a sign on the front which read: 'Beijing Railway Station District Public Security Bureau'.

Yet everyone's sense of security somehow vanished. Now, whenever you looked up in your courtyard, the first-floor windows of the police station gleamed back at you, like a row of prying eyes. A 'people's petition', for once genuinely popular, was organized in the lane; the man behind it was an illiterate old soldier, a veteran of the Eighth Route Army in the Anti-Japanese War. 'This just ain't right, Yang my boy', he told me, his face flushed and his lips trembling with emotion. 'The police are there to serve the people, not to encroach on the interests of us residents!' Everyone rushed to sign the petition. This wasn't politics, this was just a tiny little request to the government, that's all.... You won't be able to guess the outcome, of course, because there was no outcome, as was so often the case. The Municipal Government, the State Council, the Standing Committee of the National People's Congress, all those things you hear about — to the people in the lane, they were like Kafka's 'Castle'. How could you get into it when you didn't even know where it was? All you could do was to wait for orders to be relayed, one after another, from inside the 'castle', awe-struck by its all-pervasive power. This, I think, is why for so many years, the 'castle' was able to manipulate the people so successfully that they would pour into Tiananmen Square to show how much they supported it.

So that's how I lived for thirty years. Almost my entire life, from the day I was born, was stored up in the *hutong*, like a vat of fine wine in the cellar, the flavour maturing with each passing year. Again and again I sample it, savouring every nuance, soothing the heavy feeling in my breast with the wine of times past. This has become my spiritual pleasure, which I am never without, no matter where my drifting takes me. But I am well aware that it's not all pleasure — it causes me pain as well, which spreads round my body, and a terror which invades me, like a bacteria against which I have no resistance. For the more I miss my home, the more acute my sense of becoming divorced from my own history. The news my neighbours tell me in their letters is ominous: the area around my house — our *hutong* — has been completely demolished, reduced to a heap of rubble. Not a trace remains of my childhood, my past, everything I possessed. Like a shadow which has lost its soul, I drift around Manhattan, searching for my *hutong*.... The streets are strewn with its fragments; I bend to pick them up, but as soon as my fingertips touch them they turn to dust. What I'm saying is, if you've lost your links to the past, then you've lost your history, and then what's left?

The lane is preserved in a treasured photograph, the surrounding area, outside the camera's field of vision, carelessly omitted.... The road, with its length and its depth, on whose surface I used to roll my iron hoop, wrestle, turn somersaults, has been pressed flat. Thanks to a ray of light, a decent Zeiss lens and a film made in Baoding, that perfectly ordinary, insignificant moment was detached from the river-bed of eternal, seamless, constantly fluctuating time; as though knocked from a mould it fell into my palm. The picture shows a group of children aged between ten and fifteen; perhaps it was because no one had ever before scrutinized them quite so closely (though it was only for a few brief seconds), but each of their faces betrays a hint of panic. And that little boy standing, lost in thought, at the side, wrapped in a thick blue coat to keep out the wind, it never occurred to him that this fleeting sixtieth of a second out of his life would be preserved to this day, or that, twenty years later, the lane he saw, touched, walked along every day would cause him such sorrow, that he would crave possession of it as people crave vast riches. It never occurred to him that, since time could turn the world upside down, make the rivers run dry and beauty wither, nothing was beyond its powers. And now he has realised all these things which never occurred to him, and he can't help being filled with awe for the Creator.... That boy, of course, was me.

UNDER-*SKY*
UNDER*GROUND*

O

CRITICISM

SENSING THE SHIFT — NEW WAVE LITERATURE AND CHINESE CULTURE

Henry Y H Zhao

abridged and translated by the author

1 MY INTENTION

This essay is intended for a few friends who hold that Chinese culture has long been disintegrating. It cannot be saved, nor does it need to be saved. Recent Chinese literature, they hold, is another effort to totally subvert the Chinese cultural tradition.

This essay is also meant for other friends who maintain that the May Fourth Movement, the cultural criticism movement that saw the inception of *modern* Chinese literature, was too hasty in destroying the continuity of Chinese tradition, and thus actually impeded the modernization of Chinese culture. Chinese intellectuals, especially the younger generation are, it is claimed, repeating this mistake.

The present paper is not a compromise between the two positions. It only suggests a new angle from which to view the opposition of traditionalism and anti-traditionalism in modern Chinese fiction, and takes a few steps further.

2 THE THREE CONTINUITIES

Culture is humanity's most complex creation. I suggest that we regard culture as the sum of all socially-related significations (and their interpretations). Although almost all human activities can be regarded as significations, some are pure signification activities, some are partial ones, and yet others have only a marginal signifying function.

These activities of signification and interpretation can be co-ordinated because there are norms, values and ethical codes that control them. All the controlling activities merge into a cultural metalanguage, which is basically what we call ideology. There is, however, another level of activities above them all — activities which try to tidy up, to speculate on, and to modify this metalanguage. Philosophy, linguistics, literature and art are among these activities. Perhaps they can all be put under one old heading — 'Letters' in its broadest sense.

Let me borrow from Chinese historiography three concepts to summarize traditionalism in the three kinds of activities.

The Continuity of Rule (Fa Tong) denotes, in this essay, the continuity of the manner of governing, of the organization of the regime, the division of classes in society, etc. These are the most public part of cultural activities. This continuity can be claimed by any regime whose rule is maintained as valid for a sufficiently long period.

The Continuity of Truth (Dao Tong) refers to the continuity of the manner of controlling and regulating signification and interpretation. So long as the control of the interpretative codes is validated, whether the actual political practice is just or not is of little importance.

The Continuity of Letters (Wen Tong), by which I mean the tradition of the Humanities, even though there was no such concept in Classical Chinese. This is the activity that questions, speculates on and readjusts signification in society. Literature is definitely its most complicated manifestation, and deserves more careful study.

According to *The Records of History*, the Prince of Qin declared in the 7th century BC, 'China is ruled by Poetry and Books, Rites and Music, and Law and Order.' The three Traditions are listed together, and the sequence is considered.

On the large scale of Chinese history, the way these three aspects have been preserved and transformed has been very different. The Continuity of Letters seemed to be the most persistent as it usually remained unchanged as the dynasties succeeded one another.

At a glance, we can discover that the flourishing and decline of the three have often overlapped. In the so-called 'periods of prosperity' in Chinese history, the Continuity of Rule was stable, the Continuity of Truth was firmly monolithic, and the pressure to maintain the Continuity of Letters was usually so great that the introduction of new forms of literature was at least discouraged. In so-called 'periods of chaos', political and ideological control is relaxed, and literature often prospers. Indeed we may say that the May Fourth Movement was possible because the Government was made so weak by the warlords who were preoccupied with civil war that ideological control was seriously slackened.[1] The Beijing regime at the time was definitely hostile toward the New Culture Movement. It tried to confiscate books and expel certain academics from the universities, but the orders were never executed effectively. Indeed there can be found only a small number of documents about governmental suppression of the May Fourth Movement.[2]

I propose, however, that we look at these 'chaotic' times from another angle: in the periods during which the Continuity of Rule is broken, and the Continuity of Truth is in crisis, the survival of Chinese culture relies mainly on the adaptability of the Continuity of Letters, since Chinese culture at such junctures is in need not only of survival but also of reorientation. The crisis of a regime and its ideology not only creates an opportunity for reorientation but also a need for it. And the Continuity of Letters plays a particularly important role in this reorientation.

Chinese culture is the world's longest surviving culture, and is sure to regain its vitality. It is only a half truth to say that the reason for this survival is its stubborn exclusiveness, or 'super-stability'. Its ability to reorientate itself has been, I would claim, an even more important reason.

3 'NEW WAVE SENSIBILITY'?

This bold and assertive argument was put forward here only to answer one small question: What, after all, is the sensibility that has been the driving force of the New Wave of literature since 1985?

Often we hear the lament that contemporary Chinese literature suffers from a 'lack of modern sensibility', without which, it is argued, there could be only a 'pseudo-modernism'. It is also suggested that this modern sensibility could only be the product of modern existence — modern modes production and ways of life. Since these do not yet exist in a China which is still under-developed, New Wave literature, especially its avant-garde arm, is nothing more than an imported fashion. It should be considered a premature development in art, as is the

---

[1] Please refer to my forthcoming book *The Uneasy Narrator: Chinese Fiction from the Traditional to the Modern*, (Oxford: Oxford University Press, 1994) which cites examples showing the government's inability to interfere in the May Fourth cultural movement.

[2] In the Volume of Historical Documents, *Zhongguo xin wenxue daxi* (The Omnibus of Chinese New Literature, 1935) edited by Zhao Jiabi, there is a special section devoted to the government's suppression. The documents in this 'section' are too few to justify its title.

premature consumerism that is also part of China today. New Wave literature is nothing more than canned softdrink, fashionable but not yet affordable for the majority of the Chinese people.

New Wave criticism, as an important part of New Wave literature, has not yet offered a satisfactory answer to this argument. Without an understanding of this mysterious 'sensibility', the impetus of the movement will be curbed, if it has not been already.

The old challenge has a new refrain: 'The New Wave can only by appreciated by Western scholars. Chinese critics of the new school are merely slavishly echoing Western scholars of Chinese literature. Chinese readers do not like it.' I, along with many of my colleagues, are angered by this accusation, since it is totally groundless. The New Wave has been supported all along by Chinese critics, while Western scholars of contemporary Chinese literature are still very much out of touch.[3] Nevertheless, we have to answer the second half of the question. It is true that the majority of Chinese fiction readers do not appreciate New Wave fiction. But why?

4 PRE-TEXTUALITY

The theoretical ground for the argument of 'pseudo-modernism' is that literary sensibility generally grows with, if not from, the development of social conditions. This is at best an over-simplification.

There is no denying that social life has provided literature with empirical material. Yet any genre, at a certain stage of development, should be turning to itself, as a text turns to previous texts which are more or less familiar to its readers, for subject matter as well as for interpretative criteria. In the history of Chinese poetry we can see that from *The Book of Songs* (compiled *c.* 7th c. BC) and *The Music Department Collections* (*c.* 2nd–1st c. BC) to the great periods of Tang and Song, the reliance on social experience gradually fades. With the accumulation of pre-textuality, the demands on the reader's knowledge of previous literature becomes greater.[4]

Pre-textuality is actually the presence of the whole cultural tradition in the text.

---

[3] An outstanding example: the Chinese writer that interests Western critics and publishers most is still Zhang Xianliang. The only selection of Avant-Garde Fiction currently available in English is *The Lost Boat: Avant-garde fiction from China*, compiled by myself (London: Wellsweep Press, 1993).

[4] There is no fundamental difference between my conception of pre-textuality and Julia Kristeva's intertextuality. But she emphasizes more the mutual control of co-existent texts while I emphasize the accumulation of the control of previous texts.

In early 1980s, Li Zehou, the leading contemporary Chinese aesthetician, put forward the proposition of 'the Sedimentation of Cultural Mentality' which argues that the 'practical rationalism' of the Chinese nation is 'the sediment of the whole of Chinese material and spiritual civilization that presents itself in medicine, agriculture, war, historiography, philosophy … etc.'[5] This is a universal sedimentation. All cultural activities add to the sediment, and the sediment covers all areas. Li did not try to classify the cultural activities according to how they contribute to the sedimentation.

Li's proposition was severely criticized by Liu Xiaobo, a much younger critic, who refuted the proposition with harsh words, 'a theory that is supposed to be able to solve all problems is unable to solve any problem.' To replace this 'all-round sediment' theory, however, he suggests a theory of all-round negation. 'Culture,' as he puts it, 'is not an apple beginning to rot that could still be eaten after the rotten part has been gouged out.'[6] Instead culture, when partly rotten, should be thrown away altogether.

Indeed the activities of meaning-practice leave little pre-textuality. After a war that cost tens of thousands of lives, the only remaining thing might be 'a rusted spearhead picked up by a shepherd boy on the hillside'. The activities of meaning-control could leave many more traces, while the efforts to modify codes are meaningful only through the pre-textuality they leave behind. On the other hand, the three kinds of activities, when practised, experience different pressure from the past — with the last almost totally dependent on pre-textuality.

This is why the history of literature has to be constantly rewritten.

5 PRE-TEXTUALITY DURING CULTURAL REORIENTATION

Whether a treasure or a burden, the abundance of pre-textuality in Chinese culture is something that Chinese literature must acknowledge.

Chinese culture has two different phases of development — continuation and reorientation. In Chinese history, we can detect at least three periods of drastic reorientation: the Spring and Autumn and the Warring States (8th–3rd centuries BC), Wei–Jin and Six Dynasties

[5] Li Zehou, *Zhongguo xiandai sixiang shilun* (*A* History of Modern Thought in China), Beijing: Dongfang Chubanshe, 1987, p. 321.
[6] Liu Xiaobo, *Xuanze de pipan* (The Critique of Choice), Shanghai: Shanghai Remin Chubanshe, 1988, p. 14.

(AD 3rd–6th centuries), and Southern Song and Yuan (AD 12th–14th centuries).[7] Each period of reorientation is followed by a period of relative stable development, that is, periods of continuation. These were, however, also periods of accumulation of tension which would eventually lead to a breaking point, thus calling for another reorientation.

In the late Ming, starting from the mid-16th century, a reorientation was rapidly brewing following the decay of the Continuities of Rule and Truth. Among late Ming literati, there were large numbers of intellectual rebels and ideological dissidents. Many of them showed great interest in popular literature, even in 'pornographic' novels. Some of these were, indeed, written by these same scholars themselves. The realm of Letters was changing drastically.

Regrettably, peasant uprisings destroyed the weakened Continuity of Rule too rapidly, and the invading Manchus effectively rebuilt this Continuity in the mid-17th century. In order to justify their foreign rule, they tried their best to re-establish Confucian orthodoxy. A potential reorientation that might have taken place at a critical historical juncture (almost simultaneous with the Renaissance in the West) was abortive. An opportunity to make Chinese culture flexible enough to face modern times was lost.

The next reorientation period of Chinese culture is none other than modern times. Since the late 19th century, Chinese culture has been confronted with one of the most serious challenges in its history — to reorientate in order to face the modern world. This period has been dubbed, by the alarmists the 'Crisis of Chinese Culture' repeatedly, although in my view it is, rather, a period of profound reorientation.

This reorientation has been difficult. More than one hundred years have passed, with still no immediate prospect of success. Yet history tells us that the reorientation of Chinese culture always took much longer than one century. If that is the case, my pessimistic friends should perhaps be less worried.

During the periods of reorientation, old genres are often found to be too heavily burdened with pre-textuality (cluttered, for instance, with too many hackneyed expressions, allusions, conventions, etc.), and new genres are called for. This very fact causes art and literature to

---

[7] Not everyone would agree with me that the Southern Song and Yuan is a period of cultural re-orientation. The Neo-Confucianism that arose in this period was certainly an effort to consolidate the traditional ideology. Nevertheless, the rise of vernacular literature, together with the rise of Neo-Confucianism, transformed Chinese culture from one that was relatively homogenous to one that was overtly stratified.

flourish. For being new is indeed the first requirement of literature. The poetry and philosophical essays before the 2nd century BC, the five-character poetry and rhapsodic rhyme prose of the 3rd–6th centuries, the vernacular fiction and drama of the 13th–14th centuries, are all the high points of Chinese literary history.

In these periods, social conditions were miserable, with incursions of nomadic invaders, the rapid impoverishment of the people, and the collapse of social order. If literature reflects social reality, the dominant theme in those periods should have been the sufferings of the people. But in fact the opposite seems to have been the case. Accounts of the people's suffering are much less in evidence in the literature of those periods as compared with other periods of stability.

To the literature of these periods, the problem of cultural reorientation is more important than social life. Its literature emphasizes cultural, or rather spiritual, values. Their relations with the cultural tradition, i.e., pre-textuality, become the focus of attention.

That is why Chinese literature in the periods of reorientation is different in style from that of the stable periods. The former, more obsessed with speculation, is stranger, more fantastic and original in style, while the latter, more embedded in society, is broader, more magnanimous, more profound.

6 THE SEARCH OUTSIDE

Since very early times, Chinese culture has predominantly been a culture that values literature highly. Oral and other non-literate texts (music, for instance) did not have sufficient meaning power, and lacked the ability to produce pre-textuality.

Chinese culture was not ever thus. In the Classics prior to the 2nd century BC there were many passages emphasizing the importance of the 'cultural education' of music or the 'cultural supremacy' of dance. Literary domination set in at the end of the first reorientation period. The sharing of meaning power by non-literary forms of 'texts' was brought to an end, and the dependence on the literary became greater in Chinese culture than in any other .

This literary dependence may have something to do with the non-phonetic nature of the Chinese language. Perhaps it is no coincidence that the Chinese people, since those times, no longer excelled in singing and dancing when contrasted with the 'barbarians' surrounding them. Confucius' obsession with music has never been fully understood by Confucian scholars for more than two thousands years.

They only took it as a complement to Confucius' emphasis on the Rites. Even Chinese statesmen have seldom striven to excel in oratory (in sharp contrast with the statesmanship of the Warring States period of 4th–3rd c. BC) but pride themselves on writing elegant essays.

Literary culture enjoys greater capacity for continuity, since written texts can be easily preserved, reread and reprinted. The failure of the burning of books by the First Emperor proved that pre-textuality, once formed, can hardly be wiped out by political force.

The conservation of this tradition, nevertheless, leads its lack of flexibility. The ease of the production of pre-textuality naturally leads to the weight of accumulation. After a period of stability, the excess pressure of Letters combined with the inefficiency of Rule and the hypocritization of the Truth, and Chinese culture is then left with no choice but to reorientate.

Looking back at Chinese history, we find that, in literature, reorientation often includes an expansion of the generic range, that is, the exploration of new genres and new forms. These new forms can come from two sources. Sometimes the subcultural oral genres are absorbed into mainstream literature, and we can see a re-adjustment of position between centrality and marginality. Sometimes the new forms come from other cultures, and we can see a re-adjustment of the relationship between the centre and other centres. In the Southern Song and Yuan period (AD 12th–14th c.), it was mainly the oral subcultural strata that served to supply new genres; in the Six-Dynasties (AD 5th–6th c.) and modern times, alien cultures seem to have been the main sources of new forms.[8]

The adoption of new genres creates not only a rupture in the Continuity of Letters, but also an opportunity to re-examine pre-textuality and to consider a new mode of accumulation. For instance, modern Chinese poetry, beginning in the late 1910s, started to use vernacular Chinese as the new poetic language, and borrowed Western stanzaic forms. The first aim was in fact to shake off the too cumbersome accumulation of pre-textuality in Chinese poetry, because it has imposed a huge burden of allusions and poetic diction upon the writing of poetry. The 'New Poetry' succeeded in integrating the spirit of the Greek gods and goddess with the passion of *Songs of the South*, in combining Anglo-American Imagist principles with the traditional Chinese attention to images; the religious quietism of Tagore with the

---

[8] Before the 3rd century BC, the distinction between China Proper and the Barbarians was not clear, neither was the distinction between literacy and orality.

serenity of Chinese art. Many scholars hold that Chinese New Poetry was a typical subversion of national tradition by Western influence.[9] I prefer to see New Poetry as a more effective continuation of Chinese tradition — its transformation, not its disruption — because the new genres were quite successfully grafted onto the pre-textuality of Chinese culture.

To use the terms of semiotics, we may say that in periods of reorientation, syntagmatic expansion is the main form of development, with the component genres re-adjusting their relative positions; in periods of stability, the paradigmatic extension is the main form, with the genres enlarging their connotations.

It is not strange that in the literature of the reorientation periods we often find a powerful 'formalistic' tendency. Because during those periods, the development of literature is mainly an adoption of new forms.

7 LITERATI GENRES

To absorb new genres or new forms into Chinese culture, it is essential to grant them sufficient meaning power. They have to become 'literati genres'. Without this change, they remain unassimilated, to be tolerated but not respected.

Transforming a certain genre into a genre of the literati can be seen as a process of transfusing it with pre-textuality. Folk-songs of the 7th and 8th centuries remained a subcultural genre. It was the effort of Wen Tingjun and other poets in the anthology *Amidst the Flowers* that turned them into a new 'literary' genre. The popular songs of the Jin and Yuan periods (12th and 13th centuries) remained outside Chinese culture until Ma Zhiyuan, Bai Pu and others made it a new genre of Chinese high literature. The Southern Opera of 13th and 14th centuries did not enter Chinese culture until The *Lute Song* (*c.* AD 1375) turned it into a new genre. Many scholars would protest loudly — today we know at least two hundred titles of early Southern Operas. But the printed texts of those plays in the 13th century or the first half of the 14th century were all lost. The dozen or so texts we can see now were all recently unearthed relics. If the texts of a whole genre are not

---

[9] Prof. Stephen Owen's accusation ('What Is World Poetry', *The New Republic*, November 19, 1990, p. 28) that modern Chinese poetry is a poor imitation of Western Romanticism is one of the latest of almost a century long toll of unfair judgement on modern Chinese literature by Western scholars.

preserved, we can only say that the genre had not yet entered into the highly literary-dependent Chinese culture.[10]

The May Fourth writers who began to use the vernacular in literature, earlier in this century, believed that they were making literature more accessible to the masses. They may well have been sincere in their efforts, yet what they actually did was to make the originally reader-friendly popular vernacular fiction much more difficult to read. Only after being accept for use in literati genre was the Chinese vernacular, originally a 'vulgar tongue', made into *the* language of Chinese culture.

The process of privilege is also one of sinicization, during which the pre-textuality of Chinese culture is forced into the alien genres. We discussed the case of New Poetry in the last section. Let us now take a look at modern Chinese fiction. Lu Xun, the writer who was most critical of Chinese culture, and Yu Dafu who was the first to propose that Chinese literature should 'go to the world', are both extremely concerned with their pre-texts. The first piece of modern Chinese fiction, 'The Madman's Diary' has an narrative frame written in classical Chinese; The *True Story of Ah Q* discusses the subgenres of biography in the Chinese tradition, and finds that the present one does not fit into any of them. Both these two works can be seen as efforts to place modern Chinese literature within the Continuity of Letters. Many of the characters in Lu Xun's other stories are members of the former literati, who have had to readjust their positions in relation to Chinese culture since they find themselves thrown out of its power and meaning structures. Yu Dafu's intensely autobiographical protagonist, while obsessed with Wordsworth, was perhaps even more possessed by the ghosts of Chinese poets of the last century.

Indeed there was little realism of any sort in May Fourth fiction. In contrast with the late Qing fiction (1902–17), May Fourth fiction (1918–27) took a huge step back from political and social realism. It might even be said that while late Qing fiction was still concerned

---

[10] This rule of thumb is applicable only to certain periods of Chinese culture. Before the 2nd century BC, many texts of mainstream culture were passed down orally. The lack of a fixed channel for the culture's texts resulted in textual chaos when literacy became the criterion, and led to the two thousand years dispute over Confucian scriptures between the Old Character School (who hold that the texts of Confucian canons inscribed in 6th century BC characters are the genuine texts) and the New Character School (who hold that those inscribed in the 2nd century BC are the genuine texts as they had been orally passed down by generations of Confucian scholars).

with the Continuities of Rule and Truth, May Fourth literature was concerned more with that of Letters.[11]

Therefore, May Fourth literature is what I call pure literature, which arises only in a period of cultural reorientation.

8 THE FUNCTION OF THE COUNTER-CULTURE

The independence of Letters is especially important in periods of cultural reorientation, when the criticism of pre-textuality becomes a central issue for the survival of the culture.

Generally speaking, in periods of stability, the adjustment of the signification system is mainly a defence of pre-textuality, while in reorientation periods the adjustment of the signification system often assumes a subversive position, since the new codes of the signification system can only be built on a criticism of pre-textuality. So long as the reorientation is not yet complete, a critical examination of pre-textuality is the focus of the activities of Letters.

This subversive attitude gives literature a strong counter-cultural inflection during periods of reorientation . A portion at least of men of letters are intentionally violating the social norms: their gatherings of students and propagation of ideas in the Spring and Autumn and Warring States periods, their 'pure conversation' and 'unruly and unrestrained' behaviour in the Six Dynasties period, their frequenting of popular theatres in the Southern Song and Yuan period, and their megalomania during the May Fourth period. All these manifestations of personal behaviour, intentionally eccentric, are meant to challenge the norms. Naturally, these people's re-examination of pre-textuality often poses as a total rejection of traditionalism.

We have to understand that this pose of rejection is more a metaphor than a discursive statement. The best example is Lu Xun's claim that Chinese history is a history of 'man eating man', a claim that excited the whole May Fourth generation. Since Chinese history was considered more civilized than the history of any other nation, Lu Xun's statement can only be seen as a devastating metaphor, a chal-

11 This attitude was drastically changed around 1925. Lu Xun, the leading May Fourth writer, and a firm opponent of 'Revolutionary Literature' began to be involved in political disputes, and by the end of that year, he stopped writing fiction for good.

lenging pose, a signal of his hatred of the dark side of Chinese culture.[12]

Similarly, we have to view the notorious 'wholesale Westernization' of the May Fourth as a counter-cultural metaphor, a special mode of pre-textual criticism. Indeed Westernization in modern times bears a striking resemblance to the influx of Buddhism during the Six Dynasties. In the 5th and 6th centuries, Chinese culture was overrun by Buddhism to the point of turning the whole country Buddhist, something which worried many who believed that Chinese culture would be totally swamped up by the alien religion. Since there was nothing farther from Confucianism than Buddhism, this fear was taken very seriously, and many died in order to 'save the nation'. What does history then show us? Buddhism was sinicized by the 7th century, and both greatly enriched and was greatly enriched by Chinese culture.

Nevertheless, in order to preserve the metaphorical nature of cultural criticism, literature has to stay within the sphere of Letters, that is, to remain 'pure'. Because, we have to understand, counter-cultural criticism only provides a *possibility* of cultural reorientation. To use the words of the May Fourth writers, it is diagnosis without prescription, let alone cure.

Viewed in this way, counter-culture cannot be judged as a success or a failure. In fact it is destined to be failure, because its subversive power is only metaphorical. The direction of the counter-culture is never the eventual direction adopted by mainstream culture after the reorientation. If Buddhism had become the real direction of Chinese culture at the time of the Six Dynasties, Chinese history would have been cut into two scarcely connected halves, as Islam divided the history of many Middle-Eastern nations.

The often-heard accusations: 'pure conversation ruined the Jin Dynasty', or 'Buddhism and Daoism ruined the Liang Dynasty' are all politicians' scapegoating. In the 1950s many in Taiwan accused Hu Shi, the pioneer thinker of the May Fourth Movement, of 'losing China'. In the last twenty years there has been a view shared by many Chinese scholars, especially those residing in the West, that the May Fourth criticism of Chinese culture is shallow and harmful. I believe

---

[12] Lu Xun himself was aware of this metaphorical nature of his criticism of Chinese culture. When commenting on the 'anti-ritual' tendency among the men of letters of the Wei–Jin period (AD 3rd–4th c.), he pointed out, 'Those who upheld the Rites were actually destroying them. They in fact did not believe them. Those against the Rites were in fact recognizing the Rites and believing in them. [Their negation of the Rites] was only a pose.' (Lu Xun *Quanji*, Beijing: 1981, vol. 3, p. 513).

that these accusations all come from a misunderstanding of the historical role of counter-culture.

9 NEW WAVE SENSIBILITY IS THE SENSIBILITY OF REORIENTATION

After all these arguments we can now come back to our topic of Chinese literature. 'Pure literature' is not art for art's sake. Any signification is inevitably a social activity. No literature can be totally detached from society and culture in general. The obsession of pure literature with itself should be understood as mainly a disguised concern with the pre-textuality of the culture.[13]

Contemporary Chinese literature began to discard the role of political and propagandist tool at the beginning of the 1980s. Yet its main concerns remained utilitarian, as in the early 1980s Chinese literature was still trapped within immediate social concerns. It was not until the post-1985 New Wave that Chinese literature regained the spirit of cultural criticism it assumed during the May Fourth period, and became concerned with Letters alone.

New Wave literature, in its brief history of five years, has shown various characteristics typical of literature during a period of reorientation — its counter-cultural 'total subversion' (Can Xue's *The Muddy Street*, Liu Suola's *You Have No Choice*), its stubborn antagonism against existing norms (Wang Anyi's *The Century on the Hill*, Han Shaogong's *Dad Dad Dad*), its unsparing ridicule of any existing value system (Ye Zhaoyan's *The Dusk of May*, Duo Duo's *The Last Song*), its impulse to find values outside the mainstream culture (A Cheng's *The King of Chess*, Mo Yan's *Red Sorghum*), its strong disbelief in any control of signification (Yu Hua's 'Bloody Plum', Su Tong's *The Escape of 1934*), its resignation to the inevitable tragedy of the individual in the society (Shi Tiesheng's 'Fate', Ge Fei's *The Lost Boat*), its esoteric and bizarre style (Sun Ganlu's *The Letter from the Postman*, He Liwei's 'The White Bird'), etc.

The comparison between New Wave fiction and pre-1985 'Wound Fiction' is very similar to that between May Fourth fiction and late

---

13 The forum chaired by Zhu Dake on Chinese Avant-garde Literature in March 1989 seems to represent a high point in the understanding of the New Wave by Chinese critics and writers. Anyway, it was the last published critical effort to interpret the movement. At least, Sun Ganlu suggested that the Avant-Gardists should 'take the lead in withdrawing from the national arena. (*Shanghai Wenxue*, 1989, no. 5, p. 45). Such desocialization of Avant-Garde literature denies the cultural meaning of avant-gardism, reducing it to the isolated preferences of some individuals.

Qing fiction. The New Wave keeps a distance from reality. Even the Reforms which concern everybody in China, or the Cultural Revolution that no one can forget, are now placed in the distance, as can be seen in such works as Yu Hua's *1986*, or Ge Fei's 'A Trip to Yelang'. In these works, social reality is only the vehicle of a metaphor.

And, while handing over the task of entertaining the masses to popular literature, and that of educating the masses to 'Reportage' literature, it has willingly jettisoned the power to cause a popular sensation. Its persistent formal innovation has diminished its readership. It has been turned into the privileged literature of an elite.

Behind the kaleidoscopic features of the New Wave fiction, there is an obvious shared sensibility, or guiding principle, which the New Wave writers themselves may not be aware of — they are writing the kind of pure literature needed for cultural reorientation. Its critical spirit seeks to cause a rupture with the pre-textuality of Chinese culture, a temporary vacuum of values, through which the immense pressure of the cultural reorientation may surge in a new direction.

Such a sensibility can not be a mere fashion borrowed from elsewhere. Alien culture can provide Chinese literature with a few new forms but not with the sensibility of cultural reorientation.

This is a genuine, not a bogus, modern sensibility, because it is summoned forth by this entirely modern period of cultural reorientation. Whether the laurels of modernism or postmodernism suit it best is of lesser importance.

THE 'WESTERNIZATION' OF CHINESE LITERATURE IN THE 1980s

YOU YI

translated by Duncan Hewitt*

Westernization, imitating the west — these are phrases with elusive definitions and which arouse much controversy, but which are unavoidable for students of modern Chinese literature. Mainland Chinese literature of the 1980s saw great outpourings of 'anti-realism' and experimental works, and the world of literary criticism was forced, against the background of the theory and events of the preceding years, to seek a suitable response to this new — or rather perennial — problem.

All kinds of labels have been attached to these 'anti-realist' works over the last few years — 'misty poetry', 'new poetry', 'stream of consciousness fiction', 'modernism', 'pseudo-modernism', 'experimental fiction', etc. Clearly none of these epithets gives a really accurate picture. But accurate or not, the real questions surround the links between such writing and Western literature remain unclear. Undeniably, all of these labels provoked fashionable short-term debate as to whether a particular work really was, or really resembled, Western stream of consciousness or modernist writing, whether it was the real thing or just false modernism, which works were imitations, which were original creations, and where the line should be drawn. As early as the mid-eighties, a few scholars were starting to debate the question of western influence and the problem of such labels. And while reminding writers that literature should not be the blind pursuit of passing fame, critics like Huang Ziping also pointed out that the dispute over fake or genuine modernism was a trap which the critics had set for themselves.

* This is a translation of the first, more or less self-contained, part of You Yi's essay as it was published in the original Chinese.

It wasn't long before the works being produced began to display a greater depth and breadth of content to match their new techniques, yet, for the critics, the problem of labelling them still remained. The technical terms which accompanied every characteristic of Western modernist literature began to cast their shadow, seeping into the explanations, terminology and descriptions of Chinese 'anti-realism'. A few critics soon settled on the term 'experimental', with its very broad denotations, as a temporary label, yet it was still hard to get away from the limitations of the established Western usage. In an attempt to shift the critics' focus away from 'what should we call it' to 'what does this actually mean', and reveal the gulf between Chinese and Western literary terms, other critics, like Tang Xiaobing, raised the question of what 'postmodernism' actually signified in China. However, it is still possible to find oneself going round and round in circles debating whether or not 'postmodernism' can actually apply to anything in China.

But this was not all — if you start to analyse this 'post-socialist realism' in the context of global or 'international' terminology, you come up against a new type of ambiguity. Bearing in mind the world-wide spread of Western terminology in recent times — or to be more precise, based on the analysis and criticism of the language of colonialism by many third world scholars — some academics, as they became aware of the historical existence of this kind of linguistic power structure and joined the ranks of its critics, were far too quick to see certain some 'anti-realist' Chinese works simply as further examples of the 'globalization' of the West-Centrism of discourse. Whether China had absorbed 'the discourse of Western cultural colonialism', or whether works suspected of being 'Western' were actually the products of colonialism, has troubled many people .

It is my view that, on two points, the apparently plausible criticisms of 'postmodernism' by many scholars are actually misguided. Firstly, colonial phraseology is actually a kind of international language developed within modern and contemporary Chinese literature itself. Undoubtedly, certain Western modernist styles entered the discursive structure of 1980s Chinese literature in specific ways. But this fact cannot obscure several others. This is not the only area of language — it may not even be the most important area, in fact; and the way in which Western modernism became a part of Chinese discursive structure remains unclear. The second point is that anti-realist Chinese works, even 'experimental' and 'avant-garde' works, display both similarities and differences with Western modernist literature.

Unfortunately, before drawing their conclusions, very few people bothered to clarify whether or not these works were similar to one or another Western work, or to examine why they might be similar or not. Nevertheless certain of these critiques have provided a basis for further discussion. In the context of post-colonial discourse, we ought to discuss these aspects of 1980s literature, their true origins, what intertextual connections they reveal — and why they do — in order to affirm the special nature of post-realist works.

Actually, it is probably futile to try to establish whether or not the anti-realism of the 1980s is part of the reappearance of a 'global discourse' in China simply by looking at the texts and the words. At the very least, this approach lumps form and discourse together, and even mistakenly interprets the stylistic characteristics of the writing as symbols of a specific type of discourse (for example, modernist writing is equivalent to Western discourse) I don't deny of course, any of the discursive significance which history has bestowed upon certain literary forms, but for this very reason it is all the more important to clarify the specific discursive relations of the time, before judging which type of discourse some aspect of form belongs to.

Something critics often neglect is the fact that the earliest steps in this 'anti-realist' type of work were taken not after the reforms had begun but in the latter part of the Cultural Revolution, under a form of discursive dictatorship which had gradually become more and more extreme over time. As is well known, the literary form of this authoritarian discourse was 'socialist realism', with its 'three foregroundings'. In fact, even if the majority of anti-realist works only converged in a real literary movement after the reforms had begun, their discursive significance and status can often only be established with reference to the discursive structures of the Cultural Revolution. For one thing they were the products and symbols of changes in that structure. The details referred to above beg the question: what was the discourse of the Cultural Revolution, how could it produce such an extreme form of dictatorship, and, why, in the midst of this discursive rigidity, were some people able to write 'Misty' poetry? If we wish to clarify the historical context, these are questions which must be answered.

If one looks at the actual words, there is a connection between the discourse of the Cultural Revolution — the discourse of the 'proletariat' or of the 'dictatorship of the proletariat' — and certain Marxist categories, yet there's no doubt that this discourse was a product of recent Chinese history. It's perhaps worth pointing out that 'the proletariat' here does not refer to a class in the sociological sense of the word, but to the subject of a political discourse, one whose size could be varied. The proletariat refers to a standard, a classification which over 95% of the population may hope to attain by altering their world view. And so 'proletariat', as a reference to the discursive subject, became a kind of prescription or self-designation for the broad masses of society, for the body politic of the nation. And we ought to point out that it was a new designation, a new name. Following the 1911 revolution, the terms 'republicans' and 'citizens' were initially applied to the body politic of the nation. In the intervening period, huge changes had taken place in the arena of Chinese history and, particularly, politics; yet in some respects, the two terms themselves are inter-linked: 'citizens' and 'proletariat' both encapsulate the idea of 'the majority of the Chinese people, or at least over 95% of the Chinese people. And ultimately these words are no more than discursive functions — both are far removed or have even turned their backs on — the 'great majority' of the people who exist in the reality of history.

The desire to give the masses of the people a specific political discursive status can be traced back to the unprecedented historical situation with which China was confronted after the Opium War. Admittedly, changes did take place in China's social structure from the late Ming onwards, but modern Chinese history really began with a series of foreign wars — a series of duels with, and defeats by armed expansionist capitalist states. When the threat to her culture and nationhood left China with no choice but to muster the greatest social and political strength and to accept and join in this global military and economic competition, great chasms and even open conflict appeared between the ancient imperial central power and the rest of society. The 1911 revolution established a new form of the nation, yet did nothing to heal this rift. The second generation of reformers — from Liang Qichao to Sun Yat-sen — hoped that the broad mass of people, previously quite apolitical, would now assume the role of 'citizens ' in a democratic nation-state; moreover they hoped to guarantee the actions of the masses with legal prescriptions. The new culture and literature of the May Fourth Movement' was even more specific in identifying the need to speak the language of the 'great majority of the Chinese people', to write 'an everyday, honest literature of for the citizenry' — 'a national literature'; and of the need to affirm, by means of language and literary style, the discursive status of the masses of 'the people' who had always been excluded from the field of history.

However, this new 'vernacular' language of the time was not really the discourse of the 'people'. More significantly, a social mass which was 'modern' enough to support a new type of nation-state and broad enough to deserve the term 'majority' was not something which could be achieved simply by fighting a few wars or announcing a few linguistic reforms. The fact was that, under threat from the 'global' colonial powers, China's non-colonial economy was under severe threat, the nascent middle class had scarcely developed, having actually fragmented at the moment of its birth — not to mention the 'modern' political and cultural customs of the agricultural masses. Thus the construction of a 'citizen's literature' or a discourse of the 'majority' was very quickly bogged down, as a result of the insufficiencies of the people who were actually intended to speak it. Those in the vanguard had foreseen and planned a 'popular mass' role for language, in an attempt to break the historical impasse; however, the masses, themselves caught in this impasse, failed to fit in with this single-minded stance, or to exercise their allotted function. And so 'the masses' became an empty label, concealing this huge blind spot in the ideology of the May Fourth period.

It is worth noting that, from the 1930s onwards, the 'majority of the Chinese people', a phrase which had previously had no real discursive significance, became a widely accepted literary narrative mode, based on the fusion of a simplified version of Marxist class theory and theory of social revolution. And so from now on the hollow 'mass' came to have a political inflection involving social relationships, motives for action and types of plot.

Thus, the discursive roots of the political category 'proletariat' which appeared decades later can be traced back to this point. The development of this term began with a misnomer and a misunderstanding — the labelling and substitution of China's social divisions with the 'class relations' Marx described in his studies of capitalist forms of production. It was also used to explain the relationships, contradictions and clashes between China, an oppressed nation, and the capitalist nation-states — the plight of an oppressed nation struggling to develop in the modern world having been mistaken for the situation of the 'proletariat' as described by Marx. China's social and political prospects seemed somehow relevant to the original state as described in the theory of proletarian revolution. From the very start, when the proponents of Marxism began to describe China's social contradictions in terms of class, they clearly neglected the complexities which the modes of production of the two clashing parties created in the relationships between the different mass groups within society. They neglected the specifics of the relationships between various clashing groups: modes of production, the conflicts of nation-states, and between the different social groups. By the 1930s, these relationships were clarified in debates over 'the nature of society', but the simplified version of the view of class relations proposed in Marx's writings nevertheless became the basis for the relations between the characters in many literary works, and via literature became even more widespread. And so this is how 'proletariat' turned from being a category of the masses in society into one of the subjects of the literary discourse, into a national and political entity designed to reduce the 'majority' to a single entity.

This ideology, founded on a mistaken identification of the 'majority' of the nation as the 'proletariat', involved not only discrepancies between description and fact; it did more than simply play a part in describing reality at home and abroad, and in creative and discursive activities. It also played a role in the social revolution, in inspiring and defining that revolution, and even, to a great extent, in the creation of the policies of the government of the New China. From a historical perspective, it was thanks to this revolution with its unifying banners of the 'proletariat and the oppressed classes' that China was spared from the ignominy of becoming a colony or dependent state of the West. The mass of the lower peasants no longer had to go on suffering the inevitable disasters visited on them by international capitalism. But at the same time, this national political ideology, developed in response to the international threat, moulded and reflected the particular relationship between nation and society. Its discursive principle of simplifying the mass into a single entity and the state's principle of imposing strict control on society (e.g. 'smashing a handful of class enemies') worked to their mutual advantage. In fact, it was only through this discursive reduction of the masses of society to a single entity that the state was able to implement and maintain such a high degree of control over social, political and cultural life. There is no doubt that the level of control was directly linked to the potential threat which the bases and military centres of the world powers posed, during the cold war. So although the 'bourgeoisie' and the 'landlord class' no longer existed in terms of modes of production and productive relations, 'class struggle' — this mass form of discursive manipulation — nonetheless became, for many decades, the most common type of political and cultural movement. These movements were really just one 'unarmed' military exercise after another, a symbol of the nation's ability to mobilise. And, thanks to 'false distinctions and condemnations' it was always possible to find someone who fitted the role of 'the enemy' — an inherent product of this manipulative principle. The Cultural Revolution was simply the most extreme form of this kind of manipulation.

'The dictatorship of the proletariat', a phrase designed to fit 'over 95%' of the population, eventually, in a series of almost schizophrenic political movements, became a form of oppression affecting the majority of the people — since nobody was really sure who was a member of this 'majority', nobody was immune from one day becoming an 'enemy' of this 'majority'. During the 'ten years chaos', the individual, along with society as a whole, had been reduced to mere tools of this phrase. It was against this background that contemporary China's earliest batch of 'non-socialist realist' works — later known as 'Misty' poetry — were produced. Before these attempts at writing, discursive 'relations' had practically ceased to exist — the so-called 'national discourse' was accompanied not by any 'Western', 'native', nor even 'personal' form of language, but by silence.

And so, although many characteristics of the early 'anti-realist' works may require further description in terms of literary form, they can only be fully explained against the background of a history of discourse. According to strict literary categorisations, 'Misty' poetry is probably not a 'new school'. The stylistic characteristics of the poets of the *Today* group are actually extremely varied — some are nearer to the romantics, some closer to the symbolist writings of 1930s poets like Dai Wangshu and Bian Zhilin. Some use non-rhyming, free verse, others follow the formal rules of regular verse sporadically. Yet there is no doubt that together they represent a different kind of discourse, or, more accurately, a new form of discursive relationship.

In an attempt to distinguish this new form of discursive relationship, it may be of assistance to examine the 'Misty' poetry alongside the Tiananmen poetry of the April Fifth incident of 1976, not far removed from it in terms of time. This Tiananmen poetry is appropriately named for it was the product of a mass political movement which sprang from the grass-roots, a popular, spontaneous outpouring of discontent and other strong feelings following on the death of the Premier, Zhou Enlai. It should be said that its true writers — and its true themes — were what was known in the discourse of the past as the 'majority'. The poetic forms of the Tiananmen poetry (ranging from classical poetry to new poetry and even ballad couplets), as well as its style, paid not the slightest attention to the monolithic patterns of the past. Yet at the same time, these poems commonly invoke a higher discursive authority than simply that of the individual speaker

— an abstract 'people'. Examples might be a poem of mourning for the good *people's* Premier to express the desire for more moderate government, or an outpouring of hatred for those 'robbers of the *people'*, the Gang of Four — the abstract authority of the 'people' legitimizes their criticisms and the requests which the narrator makes of the government; in fact it is the only term which could legalize these poems. One could, therefore, say that the Tiananmen poems were exploiting or hijacking the 'national discourse'. In 'Misty' poetry, on the other hand, where real politics is rarely allowed to impinge upon the overall sense of the poem, the abstract authority of the 'people' is no longer invoked. Consequently the two poetries cannot be considered to be part of the same discourse. Taking a few lines at random from a collection of 'Misty' poetry, one finds phrases like: 'Let me be a kapok tree close by your side.'; 'I stand here, taking the place of another, murdered man'; 'Hidden by the storm I can slyly size-up the passers-by.'; 'Life really is this beautiful — go to bed.'; 'Autumn came, autumn had nothing to tell me.'; 'Once I was eight years old — liked bullying and begging.'; 'Hey, black night crouching at the door ... my loneliness.' These lines may not be outstanding, but they demonstrate one of 'Misty' poetry's historic contributions, which was to re-establish the specific role of the description of emotions, at the same time re-establishing a concrete, individualised discursive world. In these phrases, for the first time in more than a decade, the sense of 'I' is not defined by the collective singular of 'the people' — it must be seen within the context of a 'slyly sizing-up' in the storm, the relationship of a particular 'you' or a particular 'other' — in the autumn, in a recollection of the past, in a tiny detail, in a fleeting emotion. This special relationship existing between an everyday scene and the description of emotions, the significance of these settings and the details of a subject, had completely vanished from our discourse over a period of decades, yet they are fundamental to the poetics of 'Misty' poetry. So, in a way, the world of this poetry became the signal of another world of discourse, both individual and popular, which had been destroyed and fallen completely silent. I should probably add a word of explanation — I am talking not of the 'individual' and the 'people' in the sense of class structures or philosophy (e.g. humanism, individualism), but in an historical sense — of the individual and people who were deprived of memory and language in the name of the 'masses'. As with the Tiananmen poetry, 'Misty' poetry came from those people who had been so silent; where it differed was that it was part of a discourse that was still relevant to these silent people — it created a new discursive world, with discursive relationships designed to distinguish them from the 'collective singular'. Of course, if one were determined to trace the stylistic roots of 'Misty' poetry, one might return to Chinese translations of modern Western poetry, as opposed to classical Chinese poetry. Yet just as the Tiananmen poetry did not form part of a traditional discourse despite having sometimes been written in classical forms, and as modern Western poetry's borrowing of traditional Chinese poetics did not produce a 'Chinese discourse', so 'Misty' poetry does not amount to a 'Western discourse'. The message it contains concerning China is not, I would guess, something which can be easily appreciated by readers, no matter where in the world they come from.

UNDER-*SKY*
UNDER*GROUND*

O

FICTION — II

MOMO AND LIN HONG

AI YAN

translated by Deborah Mills

MOMO'S MISTAKE

One afternoon, the three of them arrived in the countryside outside the town. Momo was in charge of the camera, her job being to take photographs of Lin Hong and Liu Quan. They passed through a village, climbed a small hill, and spent some time in a newly-harvested field. There were photographs of all of these — that is to say, the village, the hill, and the field — but none of Lin Hong and Liu Quan.

Up until then Momo had never come across a camera, still, in her photographs the sky appeared very blue and the trees very green. At the left-hand side of one of the photographs Lin Hong's right elbow was visible. I'm sorry to say that this was sheer negligence on Momo's part. At that moment, Lin Hong had had her right hand in her trouser pocket, and her left hand high on Liu Quan's shoulder. This moving scene was forever lost to posterity.

In another photograph Momo had made yet another error. The evening sun behind her back had cast her shadow onto the field. The outlines were in focus, everything was in the right position, so she raised the camera and took a photograph of Lin Hong and Liu Quan. Unfortunately all she took was her own shadow.

There are many possible explanations. The fact that Lin Hong's blouse was of an unsatisfactory appearance was one. This blouse had been made by Momo. Before they had set out she had been praising it unconditionally — both the blouse and the wearer. In the dormitory there wasn't a mirror big enough for one to see one's whole body, so Momo was Lin Hong's mirror. It was the same this time. Lin Hong hadn't been able to see what she looked like in her new blouse in any of the pictures. Momo said that in a mirror the appearance of the blouse changed completely, so completely that it was unbearable to look at.

In shooting practice Momo scored on average 9.7 out of a possible 10. It was therefore logical that she should say that the whole process of taking photographs reminded her of firing a gun. She couldn't bring herself to point the muzzle (mirror) at her best friend.

Lin Hong leant against the bed wearing the guilty blouse, repeatedly going through the photographs in her hand. She kept putting the top photograph onto the bottom. She went on and on doing this. Momo had already said quite a lot about the affair, but Lin Hong wanted her to say more. She knew Momo was cowed, knew she was sweating. She was well-acquainted with all Momo's bodily functions. Momo had even begun to tell her about the abnormal feelings she experienced periodically.

LIN HONG'S BRIGADE

Each pair of lovers on campus had its own special place. Lin Hong and Liu Quan were no exception. As well as being private, the place had to be out of the wind, as it was already the beginning of winter. Actually suitable places were scarce, so couples often collided with each other, The campus lovers groped about in the dark, learning the art of the polite retreat. They didn't know the names of the opposition, and they didn't speak to each other. They made out their partners by means of smell, footsteps, and silhouettes against the vast canopy of heaven. Also, there was an unspoken agreement that one should always keep to the same time: for example, one place was Lin Hong's and Liu Quan's between seven and nine o'clock, and when they emerged from their hiding place another couple would be walking up in no particular rush, not ten metres away from the entrance. To this day I don't know how they managed to arrive at such a perfect arrangement. By day they were strangers, or even sometimes enemies.

Whenever night begins to fall, I think to myself, a great underground army of lovers is appearing and disappearing around the campus. They are peaceful, mysterious, even beautiful. And if you take into account the enthusiastic interference of the security personnel, the whole picture becomes full of sound and colour.

WITH REFERENCE TO MOMO

Lin Hong and Liu Quan had settled on a flower bed. Four little paths led to this bed. The paths were lined on either side with neatly clipped ilex trees (forming the first protective screen). The flower bed had no flowers in it, and was surrounded by a circle of snow pines (forming the second protective screen). Lin Hong and Liu Quan loved evergreens, and every evening they would stay in there and stare up at the sky, just visible between the leaves.

First of all they discovered some excrement. Liu Quan put his foot in it, causing the smell to spread all around under the pines. They spent all evening cleaning the place. They had no tools, and it was pitch dark, so one can imagine their difficulty. Above them twinkled the winter stars. Afterwards, Lin Hong lay on Liu Quan's breast, breathing in through her nose with all her might.

The next day when they arrived they found there was already someone at the flower bed. Seeing the silhouette of someone with his back to the entrance, they assumed there must be a second person inside.

Being defeated on two consecutive evenings made Liu Quan angry. He was the one responsible for arranging the meeting-place — all tacit agreements made under cover of darkness were taken care of by him. After they had been forced to retreat to their second place — an air-raid shelter — more than half the time they had available had passed. The school security section often patronised this place, so it was not at all safe. They had just sat down when they heard the sound of footsteps. The sound kept coming and going, but stayed in the vicinity. Listening to this sound, they guessed the intention behind it. One way or another, it involved them. In the end Liu Quan decided that it was a couple who had just fallen in love and who were still in the process of finding out about the workings of the underground world. When you connected this with the interlopers in the flower bed, it all pointed to the fact that the army of lovers had grown bigger.

After a rustling of vegetation, someone arrived on the roof. The shelter was actually a small room built of concrete, with a flat roof. In summer maybe it was a nice place for getting cool, but now the people on top succeeded only in posing a threat to those below. Liu Quan hauled Lin Hong out. They saw two people silhouetted against the sky, cumbersomely dressed in winter clothes, half sitting, half squatting.

Lin Hong and Liu Quan cut their losses and returned to the flower bed. There was no one in there now, and no strange smells, but unfortunately they had only a quarter-of-an-hour left. In addition, another couple arrived early. Five minutes later they appeared on one of the four little paths and sat down six or seven metres away from the flower bed. Lin Hong and Liu Quan were fascinated. They could not understand it. They could only sit there, looking at the two people, at the little path they were on, and at the campus, which this evening seemed even more mysterious than usual. In the end, Liu Quan denied it. It can't be them, he said.

It's Momo. Lin Hong said, Momo in love, that's impossible.

LIN HONG AND MOMO

They had agreed that neither would fall in love before the other. Of course, in the future they might get married and have children. The contradictory logic of this idea didn't bother them at all: they just admired each other for it.

There were eight female students in the dormitory. Every night before going to bed they all had to have a bath. Later they discovered that the time for each girl's period was getting closer to everyone else's. Every month in each dormitory the dried out sanitary towels were collected. Momo and Lin Hong found this unendurable. Then Momo changed to using disposable sanitary towels and introduced this method to Lin Hong. From this point on, they were set somewhat apart from the rest.

Lin Hong went running every day. The amount of exercise she took was quite staggering. She kept up her summer habit of taking a shower right into the winter. There was a shower in the washroom. The water that came out of the shower nozzle was always cold. Lin Hong would lock the door and stand there completely naked, waiting for the stimulating cold. This wasn't something everyone could do, thought Momo.

By comparison, Momo was thin and weak. There was no way she could compete with Lin Hong in terms of fitness, but she recognised the crux of the problem. Each day when Lin Hong went to have a shower, Momo washed herself somewhere outside the dormitory. Lin Hong never found out how she managed this. What she liked about Momo were her qualities of self-love, determination, thoughtfulness, and also a sort of innate mystery.

LIN HONG, MOMO, AND EVERYONE

Campus life in general is not the point of this story. There is an unalterable daily routine progressing from dormitory to classroom to refectory. What I am attempting to describe is the unusual nature of Lin Hong and Momo's relationship.

They were of course usually together. And their alliance was already something that set them apart from the whole dormitory: I might even go so far as to say from the entire campus and all its students and teachers, without being guilty of exaggeration.

Entering college gave students their first taste of independence. An unprecedented sense of freedom and of going up in the world meant that these girls, who yesterday were secondary school students, got rather out of their depth. After they had discussed their exam results, missed their families, and been quiet and peaceful, the first thing they thought about was how to take advantage of their many new opportunities. Here I'm just referring to the female students. They vied with each other in buying clothes, dressing up, putting on make-up. Before they got in the know, in fashion terms, they became temporary freaks.

Lin Hong and Momo weren't any more knowledgeable than their roommates. It's just that they didn't try to be like everyone else. So they would be seen with their hair in a mess, dressed any old how, walking around all over campus. They would shout and laugh loudly and gesticulate. Their faces were childlike and pretty, but if you looked in their eyes, there was no hint of tenderness to be seen.

This was the way things were at the beginning. Afterwards, Lin Hong and Momo both made fun of this picture of themselves, because they had grown up, and also because they had lost a very effective method of self expression. When all the other female students in the college had chosen an image for themselves, had thrown themselves into their studies and were, therefore, too busy to improve or alter the image they had chosen, Lin Hong and Momo had just begun to put on make-up and to dress themselves up.

Momo learnt how to choose material and to sew, whereas Lin Hong became the artistic director. Their two images formed one complete whole. That is to say, each image could only be examined in the context of this whole.

For instance, if Lin Hong was wearing a short top which showed her stomach, Momo's jacket would be long enough to reach her knees. If Lin Hong had flowers embroidered onto the collar and cuffs of her top, Momo's top would have tassels sewn all round the hem. If Lin Hong's clothes were bright yellow, Momo's would be deep reds and deep greens, in strange patterns. Now the two of them would walk around campus with supercilious smiles on their faces, not speaking to one another, and making the least possible movement.

It was obvious that Lin Hong and Momo would become objects of attention and concern. The hunt was on and hostilities, many of them, commenced. The surprising thing was that they didn't actually confront Lin Hong and Momo. The method adopted by the male students was one of surrounding them geographically. As a result, all the girls in the dormitory got boyfriends except Lin Hong and Momo, and in fact, the rate of falling in love in their particular girls' dormitory was higher than in any other. Lin Hong and Momo became an isolated stronghold. They were very pleased with themselves. While the other girls were busy falling in love and suffering unbearable pain, they started to study in earnest. In the end of term exams, Lin Hong and Momo soared up to first and second position in the class.

MOMO'S DISCOVERY

When she lay under her mosquito net, Momo could clearly see the outside world, but no one on the outside could see her. This little accomplishment made her keep the mosquito net on even in winter. She would lie underneath it, reading, or sleeping, or simply watching what other people in the dormitory were doing.

One morning after nine o'clock, everyone else had gone to class. Momo lay there listening to the silence in the building, the intermittent groaning of the water pipes, the gentle sound of the wind outside the windows. In her imagination, Momo experienced the beautiful sweetness of the forsaken. She was so intoxicated by this dream that she didn't even wonder why Song Xiaoyue knocked before coming in.

The key turned and the door opened. After coming in, Song Xiaoyue had a glass of water, and then locked the door from the inside. About what subsequently occurred, she wouldn't have wanted anyone else to know, but Momo decided not to reveal her presence straight away.

Recently the weather had not been very good and so they had moved their washing into the dormitory to dry. Song Xiaoyue began to pick clothes off the rack. There was one of Lin Hong's jumpers, a pair of trousers belonging to Momo, jackets, trousers and tops belonging to other people in the dormitory. Finally, Song Xiaoyue, after a moment's hesitation, took one of her own shirts.

Now there were only a few items of underwear — bras, pants and socks — left on the rack. This was the first thing for which Momo could not forgive Song Xiaoyue, stealing was the second. Momo got out of bed, and Song Xiaoyue, down on her knees, begged for mercy. The most moving thing she could think of to say was, if you let me go, I'll be your beast of burden. Song Xiaoyue came from a village full of cows and horses, so she was well aware of both their joys and their pain.

Momo was moved.

She set out three conditions: 1) Return the clothes to their original place, apart from Lin Hong's jumper; 2) Split up with your boyfriend and never see him again; 3) Only go around with me, not with any of the other female students, and agree with me about everything.

Song Xiaoyue agreed.

Momo said, I mustn't be too unfair, so you can unravel Lin Hong's jumper and re-knit it into something else.

LIN HONG IN THE MIRROR

Lin Hong had not abided by their agreement. She and Momo, after together making fun of their slovenly clothes period, had also ridiculed their frills and furbelows period. They couldn't stop themselves. Lin Hong thought that maybe they needed to do something completely different, like go out with a boy, and vanish into the crowd, or into a corner of the campus.

Lin Hong had met Liu Quan in the track and field team. He came from an external department, and therefore knew nothing of all the rigmarole which surrounded Lin Hong and Momo. This ignorance helped him in his pursuit of Lin Hong, but also of course led to his ultimate downfall. But that is another story.

Now Lin Hong washed herself openly in the dormitory every evening. She was just the same as the other girls: they all used sanitary towels that had to be washed. Now part of the great army that manoeuvred at night, she became a member of the look, listen and smell brigade. Now Momo was no use to her as a mirror for trying things on, and looking back on the way she used to be, Lin Hong thought how strained she had been, and how mad.

After the photograph incident, Lin Hong had every reason to sever relations with Momo completely. When she found out that Momo's lover was a young man in their class, she couldn't help feeling sorry for her. He wasn't up to anything much except looking good. At first she and Liu Quan did their best to avoid Momo and her boyfriend; after a week they couldn't find them even if they'd wanted to.

From resistance through desire, the course which Lin Hong and Liu Quan's affair had followed for two weeks had turned sour. They started to quarrel and these quarrels became more and more intense. Momo and her friend were not in any of the places Lin Hong and Liu Quan knew of, nor were they in any of the places they did not know of. Lin Hong and Liu Quan, despite the taboo against doing so, scoured every corner of the campus. Once they discovered a young man weeping and muttering to himself. The next time they saw him he was with a different girl. In the darkness her eyes glittered with a fearful radiance.

And finally, when Momo and Song Xiaoyue publicly demonstrated their intimate friendship, Lin Hong felt that the situation was irretrievable.

MOMO AND THE SCARF

Lin Hong's jumper was re-knitted into two scarves. Momo and Song Xiaoyue would wear one each, and walk around campus side by side. The two identical scarves became the symbols of their alliance. The bright red colour reminded them of their 'Young Pioneers' period. Song Xiaoyue tried hard to be in unison with Momo, even to the point of tying her scarf in the same way as Momo. Momo didn't approve of this, however. Every day she changed the way she tied it, and finally decreed that Song Xiaoyue could only tie her scarf in a way that was different from Momo's. However, Lin Hong had no way of finding out that her jumper was lost. And even if she had found out, it would not have occurred to her that Momo's and Song Xiaoyue's scarves had any connection with her jumper. Recently her relationship with Liu Quan had taken another turn for the worse, and she didn't have the heart to care about anything else. Because Lin Hong paid no attention and wasn't even annoyed, Momo gradually lost interest in the scarves. Instead of wearing the scarf on the outside of her coat, she wore it on the inside. This is all we have to say about the scarves.

Song Xiaoyue helped Momo to get food and water, and told her the latest gossip. At exam time, Momo allowed Song Xiaoyue to copy her answers. She left her meat on her plate for Song Xiaoyue. Before this she used to throw her meat out with the rest of the left-overs. She gave Song Xiaoyue some clothes which Song Xiaoyue thought were pretty, but which she, Momo, did not care for. Some biscuits, pieces of dried fruit, a can of condensed milk were all over three months old, and Momo wanted nothing more to do with them. The best thing she did was to go in Song Xiaoyue's place to negotiate with Song Xiaoyue's boyfriend. Momo only said one sentence, which was enough to send the boyfriend away for ever:

She is a thief, even what you are wearing was stolen by her.

MOMO'S HOME

They were all going to be split up and sent to different places for a three-month field trip. Beijing was naturally the most attractive place to be sent, but you had to pay your own board and lodging. Momo's family lived in Beijing, so it was logical for her to go home. Also, Momo agreed that Song Xiaoyue should come and board at her home. In return, Song Xiaoyue could do a few chores. Before the event, Momo wrote a letter home, instructing them to dismiss the housekeeper.

It's a long time since I've helped Mum with the housework, she wrote. This time when I come home I want to make a good impression, so that Mum and Dad will love me all the more. Doing the housework will give me this opportunity. The classmate who is coming with me is from the country; she is very strong and loves hard work, so she can help me.

Thus, Song Xiaoyue began to learn to use a vacuum cleaner on the thirteenth floor, to operate a washing machine, move the flower pots morning and evening, fetch the milk, carry the rice and wash the windows. Apart from all this she still had to go to work.

When she came back from her unit, Song Xiaoyue always brought a few things with her: alcohol, medicines, a chemistry beaker. She gave everything to Momo. Momo put them altogether in one place, and later on made Song Xiaoyue cart them all away.

Momo's house was always very quiet: apart from the noises Song Xiaoyue made when she was doing the housework, there was virtually no sound. Momo's mother and father stayed in their own separate rooms and only came out for dinner. Mealtime conversations were also very peculiar: after one person had finished speaking, a long time passed before someone replied. Momo ordered Song Xiaoyue to fetch this and fetch that. During the course of one meal she might be interrupted four or five times. She was embarrassed when she made a noise. Whenever she did, Momo's parents would stop talking as though they were listening intently. Momo would say, Can't you be a bit quieter?

After dinner every member of the family would retire to their respective rooms and turn on the television (every room had a television, which also amazed Song Xiaoyue). Song Xiaoyue stayed in the dining room to clear away. She would go past the doors, left half-open as though no-one had the strength to shut them properly, and through the cracks she would be able to see lights flickering inside the rooms. The television announcer's voice would be excited, yet restrained, and not very clear. No one else would be talking, and so the televisions conducted a mysterious conversation between themselves. Because she had things to do, Song Xiaoyue would return to reality. The noise of crockery, the noise of chairs and tables, the noise of running water. This was when Momo would come up soundlessly behind her back and say, Quieter, my father has a heart condition.

It was true that when Song Xiaoyue was not working there was no sound. The noisy racket of the main road was far beneath them. The street below seemed a very remote and faraway concept. Song Xiaoyue once tried spitting a mouthful of phlegm downwards, and although she waited for a long time, she never heard it hit the ground. There was carpeting underneath her feet, and everyone had to learn how to walk like a cat. There were no mice here, nor any other form of animal or insect life. The sound of the wind was cut off by the double-glazing. There wasn't even the clamour of the stars (the windows being covered with dark grey swansdown curtains). Here, there was absolutely no sound.

In her sleep, Song Xiaoyue would grind her teeth, talk, and call for her mother without knowing. Then Momo would turn on the bedside light, and shine it in her eyes until she woke up. Momo wouldn't let her turn the light off, nor point it in another direction. If I don't leave it on you'll just talk in your sleep again, Momo would say. She would lie on the other bed and not go to sleep at all. In this way, Song Xiaoyue would spend the whole night lying in the bright light and the silence, conscious of the fact that Momo never took her eyes off her.

MOMO'S EVENING READ

One evening, Song Xiaoyue was writing up an experiment under the lamp, and Momo was reading on the couch opposite. Eight minutes later Song Xiaoyue had sprawled across the table asleep. To begin with the sound of her snoring was cautious and circumspect, but then it lost all restraint. Saliva dripped down her chin, making the page wet. Momo looked at her without moving. Half an hour or more passed in this way. We have no way of ascertaining Momo's thoughts and feelings during this blank period. Gradually, Momo became aware of the weight of the book on her knees. It was a hardback English dictionary, unusually thick and heavy. Momo seized it and hurled it across the room. Later it transpired that this throw had made her sprain her right arm. Grazing Song Xiaoyue's ear, the dictionary spun off, hit the wall behind her and tumbled down onto the floor. Song Xiaoyue woke up

with a yell, the first thing she saw being Momo's eyes, full of uncon-
cealed hatred. As soon as Song Xiaoyue turned round she noticed a
small hole half an inch deep which had been gouged out of the wall.
She slid off the chair and sat on the floor wailing.

This event happened two weeks after Song Xiaoyue had arrived in
Beijing. For the two and a half months following this she stayed in the
guest house of Momo's father's work unit, and did not see Momo
again until the end of the field trip. The evening she left Momo's
house, Momo gave her a carrier bag containing all the things that Song
Xiaoyue had brought home from her unit.

MOMO'S REPLY

One quiet night on campus, Momo bumped into Lin Hong again.
This time she was on her own. Momo was not surprised. She sat by
the side of the road as Lin Hong came towards her. She thought Lin
Hong would probably stop. As before it was the flower bed; as before
the light of a starry sky; as before it was this particular spot. Lin Hong
came up to Momo, and said, it's a long time since we've spoken.

Is it really? replied Momo.

You're a lot thinner, said Lin Hong.

So are you, said Momo.

VARIATIONS

JANE YING ZHA

translated by Angela Geddes

Yezi turned over on the sofa for the fourth time, part of her arm catching the moonlight. The moon was brilliant white, scratched; like a flat face suspended in the air.

Wang Ju thought, 'If Yezi turns over once more I'll ...'

Yezi turned over again. But Wang Ju did not move — not even her steady breathing altered. She lay on a makeshift bed on the floor, two thin blankets underneath her, right up alongside the sofa bed — the only place in her room with enough space on the floor to lie down. They were lying head to toe, Wang Ju's feet and Yezi's head towards the window.

As Wang Ju looked at the flat, battered child's face of the moon, Yezi looked at the music-stand in the corner of the room. Lying in the shadows next to it, Yezi remembered, was a flute. She had seen it before she turned out the light; it was silver, with a delicate trail of flowers, also in silver, engraved along it. Then Yezi remembered, the last time she had come to Wang Ju's place it had been a cello next to the music stand.

Yezi raised her head from the pillow and whispered softly, 'Wang Ju?'

Wang Ju mentally shrugged her shoulders; 'Mmm?' she said.

Yezi sat up at once. 'So you can't get to sleep either!' she said. 'I'm just thinking, don't you think that old woman was a bit loopy, feeding such good stuff to the dog? And that film ... I'm still feeling suffocated from it. Films are all so terrifying these days. If blood isn't being spattered about, then the tickets don't sell.' Yezi sighed.

Yezi was sitting up hugging her shoulders; the ribbon of her white pyjamas had come untied and hung loosely across her arm. Her feet had slipped out from under the sheet and were hanging over the side of the bed, half blocking Wang Ju's view. Staring at the foot in front of her eyes, Wang Ju remembered how stunningly pretty Yezi had always been. She was still attractive, but what a stunner in those days!

Wang Ju and Yezi had been in the same class in secondary school, and afterwards had been sent to the same village in the countryside. They were inseparable in those days; but later, each went to university in a different city and for years they saw nothing of each other. Then Wang Ju heard that Yezi had become a happy, caring young wife. At that time, Wang Ju had just split up with her fifth boyfriend. From a certain perspective, this was not a predictable situation — in those days there were always far more boys chasing Yezi than Wang Ju; mainly because Yezi had such distinctive, lively eyes — they so easily gave the wrong impression. Yet Wang Ju's clear-headed and rational air made people feel far more at ease. Those who knew the two of them always said knowingly, 'Ah, you can't judge by appearances.' 'Girls change so much when they are growing up.' Two old sayings, but how true they are. Two years ago Yezi and Wang Ju had run into each other in this same town and become friends again; but of course it was impossible to become as close as before.

Tonight Yezi had stood in the doorway gripping a small snake-skin handbag under her arm, not saying a word. Her eyes were red and swollen. Wang Ju knew instantly that she had been quarrelling with her husband. Yezi had been on the phone to her with her troubles so many times before, but she had always calmed down by the time she had got half-way to Wang Ju's, or else her husband had caught up with her and coaxed her back home. So Wang Ju sensed that this time it was somehow different. This time, Yezi had made it all the way to her door.

Yezi made a grimace, as if trying to smile. Her hair was everywhere, and she stood in the middle of Wang Ju's room looking sheepish.

'If you don't get that coat off, you'll stifle,' said Wang Ju.

Yezi undid the stiff buttons obediently. It was a man's wind-cheater, cream coloured underneath the layer of grey dust. There was a fleck of oil on one cuff. When Wang Ju saw the white pyjamas underneath the coat, she could not hide her look of horror: it was five-thirty. Admittedly though, it might as well be evening. In another hour the sun would fall behind the mountains. And at five-thirty all the cinemas in the town started selling tickets for the evening show.

Yezi looked this time as if she had only just woken up. She cleared her throat and said, 'I came out in a hurry, there was no time to …'

Wang Ju cut her short, 'Shh, go into the bath room and cool down under the shower. There's a clean towel on the left of the rail.'

The people queuing up for cinema tickets snaked around the corner under the blood-red setting sun. A blind man was there with his dog, begging. He was wearing old army clothing, his chest covered with medals. The sound of his stick knocking and tapping the wet pavement was like muffled gunshots. Some people in the queue pretended to be engrossed in their newspapers or listening intently to their friends' conversations, while others looked constantly at their watches as though they were terribly anxious about the possibility of getting tickets. No one gave a single coin to the blind man, including Yezi and Wang Ju. Yezi was almost tempted to when the dog rubbed up against her shoes as if he had found an old friend; but when she saw Wang Ju staring into the sky with a preoccupied gaze she thought better of it.

Inside the cinema the smell of sweat pervaded the air. The title of the film shone out into the darkness with a faint blue light: FATAL ATTRACTION. They say people sweat more in a tense situation, and their sweat is more pungent. Right from the beginning, Wang Ju could not quite follow the plot, and besides, she had her friend sitting next to her with a slightly minty scent, wearing her dress — and that was a strange feeling. She had let Yezi choose whatever she wanted from her wardrobe, and Yezi had immediately picked out the white dress with red spots. Wang Ju was vaguely conscious of Yezi have overstepped a certain boundary between them, but where exactly that boundary was and how she had overstepped it, Wang Ju was herself not quite able to say.

At the end of the film, the woman, driven mad by her jealousy, was lying in the bath half strangled by her ex-lover. She suddenly leaped up again. Yezi and Wang Ju jumped in terror. When the woman was finally shot dead in the bath by the man's wife, Yezi instinctively clutched at Wang Ju's knee. The steam curled upwards from the bath. Bubbles of blood rose slowly to the surface one after the other.

Then there was the old woman that Yezi reckoned was a little mad.

After the film, Yezi and Wang Ju were eating in a little restaurant and a tall woman walked in, plastered in bright make-up. She could have been in her forties, or then again, even in her sixties. Without a sidelong glance she went up to the counter and ordered three cold dishes — red meat, fish and chicken. And without a sidelong glance she got a tin out of her bag and tipped the three dishes into it. She carried it outside and gave it to a large dog that was tied up underneath the tree in front of the shop ... without a sidelong glance.

That was the second dog Yezi and Wang Ju had come across that day.

Under the light of the table lamp, Wang Ju was smoking. After each drag on the cigarette she turned to blow the smoke out of the window.

Yezi said there was really no need for the light to be on. 'We can just talk in the dark, that's okay. I'll be asleep after a few words.' She was still sitting on the bed.

'Well, I just want this one cigarette,' Wang Ju said.

Yezi looked at her for a while, or rather at the black silk pyjamas Wang Ju was wearing. Black made her look older, perhaps a little mysterious.

'Wang Ju, you ought to try and give up smoking. Did you know that a lot of countries in Europe are banning smoking now?'

Wang Ju took a long drag. 'That's their affair'.

Another moment passed and Yezi said, 'Are you playing the flute now?'

'I started last month — two lessons a week. I play terribly.' A real smile appeared on Wang Ju's face for the first time.

'One time, a neighbour slipped a note under the door that said, 'Why don't you just strangle that old asthmatic you've got in your room!'

Yezi laughed too.

Wang Ju shook her head. 'It's so much fun. The flute is such a noble instrument, but I blow common people's sounds out of it.'

Yezi thought of the cello that had disappeared. But then, she seemed to remember that Wang Ju had produced some awful, squeaky jazz sounds out of that too. And she had played it with such passion, utterly carried away by it.

'Wang Ju, I wonder why my husband is holding his breath for such a long time. He hasn't even phoned.' Yezi was startled by her own words. She had obviously been thinking about the business with the cello and the flute.

'Maybe he phoned while we were out,' said Wang Ju. 'Anyway, he won't necessarily guess that you're here.'

'So much the better. Let him wonder!' Yezi sulked. 'He knows me too well though ... Men — it's impossible to be too nice to them. The more you give, the more they take you for granted.'

The table lamp was switched off again and Yezi and Wang Ju each lay down again on their different levels.

'Come on, let me sleep on the floor,' Yezi said. 'The night is getting cold.'

'Don't argue,' said Wang Ju.

'Actually, this sofa bed is big enough for two, you know,' said Yezi.

Wang Ju turned over on the floor.

'You're great, Wang Ju.'

Wang Ju wrapped her blanket tightly around her. 'Go to sleep,' she said.

'There is just one more thing I want to ask you. I've just been trying to pluck up courage to ask you for ages. If you don't want to answer then don't say a word, and we will just go to sleep.

'It's about that composer — are you still seeing each other?' After she had asked, Yezi felt the blood run slowly towards her ears, making them prick up. It was like a cat's eyes lighting up in the darkness when it is frightened.

Through the moonlight came Wang Ju's voice. 'Oh, it didn't last long with him.'

Yezi nodded her head in the dark. 'That's a relief; I was really afraid you would not be able to … get out of it. Did he go back to his wife in the end?'

'They never really split up.'

In the darkness Yezi drew in her breath. Another liar, she thought.

Wang Ju was thinking, 'If I told her how powerful that experience was, if I told her how much I loved him …'

A long string of men's faces flashed in front of her eyes. Those men had stepped into her life one by one, and one by one they had left and disappeared into other girls' lives. Wang Ju was not really interested in what had become of them. What she cared about was the particular impression that she herself had left on those men. She was sure that those impressions would make them remember her always: she had left a part of herself with those men for ever. Wang Ju's memory was being carried all around the world by a handful of men. She felt as if her life had been expanded several-fold. She usually enjoyed this feeling of being ever on the move, ubiquitous; but the feeling, of course, only came with the good weather. In dull weather it might be a completely different picture. Then she would recall another way of thinking, remember a different girl. These girls were married, or were mothers. They would emerge from the dips in an overcast landscape and smile at Wang Ju with peaceful, distant smiles. Perhaps time and depth did have greater significance and value than moment and breadth? Perhaps memories were only so tenacious and distinct for her because she had nothing else? And perhaps those memories that she thought were so special had already been effortlessly wiped away in her lovers' minds, because for them, the only real deep and special impressions were the ones that their wives made. She was just one more blurred face in the ranks of 'lovers', destined to fade away with the passage of time.

From the sofa bed came the sound of Yezi turning over.

'She's still awake. When is she finally going to fall asleep?' Wang Ju thought that Yezi was probably a very different type of woman. But what was it that made her face so unreadable? She did not seem content to just be with her own friends; she wanted to step out into wider circles. With that thought a complex, inexplicable feeling of uneasiness churned inside Wang Ju's stomach.

Yezi turned over noisily again. This time she seemed to have made up her mind.

'Wang Ju, I'll tell you something. Since you are out of the relationship it doesn't matter now, but I was always worried sick about you. I knew at the time it was no use saying anything though.

'That composer ... he accosted me once too. You know what he asked me? He said, "How does that man of yours rate? Is he good in the afternoon as well as the evening? and what about the morning? Do you know how many ways there are of cooking your eggs for breakfast? And did you know there is more than one way to cook spinach?"'

Yezi felt the blood rushing to her ears again; she heard it thundering. Her voice was sounding louder too. 'That sort of man is the pits. Maybe he knew you at that time too. Maybe he knew you and me and other girls too that we don't know. I bet he came on to all the girls with the same filth. There are such bastards out there these days. I pity anyone who falls for their words.'

Yezi was not quite sure whether she even expected a reply to such frankness. But to her surprise Wang Ju did not so much as utter a sound.

After a while, Yezi held onto the edge of the bed and said in Wang Ju's direction, 'Wang Ju ... Wang Ju, are you asleep?'

Wang Ju said 'No', but the voice that came was wavering and lethargic.

Yezi could not see whether Wang Ju's eyes were open or closed. Wang Ju used to so love talking, she thought. How the old Wang Ju could talk! Yezi suddenly remembered she had to sleep up against the wall, otherwise, if she fell off the bed she would land right on top of Wang Ju, and then they would have their feet in each others mouths!

After some time — it was hard to say how long, except that the moon was no longer shining through the window — Wang Ju heard the sound of sobbing. The stifled sobs burst out one by one, in fits and starts. It made Wang Ju think of her beloved flute engraved with flowers. Again that genuine smile spread across her face. It rippled over her cheeks and down to her chin, like a bright, shimmering pool of quicksilver.

Wang Ju finally cleared her throat. 'Yezi?'

Suddenly there was no more sound from the sofa bed. Then in a moment, Yezi's sobs turned into unstifled crying — The flute had turned into an accordion. Wang Ju sat up on her makeshift bed. The last thread of moonlight was just fading from the window.

Yezi's voice was choked with sobs. 'You know, I … when I ran out … I let him hug me … He really didn't understand … What can you do with a man like that? …'

Wang Ju stood up. She was not sure whether to have a drink of water or another cigarette. But a second later she climbed onto the sofa bed. As she lay down next to Yezi, her black silk pyjamas flashed in the moonlight.

For a long while, Yezi and Wang Ju said nothing. They now lay the same way, heads and feet together, breathing one another's breath. They both closed their eyes, and under each pair of closed eyelids appeared the image of the other just closing her eyes. All four were beautiful images, imbued with passion and grief. Yezi's breathed in and out, the fiery hot air furling round her cheeks. She wanted to run her tongue over her dried up lips, but she bore it, unable to do so. Wang Ju felt something rise up in her throat, but she suppressed the desire to cough. The four images were still silent and unmoving. Four expectant images, flickering slightly in their tensed minds.

'Hold me,' Yezi at last said softly.

Wang Ju hesitated, and then put one arm out cautiously.

Yezi felt something like a soft cooling snake coil itself around her neck. She even heard the faint rasping sound like a snake gliding over a tuft of grass. With a swift movement, she put out her hand and grasped hold of the snake.

Wang Ju's palms were cold and sweating as she felt Yezi's hand on her knee, and her heart started to thump. Her eyes were still closed, but the image inside her head kept changing. She saw the composer's long and slender body lying on her sofa bed. It was a windy afternoon and the sounds of the market ebbed and flowed in through the half open window. She saw herself going to have a shower, leaving a trail of footprints on the floor of the corridor. Under the shower, she started singing, her head shaking and bodying swaying like a fool. Then she saw herself walking down the street with the composer; the wind blew her red spotted white dress up like an umbrella. She remembered they were going to see a film. The scene in 'Fatal Attraction' appeared; steam was curling upwards from the bath, and bubbles of blood rose slowly to the surface one after the other. It was all quite distinct. There was one thing that she was unclear about: was the blood oozing from the jilted woman's body, or was she herself wringing it out of her lover's throat?

As she was wondering about this, Wang Ju noticed that her hands around Yezi's neck had gone slightly stiff. She noticed too, that Yezi's limbs had become quite limp. She even heard a faint gurgling coming from Yezi's throat; it sounded like a happy, comfortable sigh.

At last, Yezi, thought Wang Ju, you've relaxed.

TATTOO

DUO DUO

translated by Harriet Evans and John Cayley

1

As I moved outside the room, the darkness resounded with a rumble that seemed to come from somewhere deep within the earth. I raised my eyes, and under the misty curtain of the night, I saw the dunes shifting over the New Mexican desert. It's absolutely true, file upon file of low dunes were moving blindly through the wilderness. No, it wasn't the wind, although there was a slight nip in the air.

'They do this every night.'

The doctor emerged. 'It's the hand of God.'

The doctor was completely bald. With a deft movement, he prised out the left lens of his spectacles, breathed on it, and put it back into its frame, covering his blind eye. 'That's why I prefer to live in this desolation, where I spend my evenings listening carefully, just listening to every sound.'

As he finished speaking he went back into the room, to the side of the big table where he kept his instruments, rulers and the computer. His room was a bit like the cabin of a large ship, with himself the captain, who every day, with great concentration, studied his charts. As soon as he came into my line of vision the dunes stopped moving, it wasn't clear whether momentarily or for good.

I went on staring into the darkness where fairy-like creatures seemed to be following after the dunes. Or maybe they were desperately trying to fathom the depths of the earth. I heard the doctor coughing inside the room. Perhaps his own movements determined whether the dunes shifted or stopped? The bald fifty-year-old, a pencil stuck in his back pocket, yawned.

'Good evening, captain.' This is what I called him.

'Good evening, Li.'

I turned to walk down the slope. A curious feeling of satisfaction spread slowly over me, and the tips of my fingers felt slightly numb, but I was relaxed and happy, as if I'd slept with a woman I'd only just met, and hoped that the world would remain exactly as it was at that moment. The captain's main subject of conversation that evening was happiness.

'It is impossible for us to be truly happy.' The captain lifted the razor to his neck. 'No matter what you do, it's impossible.' An idea had occurred to him. He put down the razor, and carefully gathered all the hairs he'd shaved off into a little heap, leaving them, for a moment, on the bulge of his belly. His head was partly raised, his body completely naked. He lifted the razor to his neck again. His shaving sounded like a needle scratching a record. His chest was greyish, and the part of his face that he had already shaved looked like a scrubbed hide. He stretched out his tongue, 'and …', his testicles moved at the same time as his Adam's apple. Then he examined his genitals, at some length, 'and all this is because some devil' — he was wondering whether to shave his pubic hair — 'made us like this. Of course, it's not the devil's fault.' He decided to keep his pubic hair, and stood up, with his trousers drooping around his feet, 'Now I look Chinese, don't I?'

I turned my head so that I didn't have to see his naked body parading about, with his single eye and bald baby-like head. My eyes were drawn to a picture hanging on the wall. It was of the captain's former wife. Close up, it showed a naked woman lying on her side, her back decorated with large flower petals. As a whole, it looked like a big bird hovering in the air with feathers of peach blossom …

'Seven years, let me tell you.' The captain was pacing around in the room. 'I worked seven years on that. It cost me one of my eyes, but it was worth it. Creating a person is immoral unless it's done by God or by sex. But perhaps you'd agree with me that life makes greater demands — Doesn't the idea of creating someone just like yourself tempt you? I tell you, it bloody well keeps me awake at night …'

I had met the captain three days before in a gallery at Santa Fei. I was enjoying looking at a painting by D. H. Lawrence. It showed a group of naked men emerging from a clump of soft downy flowers. There was another painting as well. Rays of light on its surface revealed another group of naked men who were about to haul a glistening golden sun onto their backs out of an abandoned coal mine. The captain stared at me with eyes that looked in two different directions, and told me that he was a doctor, although not in the usual sense of the term. He invited me to go and stay in his house, in the house of his former wife — a house that he had built — which she had left a long time before. When he saw that I was carrying an easel, he also

202

mentioned that he was an artist, although not in the usual sense of the term. All along the road, he kept stopping the car, encouraging me to look at the bell towers of various churches. 'You must look at the very top storey.' At the top of the *adobe* towers there was an empty space, through which you could see the sky, but it concealed a bell, the clapper of which hung down as if it wanted to spit out the inner language of the building. I followed the direction of the captain's finger and picked out a shape protruding from the corner of these white Indian-style churches. It looked like a nipple that was being moulded into shape by two enormous hands, or perhaps simply like the two fleshy hands themselves, left forgotten on the corner of the building.

'Do you know that I'm also a fisherman, although not in the usual sense of the term.' The captain used the hand he had used to shave his pubic hair to make a sandwich. 'Drinking gives you a day's happiness. Getting married gives you a week. But what you get from fishing is a lifetime of happiness. You need happiness,' the captain gave me a cracker with a slice of cheese, a slice of cucumber and extremely finely sliced mushrooms, 'but not in the usual sense of the term. This is our supper, but it's not the last supper. It's when you begin to feel the days getting more and more miserable,' the captain swallowed the other cracker whole, 'that's when you need some mushrooms. At least you should try it once.'

The captain's house was Spanish style, made of *adobe*, and extended right into the depths of the mysterious wilderness. The ranch of his former wife was only half a mile away, just down the hill and over the next. For the time being, I still couldn't pronounce the name of the small town, but I knew it was near an Indian reserve. The scale of this wilderness reminded me of north-west China or Tibet.

As I turned the door handle to the hall of the captain's ex-wife's house, two large dogs began scratching desperately at the glass with their claws. I rushed across the hall, fending off their eagerness with my elbows, and soon found a board to block the door frame between the kitchen and the dining room. The dogs jumped up helplessly, but without barking — perhaps their vocal chords had already been cut out, by the captain. Hurriedly, I made for the bathroom to wash the hand that the dogs had licked.

It was just then that I heard the sound of a piano.

2

I stopped dead in my tracks, foot raised. The music was coming from the conservatory. As I was wondering whether to go on, the sound stopped. I lowered my foot and went into the living room.

'Ah, Li? Henry's Chinese friend?'

'Yes, that's right, but I didn't realise that ...'

'My name is Susan. I'm pleased you've come to stay.'

One glance was enough to tell me that this was the captain's ex-wife, looking very like what I had imagined. The picture of a tattooed body was still vividly before me.

'How do you like the house, Li?' Susan stroked the keys of the piano with the back of her hand. 'Do you like all of this?'

'Of course, it's beautiful, but that's not all, it's also rather strange.'

I remember that the first time I touched the walls of the room they actually trembled, like flesh. The wall was spongy. The structure of the house was evocative: entering the kitchen by crossing the corridor from the front door, you were faced with a wall hung with hams, without being able to be sure what kind of meat they really were. And the kitchen — if you can call it that — was no more than a counter inside the drawing room, which was enormous, and from the drawing room various doors led off to the bathroom, the bedroom, the study, the conservatory, and the guest room. Hidden at the far end of the drawing room opposite the main door, there was a small room. There, on a marble bench, was an instrument that shone like crystal. Through the glass you could see a golden liquid slowly turning, like a brain from outer space. After three days I came to the conclusion that the house was made in the image of a woman's body.

'Strange? That's interesting. Have you any other thoughts about it?'

I moved towards what was my hostess's bedroom with the idea of hastily tidying it up, since I had taken the liberty of moving from the guest room into her bedroom. A rug was untidily spread across the big bed. Susan followed me in. 'I'm sorry, I didn't mean to ...' I tried to explain.

'Do you like the bed?'

I smelt a familiar smell — like a mixture of kerosene and washing powder — sexual desire with a trace of malice. Before, when I had been in the kitchen, I had examined the bits of bread, the raw meat, the greasy traces on the plates, the onions that hadn't been eaten, the pepper scattered over the counter, and the hams hung on the wall. But this was not the smell of food. It seemed to come from flowers. A deep draught of it was intoxicating, but just as it was becoming so strong as to overwhelm the senses, it's particular source eluded me. It was everywhere, the floorboards, the cracks in the wall, the wardrobe, the cushions of the sofa and the rug spread over the big bed, on the top of which were dog hairs and a dent where the dogs had been lying. But in the bathroom and in the wardrobe, where there were hundreds of clothes, the only smell was of extreme cleanliness, the sort of smell which often used to wake me up in the middle of the night, and force me to open the window and let the clear air of the wilderness penetrate the room. I used to stand in that mysterious little room, holding the container with the gold liquid as if it were a scent bottle.

'Yes, I do.'

I finished washing my hands and came out of the bathroom to find Susan holding a glass of wine and wearing a night-dress. She turned the lights off in the room, one by one. She began talk, and nearly everything she said was a question. 'Did you see the cow's horn in the tool shed in the garden? Did you step on the snakeskin? Do you know where the drinks cabinet is? It's hidden in the wall cupboard. Have you just come back from Henry's? So you must have seen the dunes shifting?' I didn't have time to answer, or I held back from answering, because I was examining the line where her neck joined her chest. She crossed over to the doorway of the bathroom and, with one hand on my shoulder, took off silk stockings from under her night-dress with the other. She let them fall to the ground.

'Li?'

'Uh?'

The soles of her feet were pink, and her toes were very smooth, like …

'Can I ask you a stupid question?'

Facing the mirror above the wash basin, she gently shrugged off one of her sleeves and turned the hot tap on. Her silk night-dress slid off her shoulder, and hung momentarily on her oppressively fat buttocks before slipping to the floor. I took in her body — the body of a middle-aged woman — at a glance. She wetted her face some water, and opening her legs, started to wash her entire body, from the ankles upwards. There was no sound from her joints as she moved, no expression on her face. She was staring at something behind me in the mirror, but to me, she seemed to be looking at my ear …

'Why don't Chinese men have hair on their chests? And is their skin really as smooth as a thousand dollar leather jacket?'

Head bent forwards, she grasped the wash basin, slightly raising her buttocks and opening her legs even wider. Once again, I caught the same persistent smell. The petals tattooed on her back began to move in waves and I closed my eyes. The decoration of her body was that of some unnamed bird, perhaps a bird of paradise, enormous, with wings spread, and peach blossom for feathers ...

'So, have you ever seen them collecting bulls' sperm? ... Of course you haven't,' she went on. 'They ... a group of men tie the cow to a specially built stand, and before the bull mounts her, they put something between them a bit like a plastic bag which the bull can't see. In his excitement he tries to mount her again and again. Sometimes he is cheated into doing this more than twenty times in a day.'

I opened my eyes wide. The bird of paradise had disappeared, and an evil dragon was entwined around her body. The dragon's scales shone like armour and covered her body from shoulder to foot. The dragon's head swept down between her legs from the base of her spine, its evil kiss just touching, surrounding her vagina, its black lips like two dried mushrooms ...

'Stroke it.'

The swaying of her buttocks stopped. They looked like two large grindstones made of cheese.

'Stroke it. Stroke it or turn your back.'

I turned and found myself facing a large mirror hanging on the wall in the corridor. In it I could see countless images of Susan and myself in the bathroom mirror receding into the apparent infinity of the two mirrors' reflections. I saw my face, countless times over. I saw my T-shirt with Mississippi Catfish printed on it. I saw Susan in the mirror, looking much like any other middle-aged woman who had too much fat on her — over-eager, rapacious.

'You know, Henry isn't an artist in the usual sense of the term, nor am I a wife in the usual sense.' She turned around. 'And I imagine that you are not his friend in the usual sense of the term either. Do you think that I'm going a bit too far? You know, Henry doesn't like women.' Her hands touched my shoulders and opened the second button of my shirt. 'Are you his house guest or his model? Or his ... You know, he won't let you go.'

Her fingernails dug into my flesh as if they were trying to extract a bee sting.

'I'm not going to let him fuck me about,' I said in Chinese.

'What? What did you say? I just wanted to have a look ...' Her hand moved easily up to stroke my chin. '... to have a look at Henry's

206

work. Perhaps he's fallen in love with you, or perhaps he's just in love with your skin. But no matter what, you should be pleased with yourself. Your skin is enough to make any woman jealous …'

I no longer wanted to pay any attention to the images reflected back and forth by the two mirrors. They had been observing each other like this for hundreds of years. That was long enough, they'd already made me dizzy. I was simply an image between them. They were like two trains coming in opposite directions, and I was no more than the instant when they passed one another. So, I repeated myself in English,

'I'm sorry, but I'm not a mother fucker.'

'Get out.'

I stepped out of the bathroom and heard her turning on the shower. The wild New Mexican landscape was like a leopard skin discarded in the darkness. I walked out from the conservatory and tried to think back. 'When I …' I closed my eyes only to open them again at once. I ignored these futile summons and walked blindly into the darkness. It seemed to me that something soft was growing under my feet, something like a plant, but moving, and covering the ground. They were mushrooms — poisonous or otherwise — evenly spread everywhere, near and far. At this very moment, I caught the scent of that familiar smell. It was coming from the mushrooms. Their exhalations were not inhibited by this vast and barren wilderness. In the distance, I could see the house, ablaze with lights. From it came the strains of Caruso singing 'The Pearl Diver' on an old gramophone. The deep notes of the song sounded desolate, and the starry sky seemed about to collapse. I was aware of some things that I could not grasp. The desert was summoning something or someone — but not me. So I made for the ranch.

As I went in, the captain was lying completely naked on the floor of the sitting room, with beads of sweat oozing from his forehead. His legs were raised as if he were giving birth, and his testicles hung in between like two date stones wrapped in toilet paper. His mouth was wide open, exposing his bad teeth. It was hard to say whether he was gritting his teeth or laughing. He lifted one hand to turn the handle of the old gramophone so that the record would go on playing.

'Too much, I've had too much.' He gave a soundless hollow laugh, and his feet convulsed into the shape of a chicken's claw. He pressed his knee against his stomach. A large quantity of mushrooms, inside his stomach, were getting to him badly. He fixed me with his one good eye. The crystal of the other looked like a wasp's eye, divided up into countless little chambers.

'Let's have some fun. Let's have some fun.'

He looked like a small bundle which had tied itself up in knots, tossing and turning this way and that on the floor. 'I'm hooked. I want more. I've got the craving!'

He tried to crawl but stumbled. 'Let's have some fun. This is the sort of person I am!'

I turned away and took my clothes off with my back to the captain

The captain stopped thrashing about and quietened down. Caruso's song came to an end. I turned around to find the captain had twisted himself into the shape of a beetle. He looked like a strange drawing of a poisoned North American cockroach. I stepped over him and went into the bedroom.

I could hear the water in the bathroom all night long.

3

The sound of the two large dogs banging against the door woke me up.

The room was pitch black. When I opened the curtains the bright sunlight was dazzling and it shone on my body, entwined in the embrace of an evil dragon. I got up quickly to put my things together, and unbutton a new shirt. New shirts are always covered in pins which I never manage to remove entirely. Every time I put on a new shirt I always have to check it extremely carefully, several times, feeling over it with my hand, right up until I put it on. The fabric is so stiff and scratchy that you can't tell when it's going to happen. Perhaps while fastening the last button, just as I suddenly turn around — I'm bound to come across a pin hidden in the cloth. It happens all the time, as if it's fated. Today was no exception —

'Good morning, Li.'

The captain stood at the door and even though his clothes were creased, he looked quite calm, not at all like the morning of the day before when his mouth was glued to a beer bottle and he plucked his false eye out before blowing on it and putting it back in. In fact he looked rather like a vet who has just delivered a cow. 'Did you sleep well?'

'Very well, thank you.'

'It seems …' He was considering, considering what he should say. 'It seems you're all right then?'

'Of course I am. What about you?'

'Didn't you feel that it went on for a very long time? In fact it was only two hours'

'No, I didn't think about it.' I lifted my rucksack. 'But anyway, thank you both very much, for your warm hospitality ...'

'Both?'

He came right up to me, and said, 'Are you saying that you saw her? Huh?' He clapped me on the shoulder. 'So that's it. You're right.' And then he embraced me. 'You must definitely come and see me, often.'

'Definitely.'

I lifted up my rucksack, stroked the ears of the two dogs, one after the other, and left the ranch.

We embraced and shook hands again. The captain stuffed a tube holding a painting into my backpack. 'It's a present for you, that I made just last night. One day I'll have a chance to tattoo it onto a woman's body. Believe me, I will ...' He made a gesture with his hands, over and over, as if to say it was forever.

I kept turning back and waving to him. He was still saying something out loud, repeating it so often that it had become mechanical, one minute turning to the sky and the next to the ground, telling the world their secrets. He really was too lonely, a man whom women had abandoned, an artist abandoned by art, in many ways a bit like me. But I wasn't up to him, because I knew nothing about this strange wild land. I no longer heard the captain's voice, but doubtless he was still talking, gesturing, facing the sky and then the earth, and far in the distance he looked like a road sign in the desert. It was only when I had walked a long way and had nearly reached the Indian reserve that I felt a real longing for him. And straight away I remembered that he was a doctor, and a tattoo artist, and into drugs. I then forgot him, and took out the drawing and opened it up in the wind.

Like the previous one, it showed the captain's former wife, lying down, naked, a young man tattooed on her body. Encircling the young man's naked body was a black dragon, with scales like millions of eyes, set close together. The young man's head was held high. He look up at the sky despairingly, his eyes and mouth awry. One hand was stretched upwards as if parting from something in the heavens, and the other buried shamelessly in his lower body ...

'Ee ee, ya ya, ha ha, ge ge ma ma mi mi ...'

Humming tunelessly, I walked on ahead, and drove my memory — as if I were herding cattle — into the clouds.

HITCHHIKING

DUO DUO

translated by Harriet Evans

As dusk fell on Christmas Eve, I was held up on a roadside — near a petrol station in northern England. Every time the shadow of a car appeared from behind the hill I started signalling, thumbs down. Four hours went by. I had probably signalled to about ten cars. Let's get going, let's get home, let's get back together with our families: this is what I thought the gesture meant.

I had left London very early that morning all because of a telephone call during the night. It was Xiao Feng again, a Chinese student studying in Scotland. Big brother Li — that's what she calls me — I'll die if you don't come to see me today. And then she hung up. I set out as soon as it was light, because I knew all too well what her words meant. But you needn't consider her ... look at me ... Two weeks ago, every single one of the two hundred people who live in the thirteen storey student hall of residence had gone away, leaving the place deserted and me like a ghost pacing up and down the corridors listening to the big bunch of keys jangling in my pocket. With every step, the keys let me know that I was the only person around, that there was only one of me, and no matter where I went there would only ever be just one of me. Every step I took told me that this would never change.

Anyway, Xiao Feng was a girl with a mouth full of yellow teeth, born in North-eastern China in the 1960s. We had only met once, last year, when I went to make some arrangements for something in a small country town in Scotland. She picked me out at a glance just as I was passing the entrance to a theatre. She was carrying a *pipa* case, and was performing with an amateur theatre group. 'Are you Chinese?' 'Too right I am.' Just a simple phrase in a local Beijing accent was enough to bring tears to her eyes. She had not seen a single mainlander for two and a half years. After that there was no end to her phone calls. 'Big brother Li, come and see me, I'll make stuffed dumplings for you.

Help me, big brother Li, it's like being in prison here.' Occasionally, I would add, 'Why not find a Scottish boyfriend, then?'

So, to save the thirty pounds coach fare, I had to hitch a lift to see her. I knew that she wouldn't jump off a building if I didn't go, but if she stayed up all through the night of Christmas Eve, she might turn into another kind of person. I wanted her to remain as she was at our first meeting. I didn't want her to change, but change was the only possible direction she could take.

By midday, I had already hitched almost as far as York. I thought that hitching any further would be totally impossible. On Sunday mornings in London, as I recalled, there was never anyone about except for dogs shitting. I was just kidding myself trying to hitch a lift on Christmas Eve. Still, it was okay, and eventually I got a ride in a police car, with a really young, kind policeman, who in less than an hour, left me nearer London than Scotland.

'I want to go to Scotland.' He shook his head.' I don't care where you want to go, but hitchhiking at a petrol station is totally illegal.' So, I left the police station of a small town, and found another petrol station, the one where I found myself now. Where else were cars likely to stop except in petrol stations?

It was wet and cold, and my hands were so frozen that they were red and swollen. My thumbs were already sticking out from the other fingers. Occasionally, as a car window flashed by, I saw someone making the thumb down signal to me, but only when the car had gone a long way past did I hear the 'Sorry, but Happy Christmas!' The last pale light of the English winter disappeared, and church bells resounded all over the hillside, affirming the message that you will, ultimately, meet with what you believe in.

A big truck full of straw emerged unsteadily from behind the hill. It was moving very slowly, probably the driver had already had a few drinks. I changed my gesture, and moved my thumb up and down, and even though what I meant by this was not particularly clear, the truck eventually stopped.

The driver had a broad face and a greying beard. He stuck his hand out of the cabin window, thumb up.

'Sorry, but I wondered if you would give me a lift ...'

As soon as I opened my mouth he put his thumb down. But when he heard that I wanted to go to Scotland, he put his thumb up again, and said that he was Scottish. 'But you'll definitely have to get another ride because this truck may not make it until early tomorrow morning, and anyway Scotland is very big. You'll be lucky to come across someone driving about on Christmas Day, you know. You're very brave ... but I'm sure you'll have some luck. Are you Chinese?' Once I had agreed to pay him eight pounds, I climbed into the truck. A boy and his large black dog were already occupying the front seat, so I climbed into the back, and tumbled straight away into a pile of straw.

'Hey ...'

In the straw was a fair-haired girl with ear phones on, hands behind her back. She greeted me, so I said hello back to her, and just managed to see that her face was heavily made up with powder, and big black rings round her eyes. 'Hey.' Another sound came out from the pile of straw. A second fair-haired girl raised her face, and quickly buried it again in the lap of the first. The truck moved off, and the earrings of the semi-reclining girl began to swing.

It looked as if it was a farm truck. It was piled high with straw, bundled into bales by machine, for animal fodder during the winter, or fertilizer. I'd just managed to squeeze into a crack between the bales, when I heard the clear sound of the girls kissing. It was just like the sound made when you peel back the foil top of a carton of fresh cream bought from the supermarket, or when you dip oat biscuits into hot milk. I was half buried in the straw, inwardly thanking the Scottish farmer who was driving the truck. Perhaps his wife had left him, leaving him with nothing but the child and the dog, or maybe it was just the opposite, maybe he was on his way to join up with her. Whatever the case, I hoped that he would be able to return to a warm home, just like people everywhere who believed in Jesus Christ would be doing on Christmas Eve, sitting down to eat together, the man opening the champagne, the woman carrying in the roast, with the child the first to say 'For what we are about to receive may the Lord make us truly thankful', and the dog the last to sleep. I really hoped that everyone would have a Christmas Eve like this.

One of the girls was sitting on my left hand, and every time she bounced up and down as the truck jolted, the buckle of her leather belt bit sharply into it. The trembling tip of a patterned leather boot came into my field of vision. I closed my eyes, and felt my face glow at the touch of someone's thighs. I don't know whether I heard wrongly or not, but their words kept following the same order. Are you cold? Are you? I love you. Not cold? Aren't you cold? I love you. You're cold. I'm cold. I love you. The clean smell of a mass of girls' hair mixed with straw ... the empty fields of grain at the sides of the road were completely immersed in darkness ...

As I stared at the starless sky of northern England, I started to count: seventy-six. This truck of straw was the seventy-sixth bed I had slept in since leaving China. I had walked everywhere, sometimes when I was looking for work, and sometimes to avoid getting into a bed altogether. Sometimes I slept on floors, sometimes on a sofa, sometimes in a bed, and even occasionally in a double bed. I once told Xiao Feng on the phone that I had slept in more than seventy beds. She laughed. 'What do you want to count beds for?'

The rock music coming out of the girls' earphones was like the noise of a large factory, like the harsh sound made by the foundry of a steel-works. As they followed the music's rhythm, they looked like two birds looking at each other, long necks outstretched, shrugging their shoulders, stroking each other's cheeks, and in the brief moments when their lips parted, they emitted warm air and muffled sounds: it's you it's me it's us we're two it's one it's all … With every jolt of the truck, the half-naked bodies of the two girls, stuck closely together, il-luminated the dark countryside of England, like moonlight …

'Big brother Li, you should take of yourself, because if you don't, no-one else in this world is going to look out for you …'

I shifted my position. 'Big brother Li, I'll make stuffed dumplings for you. Come soon. We'll make them together, we'll roll out the dough and chop up the filling, and we'll get together enough people to fill the table, and we'll eat and drink and talk non-stop, and we'll have fun right up until dawn …' I shifted my position again. I became less and less clear about where I'd come from. Was it the place that Xiao Feng, with her North-east accent, described?

A big golden threshing ground gleamed in front of my eyes. The beginning and end of the story were missing, but there were some old women in the scene, faces looking purposefully downwards, as if ig-noring my existence. Their movements were rigid and unyielding. They seemed to suggest some pact which would not allow history to advance. I saw a boy, me, when I was eight years old, my mouth wide open and about to cry out at the group of old women, but there was no sound. It wasn't until today that I heard the sound: I am a citizen of the world.

I laughed out loud.

I laughed not because I had understood what it meant, but because I had become one, and because I had exhausted its meaning in England. So there I stood, still eight years old, in a golden landscape facing a threshing ground, with my mouth wide open. No matter what kind of life I'd had, the eight year-old would live on forever, allowing me always to remember this event in my past. Later on in my life I had agreed to another meaning of this event, with completely different scenes: a group of bare-backed young men with shaved heads, and black cotton trousers, sweat pouring off their bodies, carried a brightly coloured sedan chair across the yellow earth, and from inside the sedan protruded a pair of bound feet in embroidered shoes. There was a cry as well: 'Help me, big brother Li.' I slowly sunk into asleep, until the moans of the girls woke me up again.

I remembered that I had just entered a cemetery, I'm not sure exactly where, and spent a long time leaning against a statue, not wanting to leave. The statue was the headless torso of a big, strong woman, whose right arm must once have been much longer than her left arm, because you couldn't see half of the right arm — it was buried inside her body — the whole of her forearm extended up into her abdomen from her vagina, making the way her belly protruded look just like a fist holding a pistol. Her left leg was bent upwards, corresponding with the stretching of the right arm. The toes were all tensed up, and wrinkles showed all over the waist and buttocks because of the downward tension of the right arm. I walked around the statue three times and realised that it was, in fact, a gravestone, but I've already forgotten the words that were carved on it.

The panting of the two girls brought me back to Christmas Eve. Their doing the same thing with such concentration for so long made me realise what it really meant: people should do for each other at Christmas. Girls who, on this night, had hitched a lift from a truck carrying straw could not be particularly fortunate in life. They had no family, no place to live, and made love, tirelessly, just to get through this night. Just like me, but all I could do was dream. But my dreams had been cut short ever since I had gazed upon all those girls sunning their breasts or standing with legs apart, in London swimming pools. These two girls, making love as if there was no-one around, reminded me that in the dreams I had, English girls never saw me.

'Happy Christmas! Happy Christmas! Happy Christmas! Happy Christmas!'

The two girls sat up and shouted to each other, clapping each other's hands.

It was exactly twelve o'clock.

The sound of 'Happy Christmas' came from inside the driver's cabin as well, and a bottle was tossed through the window into the pile of straw. The girls rushed to look for it, their breasts facing downwards as if assisting in the search. The distant, drawn out sounds of many church bells came across to us, whether or not to bless this world I don't know, but this world really needed blessing. The girls didn't kiss me, they kissed each other, pressing and squeezing each other hard. Their gleaming painted finger nails shone, like eyes.

I toppled over, and heard the excited barking of the dog in the cabin. It barked for quite a while. I really felt like bringing him into the back of the lorry, to stroke his head and read the deep things in his eyes. I have never truly understood the mind of a dog. Crossing my hands behind my head, I repeated again and again the words of an old friend who had been living abroad for many years: I want to close my eyes and hibernate for several decades. Perhaps I won't want to open my eyes again, even after I re-emerge. The alcohol had calmed the girls down, and they fell asleep, looking like two planks of wood. Their bodies had already separated a bit, and the fingers of one of them was touching my leg. The truck seemed to come to a halt, and I faintly sensed that the driver had jumped down from the cabin, and was stamping his feet and talking. The cold night had arrived. I think I must have fallen asleep for a while, for when I felt my hand being grasped by another's, the truck was already moving again.

Which one of the girls was it? They were very much the same, both with long legs, both vigorous and healthy, with the cold, strong expression of a horse. I thought, that's the one, the one whose nose always twitches when she speaks, as if it were trying to help her get her words out. She had simply mistaken me for the other girl. I withdrew my hand. Her hand continued to pursue me, to stroke my jaw, my nose — she stroked the bridge of my nose for a long time, as if she was concentrating on some kind of a puzzle. I wanted to turn around to look at her, but her hand covered my eyes. She might have felt a bit embarrassed. Was she scared to see my face? Her body nestled close to mine. It was, actually, very still, almost too relaxed. I felt as if I was blind, I had forgotten what a woman's body felt like long ago. Before this, I hadn't realised that there were real human bodies in England ... Even though there were countless numbers of faultlessly beautiful legs on Oxford Street, I preferred to look at the bare-headed, unclothed wooden mannequins in shop windows. I dreamt about them. I never had any dreams about living people. The boundaries set out for living people in England are absolutely clear. In the English school I attended in London, the twenty odd students in my class divided totally naturally into two large groups, always sitting at the same two separate tables. One group had fair hair, and the other had black hair. No-one wanted to sit in the wrong place.

But her body, here, seemed to be telling me that this wasn't real.

I couldn't smell the sweet scent of the hair mixed with straw, although I really tried to. All I sensed was a kind of worn out sadness. The sighs filling her body were squeezed out by our embrace, as if they had been waiting to be released for a long time. And this moved me; it was a shared experience, and I didn't once feel that I was lying down with a simple, foolish young girl. Perhaps I was already too old, for this body conveyed the exhaustion you get from long distance flights, and which I knew well. Or perhaps I was too young, for this body no longer seemed to hold any dreams. But it stayed close to mine. That was already enough. People only give a little to others. The demands we make on others are not great, either. But as long as there is something, no matter how small, it's enough. Her body didn't indicate a desire to toy with mine; all it wanted was to give me some warmth, to tell me that this was how people should behave. We stroked each other's body: thank you. And thank you, too. The embrace of these two bodies was a way of getting us through the cold night. Her body made my heart beat with the meaning of Christmas. It signified that it was not right for a soul travelling across England on Christmas Eve in a truck carrying straw to be left completely alone.

I was beginning to realise that her constant stroking was a kind of blessing, when her tongue touched my lips, and she clasped her legs tight around me. Her hands were dry, her lips seemed maternal, perhaps because they lacked moisture. An uneasy premonition came into my mind: the sense of calm after being blessed by a person is never is as great as being blessed by god …

At sunrise, I heard the sparrows' call becoming English again. The two girls spoke hurriedly, in muffled tones: 'She was forty, fifty, fifty-five? No, more than sixty.' In the early morning, their voices seemed coarse and raucous, like two schoolgirls. 'An old cow from the back of beyond.' 'You're right.' The only sentence I heard clearly was: 'Is he Chinese or Japanese?'

'Chinese.' I stretched out my hand.

Three fingers, I guess, certainly no more, three icy fingers picked up my thumb, and put it back on my crotch, where it had come from. Another burst of English followed: 'Shit, that old cow, she stepped on my hair.' 'An old lady from the countryside, with bandy legs.' 'When did she get off the lorry?' 'Shit …'

Dawn had already spread across the horizon, like a big knife clearly delineating every boundary, leaving nothing indistinct. 'You there … we're already in Scotland', the driver shouted loudly. The lorry stopped. I stared at the sky, a Scottish sky, and the bags and boots of the two girls clattered against the sides of the lorry. The sound of their heavy jump onto the ground, the sound of money being counted, and the sounds of farewell — I heard them all really clearly. 'So long, you're all right, you are.' 'Happy Christmas, boys.'

The driver knocked on the back of the lorry with his pipe. I was half kneeling on the pile of straw, watching two young men set off towards the Scottish countryside into the dawn. Their long fair hair was swinging and their arms were around each other's waist. Stepping out on their long legs, they took the way ahead without looking back, the tassels on their leather jackets swaying all the while. I felt flat, and realised that the adrenaline injected into me that Christmas Eve had already ebbed way by Christmas Day

With ten pounds in my hand, I too jumped down from the lorry.

'Thanks, you were a Godsend.'

'Don't mention it.' The driver pushed my hand back, and holding his pipe in his mouth, climbed back into the cabin. 'You've already been paid for.' He twisted himself back into his seat, and closed the cabin door. 'She was a kind-hearted old person; thank her, not me.' He turned his thumb downwards, three times. 'You'll have to go on hitching.'

The driver started up the lorry, and, as he did, the boy and his dog turned towards me.

'Happy Christmas, my old China!'

INTO PARTING ARMS

DU MA

translated by Helen Wang

1

On Saturday I had a long distance phone call from my sister.

'Can you come home?'

'What's happened?'

'Mum and Dad are getting divorced.'

'What! What on earth's going on?'

The line was silent for a while, except for the buzz of the electricity. Then my sister told me it was all very complicated, it seemed to have started with an argument, and it was impossible to explain right now. Anyway, everything at home was in a complete mess. She was phoning from home, she said, charging the call to our father's account at work. Dad would be back soon, we could talk more when we met. Then she hung up.

I didn't dare waste any time, and immediately asked for leave from work, and went to the station to buy a ticket to travel the same day. My girlfriend made it to the station platform to see me off. She's very thoughtful, even in the hurry she'd managed to buy me a bag of food and drink. But time was short and I only got to have a few words with her.

The departure bell sounded and the train began to move off. She ran alongside the train, waving, and urging me to come back as soon as I could, and on no account to argue with my family. Then she and the platform disappeared. Ten minutes later the train had left the city. I glanced at my watch, it was half past two in the afternoon. Usually at this time I would be sitting in the office staring out of the window at the traffic on the road below. But now, through the carriage window, I looked onto vast fields and hills rising in the distance, and clouds in the sky, so different from what I normally saw. It made me feel, truly, that I was on my way home.

Relations with my family had been bad since I started university. My parents were both from science and engineering backgrounds, and had hoped that I would go on to do scientific research. But I'd acted on my own authority, and moved from the chemistry department to the Chinese literature department. They weren't pleased. After that, a series of arguments had begun. I would often shirk obligations, my grades were bad, I didn't want to sit the exams for postgraduate entrance, nor did I want to have to return to live with my parents. My girlfriend wasn't what they'd hoped for, she wasn't pretty enough and she came from a farming village. With all this, and more, every time I went home during the vacation we'd argue and part on bad terms. More than once they'd said I was no longer their son. So, in the two years since I started working, I've seldom written to them, and haven't been home, even at New Year.

Nonetheless, my sister's phone call had taken me by surprise. Perhaps because I thought of them as like most of the educated families I knew, where you couldn't say relations were either good or bad. I'd never seen them show affection in public, nor could I really remember them ever arguing. Intuitively I felt it was my father who had brought up the subject of divorce. I tried to picture his face, hoping to find a clue there. He was very good to my sister and me when we were little. He had taught me to read, and when I was five I was reading full length stories. There was one book, I remember, *Angry Tide on Fishing Island*, which I have to give him credit for. My sister and I used to love sugar cane, but we had bad teeth. My father would cut the sugar cane into slices, then cut each slice into four pieces, and put them in bowl for us. It was a shame that the arguments at university had wrecked our relationship. All that came to mind now was his fury and animosity. I didn't know much about his life during the last few years. All I knew was that he had transferred from the university to a government office, and had been sent to the Hainan branch to do business there. As my sister put it, he'd gone 'from the academic world to the political world, and from the political world to the business world'. Not long ago, I heard that the business had gone under, and he'd returned to his post in the government office. And now for some reason he wanted to get divorced. Perhaps he was going through the menopause? Or having an affair? It made me realize how little I knew my father.

I felt my reaction was somewhat ridiculous. After so many years feeling distanced from my family, I had suddenly been summoned home by a phone call. I was just like those patriotic Chinese years ago who had initially lost hope in the motherland and gone abroad, only to pack their bags and come scurrying home as soon as they heard that there'd been some sort of disaster, even though it really wasn't clear what they would be able to do about it. My situation was exactly the same. If my parents really were going to get divorced, I didn't think I could do anything to help. I might make matters even worse. Perhaps the phone call was no more than my sister over-reacting.

The train sped on southwards, further and further from the city where I lived, nearer and nearer to my family. I decided not to think about it too much; as my sister said, we could talk more when we met. By now the sky was growing dark, and the scene outside the window was becoming blurred. I turned back inside and opened the bag of food my girlfriend had packed. Inside were the beer and cigarettes I loved. I lit a cigarette, drank the beer, and felt very content. The evening news came over the loudspeaker in the carriage and I remembered that it was the weekend. I had arranged to go and see a film with my girlfriend. But now, everything had changed.

It was a long journey, and the train was swaying from side to side, and I was beginning to feel restless. I regretted not bringing a book to read. Then a middle-aged woman sitting beside me tried to start a conversation. Perhaps it's a bit strong calling her middle-aged, only the clothes she was wearing and her style of conversation were all so staid, and she looked married. Actually I knew she'd been looking at me since she got on the train — perhaps because I'm good-looking? We got talking. She spoke very slowly, with a beautiful voice, and her conversation was interesting. I learnt that she wasn't married after all, and she was the same age as me, so she certainly wasn't middle-aged. By chance we were heading for the same destination, she was travelling on business. We chatted about everything under the sun, and really enjoyed ourselves. But as it grew late, and the lights were turned down, the passengers around us began to drop off to sleep, any way they could. I'd been busy all day, and felt completely exhausted. We exchanged telephone numbers and promised to be in touch when we got back home. Then I dropped off too.

2

It was Monday afternoon by the time I reached home. My parents were still at work, and only my sister was there. She was delighted to see me, said she reckoned I'd arrive the next day at the earliest. On the way I'd made up my mind to give a better impression this time, to be more like a grown-up son. I put down my bags and asked about my parents.

The argument had happened over a month earlier. My father had gone to Beijing on business, and had promised to buy some clothes for Mum. Mum had written to him there, telling him not to buy any clothes as money was tight at home just then. But as soon as Dad walked through the door, Mum asked him for the clothes he'd bought. My father said didn't you tell me not to buy them? Mum kicked up a fuss, said my father never thought about her. They had a bad fight, said many unpleasant things, and Mum suggested divorce. Although afterwards she said she regretted it, my father got hold of the idea and wasn't going to let it drop. He wanted a divorce. I was perplexed at what my sister said. Surely the divorce couldn't be over something as small as this? My sister didn't have anything else to say about it, except that recently our parents' relationship had been very strained. Dad would go out every evening, saying he had obligations at work, then come back very late, and Mum would stay at home on her own crying.

I felt like an incompetent detective, faced with a suspicious case and not a thread to go on. I decided to leave the subject for a while and talk about something else. My sister had obviously been under a great deal of pressure, and her face was pale. She was wearing a flashy necklace around her neck. I asked her about it. It was only a gold-plated necklace, she said, not a very expensive one. But it was fashionable in their class to wear rings and necklaces. She was a third year student in the modern languages department. Their foreign lecturer had an enormous wedding ring and all the girls kept their fixed glued to it during his classes.

We talked about her life. She said she hadn't found a boyfriend she was happy with. The intelligent ones were too poor, and those with money were too stupid. A lot of people asked her out though, and every evening someone would invite her for a late evening bite to eat. Well that's OK then, I interrupted. What do you mean? my sister contradicted, if I was doing well, I'd be getting an expensive breakfast!

She carried on off-loading anything that was on her mind. She wanted to be a party member, and to be given a recognized position in her class, as this might be useful when it came to being assigned a job. Otherwise she'd try to be an organiser of evening activities at the school, and gain some popularity. My father had promised to buy her a gold ring, but now, with all this business, there was no hope of that. I felt very sympathetic as I listened, but there was nothing I could do to help.

After a while Mum came home. She burst into tears when she saw me, saying my father was going to leave her. It was all very embarrassing for me, because I wasn't used to this kind of show of emotion. I said a few words of encouragement, then pulled myself together, and asked her what it was all about, but like my sister, she was unable to say anything specific. She cried and complained how cold Dad was towards her, and how he didn't do enough for the family.

I'd only been home a few hours and already I was feeling irritated by Mum and my sister. I was almost losing patience. I simply kept my mouth shut and waited for Dad to come back.

Dinner time passed, and he still hadn't returned. My sister said he might be eating at a reception. I went out and bought some beer and pickles, and helped Mum make the dinner. When we'd eaten, we stayed in together waiting, but Dad still didn't come home. Mum started to cry again, and said he was always like this, if he was *out* he wouldn't be back before eleven. It was amusing how she used the word 'out'; it's usually used to describe a kid who doesn't know any better.

I was in the sitting room, flicking through the telephone book. On the cover were the telephone numbers of some of my old student friends. I tried dialling the numbers, and was lucky — two of them were still there, and they invited me out for a drink.

My family lives in a city in the south, where the climate gets extremely hot. I washed and changed into a T-shirt and shorts, and walked out of the building just as my friends were arriving. We cycled down to a street nearby that was full of small stalls and private businesses and very busy. The cafe had moved the tables and chairs out on to the pavement and the roof, and even had little fairy lights flickering on and off. We found some seats, and my friends ordered 'fashionable' fruit-crush and some other drinks. Fruit-crush is really just crushed ice with some fruit juice, only it's fashionable, so it's expensive. They told me the latest news and gossip, how the boss of some dance hall or other had been murdered, how a young lad of such and such a work unit had married a forty year old woman, and about our old student friends who were now married. I asked how the two of them were: one was preparing to get married, buying the things they'd need for their new home, and the other had had a number of girlfriends but still wasn't ready to settle down. He said he'd met a girl from Taiwan on a train once when he was travelling on business. They'd got along well and had even corresponded for a while. But when he went to check the regulations he discovered he wouldn't be permitted to go to Taiwan to marry, and he felt utterly dejected.

I wasn't feeling very sociable and didn't say much, but they didn't notice, they were happy enough. Naturally the conversation soon turned to their particular familiar topics. I couldn't join in, so I started watching the nightlife on the streets. I noticed that there was an extraordinary number of people on bikes, all in a hurry, as though they were all going some place. I'd arrived home in the afternoon, just at rush-hour, but there hadn't been as many people as there were now. What's more, this street wasn't exactly the liveliest part of town. I knew everything came to life at night here, and there were many places you could go: cinemas, video-clubs, dance halls and bars, all there to entertain. But there weren't enough places for all these people. I watched for a while, and it was quite interesting to see how many old men and young children there were in the flow of people. I wondered about it and asked my friends, but they didn't know the reason either.

Then, suddenly they began a heated argument. There was a motorbike outside a shop across the road; one of them thought it was a Honda, the other insisted it was a Chinese 'Wild Wolf'. Each stuck to his guns, just like two mechanics insisting on a technical point. But it was too dark and there were too many people on the street to see clearly. Neither could get the other to change his mind, and in the end, they decided to bet on it. The loser would buy the next round.

They got up, shook out their hands and feet, like two swimmers preparing to race across a river, staggered forward and disappeared into the flow of bicycles. I could barely make them out. It was so hot, and though I'd washed before I came out, my T-shirt was soaked through and sticking to my back. As soon as they left I became aware of all the noise around — the loud chatter and laughter at the next tables, the cassette player in the café, the bicycle bells in the street, the motorbike engines, the car horns, and the coloured lights above flashing on and off. I called the waitress over by clapping my hands and ordered three cold beers.

3

I kept the real reason for coming home from my father; I told him I was on a business trip, and he didn't suspect anything.

I could see that my parents' relationship was strained. When they did eat together they hardly spoke, they did everything coldly, like two guests in a hotel. Yet I also discovered that since I'd turned up, the whole family had relaxed a little. They lived in an atmosphere of heavy pressure, which my presence seemed to lighten. It was as if I was the head of state, whose role was to let everyone get on with their own things without having to worry. The phone would ring non-stop every day at meal times, mostly people asking if my sister would go out with them. Then my father and sister would go out, one ostensibly had work to do, the other had a date. When they left me watching television with Mum, everything was peaceful and reasonable. The phone calls would keep coming, and each time I would answer politely that my sister was not in, then hang up quickly, so that I wouldn't have to listen to the boys' murmurs of disappointment. Mum was not as dejected as she had been when I first arrived, she had regained a strange calmness, even getting interested in the television programmes. I remembered how she never used to like watching television, but now when I watched the football, she would switch channel and insist on watching the two episodes of a Taiwanese serial that was on every day. I gave in. I knew that although I could now be considered the head of the family, this was merely symbolic; I was no more than a puppet. All I could do was watch television with Mum.

But during the long hours of daylight, my life became extremely tiresome. My parents went to work, my sister went to college, and I was on my own at home with nothing to do. I wanted some company and to go out, but my old student friends were at work. To be honest, after seeing them that day, I couldn't be bothered with them any more. I'd go out on my own, see a cheap Hong Kong video, have a few goes on the games machines, till there was nothing more to play with. I went into the bookshops, and found there was almost no serious reading. I looked all over and saw only one book, Hemingway's *The Sun Also Rises*. I'd read it several years earlier, but I bought it all the same. The sun was really fierce and I went into the first opticians' I came across and bought a pair of sunglasses, and then thinking about it, bought another pair for my sister. Back home, I noticed my legs had caught the sun.

Since I started university I'd wanted to be a writer, which was why I switched from chemistry to Chinese literature. After work I was always complaining about having to go into work every day, and having so little time. Now suddenly I had all this spare time, but whenever I laid a sheet of paper in front of me, it became a letter to my girlfriend. In the letters I'd complain about the situation I was in. I knew there was little sense in my complaints, there wasn't actually very much difference between the city I lived in and here, except that my girlfriend was back there and so were my friends. I hadn't realized in the past just how much a part of my life they all were; I couldn't do without them.

But I'd complain wherever I was; it's a fault in my character. In a way I'm psychologically dependent on them, just as my family is now psychologically dependent on me. In fact, their situation is much the same as mine, and it's very hard for them to share my troubles, the result being that I often got into arguments with my girlfriend or with other friends. Now I was conscious how important they really were. The letters I wrote to my girlfriend were very long, I told her I loved her, and how much I was missing her. Sometimes I wrote two of these letters in one day. But, at the end of every letter I would write that for the time being I still couldn't go back.

This afternoon, I accidentally came across the telephone number I'd taken down in the train. I rang the number and it was the same woman who answered. She was delighted to hear from me, and asked what I was doing at home, and if I would be free some time. I said I couldn't make it in the evenings but that I was free during the day. She invited me to go over and see her. Her work wasn't very hectic, and their company was not far from my home, in a tall building nearby.

I cycled over and she was standing at the main entrance waiting for me. She was wearing a T-shirt and a faded denim skirt, she looked so young and pretty in the sun that I only just recognised her. I was wearing sunglasses and she almost missed me. There was a bar quite close, she said, where we could sit down. The bar was air-conditioned and quite cool, with the blinds drawn tight, as though it were evening. It was office hours so there were hardly any other people. We had just sat down when a waitress appeared from nowhere and asked discreetly: 'Sir, a millionaire or a powdered beauty?' Both were cocktails. I ordered a coffee and a grapefruit juice for her and a cold beer for myself. In the hazy light the outline of her face looked soft, like a young girl's, and compared with the woman on the train she could have been an entirely different person. She asked why I hadn't called her before. Didn't *she* have my telephone number? I answered. She smiled: she'd have been too embarrassed to call me first. Yet, she added, she had been waiting for my call these past days, and had been looking forward to seeing me again. She spoke in that slow, beautiful way, not at all affected, and was quite frank in her manner, not going round and round in circles. I liked this, and suddenly felt very close to her. She looked beautiful today, I said, a pleasure to look at. She smiled again. She was pleased to hear it, she said, because I had said it. I could see she was very happy. Then she said she enjoyed being with me, and when I asked why, she said because I was good-looking and because I was kind. It was my turn to smile.

I stayed until she'd finished work for the day before going home, and on the way I passed a market and bought lots of food. I thought I'd make a very good meal for my family. I was busy in the kitchen when Dad came home grumbling he was hungry. He made straight for the kitchen, saw the spread in front of me, and frowning, asked how long it was going to be, and couldn't I speed things up a bit. I raced to stir-fry a couple of dishes, then there was a fish that needed to be cooked with care, but he couldn't wait and served up the rice. He and my sister began to eat. By the time I brought the fish to the table they had already finished, she was hogging the telephone, talking with her admirers, and from my father's room came the whirr of his electric fan. I was a bit put out, and poured myself a beer, and silently ate the fish. Mum ate with me, praising my skills in the kitchen. After we'd eaten, Mum said I'd done enough for one day, and she cleared the table and did the washing up. After a while my father came out of his room, all spruced up, his hair stylishly blow-dried, and he was even sporting hair-gel. He must have been quite good-looking when he was younger, I thought, certainly no worse than I am now. However, he was in no hurry to leave. He looked up at the quartz clock on the wall and sat down on the sofa and began to read the paper. My sister put the phone down and went to her room to get ready. Mum was in the kitchen washing up. Dad looked at the clock again, suddenly folded up the newspaper, sort of half-looked at me and made straight for the door. Generally, he doesn't move very much, as though he's trying not to attract attention, but he's a tall man and well-built, and now with his scented hair, and his furtive parting gestures, he looked really quite farcical. Although I did say earlier that I had my suspicions, I was now more or less sure of it. My father was having an affair.

4

One day passed after another and my life was beginning to have less and less purpose. I was writing less and less to my girlfriend and each letter was short. In contrast, her letters were getting longer and more frequent, and she asked when I was coming back. I kept her letters under Hemingway's *The Sun Also Rises*, which I hadn't looked yet.

On the other hand, there was beginning to be more and more routine in my life, as though I was going to be there for a long time. My feelings were no longer as confused as when I had first arrived. Every morning I was able to settle down and write, and in the afternoon I would cycle over to meet my new girlfriend, usually in the bar on the ground floor of her office block. Sometimes we'd stay a long time and sometimes not. The waitress began to recognise us and would serve us coffee and cold beer without asking for our order. Once, one of my girl friend's female colleagues bumped into us and started teasing her, saying she wanted to be introduced. However, our relationship wasn't as you might expect. There may have been some warmth between us, but we were certainly a long way from being lovers. When we met we'd talk about easy, relaxing things, or joke with each other, and we never got on to serious or deeper things. There were four in her family, her parents, her teenage brother and herself, though she seldom went home. She lived in accommodation provided by her company for single people. That was all I knew about her. I knew, though, that she wasn't the sort who'd stay in of an evening after work, or go home and watch television with her Mum like me. Like other young people in this city she must have ways of spending her spare time, and have places where she went. But our relationship was no more than our afternoon meetings, and I never asked what else she did. Because, apart from the relaxed happy chatting, I never asked myself if I wanted anything else. There seemed to be a kind of tacit understanding between us. She must have seen my girlfriend on the station platform seeing me off, yet she never asked about her. And she had never asked me why I had come home, or when I was leaving. It was as though both sides knew that our relationship was a straight chalk line drawn on a blackboard which has to finish before it comes to the edge. All we could do was keep the line as straight as we could before it was rubbed off.

One day, while we were sitting in the bar, a man came in looking for her, and they stood chatting by the door for quite a long time, fairly intimately it seemed. At the time I thought nothing of it. I paid them little attention, certainly didn't take offence, and concentrated on my beer. She didn't even begin to talk about it when she came back, as though she'd just been to the ladies, and we carried on the conversation where we'd left off. After that though, our meetings were not as pure as they had been, and both of us became a little unnatural when we were together.

At home I felt I was gradually losing Mum and my sister's trust. My home-coming was like an analgesic, which, having killed the pain for a while, was now less effective. Mum had started to lose hope again, and every evening, in front of the television, she'd start her endless complaints about my father. Mum and Dad had met when they were at university. Mum was from an upper-class background, she was an only girl and had grown up used to being pampered and spoilt. My father's family, on the other hand, had fled south with the Nationalists on the eve of liberation, and times had been hard for them. Mum's family had objected to the match on the grounds that they came from different backgrounds. My mother wouldn't have cared about that at the time, I thought. But now, her aristocratic airs were coming to the fore again. She blamed him for leaving teaching, and ruining himself in business and officialdom. He'd become hollow, she said, paying attention to his clothes, which made him even more common, but he'd never be able to shrug off his country origins. Dad lacked a proper upbringing, and northerners were naturally coarse anyway. She said my father's relatives, his brothers and sisters were all the same. She analysed my father the way a classy young lady would talk about an inferior, and I found her superficiality astonishing and absurd. I had seen those noble relatives Mum talked about, and apart from liking to go calling on each other, they were no different from anybody else. The blood of both my father and my mother ran through my body and I couldn't go along with Mum's views. It would be like one half of my body mocking the other half. I reminded her that he was a very capable man. For so many years it was he who had taken responsibility for our education, and looked after the older relatives. Mum weakened at once. My father had taken care of most of our family matters. And leaping from the school to being an official at least showed he had ability. This only made her more dissatisfied. He didn't give a toss about the family now, she said, and never a moment's thought for her. Each time we talked it would end with Mum sobbing hysterically. She had countless grievances and felt everyone had abandoned her, including me. Apart from being a critical listener, I hadn't been any help to her so far. As she calmed down a little, I once hinted that Dad might be having an affair. I expected her to be shocked, but she seemed to have thought about this long ago. She didn't cry either, was simply more excited, in a different way. She said that if he — with great formality she used his full name as she spoke this words — really had the nerve to get mixed up with a woman she'd go and raise hell at his work unit, and give him such a bad name that he'd lose his official position. No way was she going to go through with a divorce, she'd fight it out with him to the end, because nothing he said or did resembled in any way the behaviour of a member of the Communist party. She urged me to be Steadfast in my Standpoint and, when it came to the Critical Moment, to beat the West Wind with the East Wind. I realised how weak Mum's power of expression was. She had started her attack, unaware that everything she said was straight out of the Cultural Revolution. What she had in mind did, nonetheless, give me a bit of a fright.

My sister had been encouraging me to talk to Dad. Today she raised the subject again. She'd been busy recently, dealing with all the phone calls, and had treated the problem too lightly. She reckoned our parents were just feeling piqued and that if we intervened they'd get back together again as before. She was stunned when I told her what I thought was going on. She didn't believe such a thing could happen, or rather, she didn't want to believe it. She became more determined than ever. If that was the case then Dad was really out of line, and there was all the more reason for having a serious talk with him. She was so sincere in the way she told me to talk with him, that I didn't know how I was going to set about it. If my father was having an affair, then it was up to him to change things if he wanted to, and there was nothing we could say that would be of any use.

My sister was adamant that talking was always better than not talking, and spent ages going over this point with me, extremely seriously. In the end I couldn't help joking that there was no point our parents carrying on as they were now, and that we might as well rip up whatever face we had left, and let Dad go and marry his lover. Mum wasn't old, she could still marry an old official or somebody. I'd obviously well overstepped the mark — my sister stared at me in disbelief. She could have been looking at a stranger. I promised to do as she asked, but suggested it would be better if the two of us both had a word with him, if we combined forces to strengthen our case. If the first talk fell through, it would be so much harder the second time.

That evening, my sister didn't go out, and the two of us sat at home, just like a funeral scene in a film. Dad was home early. He was carrying a bag, and went towards the bedroom, barely noticing us. My sister called out that she wanted a word. Dad obviously wasn't prepared for this, and looked blank for a moment, then moved off saying he was going to his room. My sister stopped him again, and said she wanted a word with him in her room. He must have sensed something was going on, and didn't resist, and followed her over. I admired my sister's nerve. But I hesitated a while in my seat. Perhaps I was hoping my sister would be able to sort the problem out single-handedly. Though I knew this was improbable, since my father had a foul temper at times. I glanced at Mum beside me; she was looking tense and pleased with herself at the same time. That evening my sister and I were openly on her side, two generals in a marshal's palm. But her opponent was on his own, exactly as she'd hoped.

Soon my sister came out. She shook her head in disappointment, and said that Dad was still the same, using the old excuse that he was too busy with work, and unwilling to say more. Mum's face was growing pale. I realised I could no longer escape my turn to step into the ring.

I went into the room. Dad was sitting huffing and sighing on the edge of the bed, like an obstinate child. I sat down facing him, and for a while kept my mouth shut. For so many years it had been me in his place, waiting for him to tell me off, and now it was the other way round. Although I was an adult now, my father's stature was still so much greater than mine that this change around felt quite strange. For a while I was quite intrigued and I believe he felt the same way. We were silent like this for quite a long time. Then I thought of Mum and my sister outside the room, both their hopes resting on me, waiting for me to begin the attack. But I hadn't moved an inch, as though waiting to be surrounded, and raise my hands in surrender. It was quite comical. I took out my cigarettes and handed one to Dad, then lit it for him. It didn't make me feel much better, in fact it was more like two strangers meeting for the first time.

It was Dad who spoke first and when he did it was as though he had lost control and couldn't stop the flow. He said I'd been home for some days now and must have noticed his relationship with Mum. Well, it hadn't been like this just for a couple of days, it was just that my sister and I had been too young to know about it before. They hadn't been married long when the Cultural Revolution started, and, because our grandfather was an officer in the Nationalist Army, his name had been on the wall-posters and he had been 'locked in the cowshed'. Other people's families had brought food for them, but Mum didn't even show her face. He knew Mum wasn't very brave and was afraid of things, and he could forgive her for that. But she'd gone all over the place, crying and causing a stir, with me, newly born, in her arms, saying she hadn't known he was such a reactionary, and she wanted a divorce, and to draw the line clearly. Fortunately, he was later released. He'd put up with all this, he said, hoping that things would go smoothly from then on, as the children were still young. But Mum never got it out of her system, and took the opposite stand on everything. In the past few years life had improved for everyone, and all day Mum would nag him, so-and-so's family had bought a colour

TV, so-and-so's husband had been promoted. He'd just transferred from the school to the government office and was about to be sent to Hainan. At first Mum was really pleased, but who could have known that the business would collapse. Being realistic about it, if it had happened in another family, the wife would have been the first to console her husband, but Mum had turned her back on him, saying she'd known from the beginning he wasn't cut out for business, she'd pleaded with him not to take risks, and if only he had listened to her, things wouldn't have turned out so badly. Dad asked me to think how anyone could rely on such a woman. She'd abandoned him in his moments of crisis. If something else were to happen, God only knows what she'd do. Anyway, my sister and I were older now, and if they really were going to get divorced, then the sooner the better.

When he came back from Hainan, he said, it had been hard: he had dozens of people working under him, a mountain of work, and any number of receptions to attend, in addition to all the talking that was going on behind his back. Every day he'd come home exhausted to see that same expression on Mum's face. He made himself sound so sad, as though he had so much bitterness sealed up inside him, like a criminal giving his own defence. But he was playing a clever game, and never once gave away whether he was really intending to divorce Mum, or whether he was having an affair. I didn't want to press him on these matters, because even if he was hiding something, everything he did say was truly straight from the heart. It sounded quite reasonable. I almost began to feel sorry for him, to feel moved by him.

Suddenly he stopped, and looked at me as though waiting for my response. In all those years this was the first chance I'd had to sit with my father and talk about ourselves. I was quite upset by his excited emotional state, and wanted to say something, and I'm sure he wanted to hear what I had to say, but I couldn't say it. I knew I was letting the opportunity slip by, letting my father down, along with Mum and my sister outside. Both Dad and Mum wanted me to understand them and take their side, but I couldn't take one side. I blurted out that I loved Mum very much, and that I loved him too. It was the first time in all these years I'd let my feelings show in front of my father. Dad's face reacted in a peculiar way to these words, the way spilling hot water over ice changes its shape. It was the wrong thing to say. That evening we'd revealed our true feelings and there'd been a willingness to give and take on both sides, but neither had really been able to take anything, and that makes you feel awkward. I knew I should have pressed on in this vein, pushed him further, but I felt that he'd said what he had to say. On the other hand, I'd interrupted his flow and neither of us really knew what to do next. Having reached that height of emotion we were suddenly tied to one place, making it difficult to go forward or backward. Like two swimmers standing on the shore, both uncomfortable at seeing the other's bare flesh. But between us, the huge breaker had already receded, leaving a space just as big, but impossible to fill.

5

The next day, I didn't write anything and didn't go to meet her. I felt I was splitting away from the family, that I couldn't do anything. I spent the whole day standing by the window, making plans, thinking things over, but my eyes were fixed on the high block not far away. It had a glass exterior, like a mirror, and my girlfriend was working inside. I stared at the calm blue sky and the clouds moving slowly in the mirror, then looked up at the real sky. By the time everyone was finishing work, I couldn't stop myself phoning and, making an exception to our rule, asked her to meet me that evening.

After dinner, I rushed out before Dad and my sister. She was leaning against her bike, waiting for me at the end of the street. She asked where I wanted to go. I didn't know. So we cycled along aimlessly. I didn't say anything. At first it was still quite bright, then as the sky began to grow darker more people appeared on the streets. I wasn't paying much attention as I cycled and we kept being parted by gangs of young people in high spirits. At one intersection I braked at the red light and was overtaken from behind, by someone racing to be first in line. I realised I'd lost her. After a while, she caught up, she'd jumped off the bike and was looking for me in the dark. Was I about to leave the city, she asked. I thought about it and said maybe. Then we carried on cycling until we stopped at a bar by the side of the road.

The lights in the bar were quite low, and the noise level of the people inside was high, like the cinema just before the film starts. We sat down and I noticed how large it was, with a dance floor as well. She and I both ordered a beer and then she asked me to dance. The floor was packed, as crowded as a swimming pool in summer. People were bumping into one another, you really couldn't move. We were crowded into the middle of the dance floor where we could move even less. It was a good thing the music was slow; couples were swaying slowly with their eyes closed. I looked around and saw that most of them were quite young, though there were a few middle-aged people.

All of a sudden, I had a funny feeling, as though I was in a crowded train carriage with the lights down low, all the passengers nodding off in the sway of the train. It made me think of the trip home, and in my subconscious, I was looking for her. Then there she was in my arms, close to me, as though she was sleeping too. As the song neared its end, it was as though she could sense it, and she suddenly shook herself awake. She looked up and fleetingly kissed me.

Song after song we danced without a break. Although there was air-conditioning the atmosphere was still thick and heavy. Between each dance we'd take a gulp of beer to quench our thirst. Our faces were boiling. On the dance floor she kissed me again. I held her closer; I didn't really want to dance at all, it was as though we were going to part for ever, and I couldn't bear it. When we returned to our seats I said I could always not leave, I could stay. It didn't have to be our last meeting. There was really no need for her to be like this. She stared at me for a while, as though nothing I said had any effect. But just saying it made me feel so much better. The next song was disco music. She said she was getting tired. I looked at my watch, it had only just gone nine. It was still early, and these places usually stayed open till midnight. I went up to the dance floor, and this time it was mainly men dancing. I'd had a lot to drink, and though my head felt heavy my feet were light. I was very content. I was looking at her in the light of the mirrored globe as I danced. I may have been a little drunk and kept facing the wrong way. Then, just as I was turning round to face her, I saw my father and a woman walk in through the door.

Although the person I was looking at kept swaying from side to side, and the light was low, I could still make her out. She was in her early fifties, dressed very plainly, no different from any ordinary woman of her age you can see in the street, nothing remarkable about her at all. I'd tried to picture my father's lover more than once. I guessed she'd probably be forty or so, or maybe in her mid-thirties, and very stylish and coquettish if she was going out with my father. But what I saw now was an old woman, nothing out of the ordinary. What can I say? A woman in her thirties is still young, a woman in her forties is getting on a bit but so what, but a woman in her fifties is past it. Apart from affection perhaps, it was difficult to imagine what he saw in her. I was muddled up inside, astonished and yet disappointed. My father and the woman found a place to sit. I danced my way back to my seat and carried on watching them. They didn't dance, just stayed in their seats the whole time, and appeared to be talking in an intimate gentle way, just like a real married couple. Then, before they had stayed very long, perhaps because they weren't used to this kind of atmosphere, or perhaps because they'd only come in for a drink, they left.

She asked me what I was thinking, with my eyes gazing so far into the distance. Nothing, I said, I'd just seen my father, that's all. Really? Who had he come with? She looked up to see. I told her he'd already left. I told her the real reason why I'd come home, something I'd never spoken about before. I didn't know why I was telling her all this, she wouldn't be able to help me make any decisions, and I didn't want her to. I grumbled away like someone in pain. The truth was I had no troubles I wanted to tell her about, but I just kept on talking. I talked about my life back in the city, about my friends, how we all depended on one another and yet drove each other mad, how we'd fall out over the smallest things. I told her about my girlfriend, how she'd had an abortion because of me, yet I still wasn't always faithful to her. I even told her I wanted to be a writer, and that for a long time I'd been working hard at it, but nothing I'd written so far was particularly special, like my life really. I said a lot of things, and carried on drinking, beer after beer. In the end, I didn't know what I was talking about. I felt I was ruining my image, and also the subtle relationship that had grown between us. I felt I shouldn't be saying so many things off the top of my head, these were all very serious matters, but I thought I spoke very well anyway.

Her expression changed as she listened. Then, cautiously, she said you're drunk. I said I am, I'm drunk, but I haven't finished talking yet. She stood up and pulled me up towards the door, saying she was going to take me home. On the way I breathed as deeply as I could, to get my control back, but it was dark and I bumped into a few people. I got off my bike and apologized as politely as I could. Perhaps it was the smell of beer on my breath but no one took it any further. Soon I got fed up with myself and all these accidents, and, not being able to work out which direction I was going in, I took to cycling slowly behind her.

I followed her up to a block, that didn't look like where I lived. I asked her where we were. At her place, she said. I'd scare the hell out of my family if I went back in that state, better go upstairs first and sober up. She helped me up the stairs and into a small room, and let me sit down on the bed, then turned round and made some tea. The tea never made it past my lips; I threw up. I didn't have time to look for a bowl, and it went all over the floor, most of it hitting me first. I didn't feel awful, I told her, I was just really drunk. She made me rinse my mouth with hot tea, and cleaned the floor, then helped me out of my dirty clothes. I was only wearing a T-shirt and shorts, so without hesitation she stripped me bare, just like a nurse and a patient. Then she fetched some hot water and washed me. The touch of the towel against my flesh made my body feel so real it sobered me up considerably. My body may have been somewhat numb but my thoughts were beginning to liven up. I'd been at home so long now, yet my brain was as clear as when I'd first arrived, and I could really think about matters at home. Everything was clear now, I shouldn't lose this opportunity to think over everything on my mind. There were so many problems I had to think through. Suddenly she knelt down at the side of the bed and began to speak. She loved me, she said, even though I already had a girlfriend and she had no shortage of people interested in her, yet still she loved me so much. If I wasn't happy she'd marry me and do her best to make me happy. Her words brought along another set of questions. Was my life really so miserable? If I really did love her would I marry her? I hadn't thought about these things much before, and now here they were all at once. I had to face my family and her at the same time. I was beginning to feel that my brain wasn't big enough. My head was heavy as well and the face of my father's lover kept appearing before my eyes. She got up and turned on the stereo in the corner, filling the room with slow music. My body was floating all the more. She began to undress, and I watched her naked body, so beautiful. All of a sudden, my thoughts vanished into thin air, the problems no longer bound me, and all I could feel was absolutely perfect. So perfect that I felt so clearly that if happiness and love still existed, I knew them both. I longed for it to last, for this night to become eternity. Let the sun never rise again, let everyone sleep deeply forever, let the dust particles in the air be still, let our naked bodies stay as they are.

How I longed to express these feelings, but my head was so heavy. I looked at her and lost consciousness.

6

Afterwards I really did think about things. The next day I opened Hemingway's novel. On the title page was written: we are a lost generation. I knew those words so well. Just as I understood the background to Hemingway's generation. They had been through war, war had destroyed their ideals and their belief in beautiful things, and they did not know how to go on living. It had been a trend among us to give such a name to ourselves or the young people around us. So there was the angry generation, the lost generation. I remember a friend of mine once saying they were the embarrassed generation. He was in his thirties, one of those who'd been sent to the countryside in the Cultural Revolution, and who had been through all the political changes. It meant that they had known idealism for themselves and had known its destruction. Yet, the destruction wasn't thorough, and no small number of things still survived: they still liked to question things, and discuss a person's moral character and purity of spirit. These things contradicted their attitude to life, like standing at the river's edge, wanting to have fun in the water yet not wanting to get their clothes dirty. Sometimes they detested the world and its ways and felt none of them could join in with society; sometimes they longed to be accepted and to do something people approved of.

But, I didn't have the same troubles they had, and rarely felt lost or angry, or embarrassed in life, and had never had any shattered ideals. People like me had had a very smooth transition from studying to work. Society had never abandoned us and we'd never thought about wanting to leave it. I thought my problem was that I was too greedy; maybe we were the greedy generation. Love, friendship, money, fame, status and pleasure were the things we hoped for, the things we wanted. We wouldn't swap money for love, or abandon pleasure to chase after money; we could only forsake one love for another, looking for a new pleasure when we grow tired of this one. The significance of this is that we are more intelligent than the generation now in their thirties. When they were young they believed in themselves so much, they thought the world of themselves. Insisting this, resisting that, they had to be different from the rest. They loved going to extremes, you can see that in the works they wrote. Just dip into the books of younger writers like Zhang Chengzhi and Xu Xing. One had the main character following one river until he got to the next, looking for some unfathomable spiritual strength. The other's main character spent all day grumbling and moaning, uncomfortable with everything. Their lives were like their works, very moving, maybe very real, maybe even right, but with no meaning. And now apart from a fair number of them who did find success, most of them really aren't having an easy life. Not that they're ridden with anxiety, or that they've numbed into slow middle-age, and reverted to the typical life they once resisted. They paid too high a price for life. I don't think we could be like that. There is nothing so special in our lives worth that kind of insistence, we have so many beautiful things, why should we abandon something because we like something else? But this is exactly where the problem lies. In reality, we won't be able to have everything we want, we may even end up with nothing. Because we lack the courage of that generation.

When they were young, they did after all do some superhuman things, they dared devote themselves to something pure, and put that devotion before everything else. The most characteristic behaviour of our generation, however, is going to study overseas, or giving up an assigned job to go Shenzhen or Hainan. Neither of these requires very much courage. Our intelligence has given us cunning, and being cunning, we lack courage, and lacking courage, we wither. Because we have always belonged to society, we do our best to keep time with society. We want to go to work every day and because we want to live peacefully and enjoy life we don't think about anything, we don't argue with our leaders, we try to get on with people we don't like. We go after beautiful things, but everything is hidden, in our spare time. What's more, we get entangled in all kinds of complicated matters and all kinds of human relationships, but so often things go wrong. In reality, we are still quite powerless.

All day I was thinking about my writing, about love, about my family, endlessly negating myself, then reasserting myself, reaching a conclusion that turned everything upside down, then distancing myself from the problems. Eventually it became clear, my problem was precisely that: indecision and excessive worry. In fact, what I needed wasn't a *laissez-faire* approach to thinking, but some positive action. So I went to the station and bought a ticket back to the city.

7

I was in my room packing when Mum came in. All excited, she told me that she and Dad had had a serious talk and they were back together again. She had promised him she wouldn't make a fuss about trifles in the future, that she'd care about him more, and that things would be better. Dad also made promises. I found it a bit strange, like hearing a murderer has given himself up, but I didn't know which parent had made the first move. Had my father's true conscience been revealed? Had he been unable to confess about his lover? I would have loved to ask. But Mum was so happy, because in the end she was victorious and she was the one who had most to lose. Maybe she felt I had been on her side all along, fighting for her, and wanted me to share in her pleasure.

I didn't ask any more. I thought there were two possibilities: that Dad was cheating Mum or that they really were back together again. Whatever, I was no longer any use there. I was the only person who'd set eyes on Dad's lover, but I'd long since forgiven him in my mind. I was standing in Mum's and my sister's camp, at the same time as I was my father's accomplice. Whether my parents' making up would be long term or not didn't really matter, one thing was certain, my attempts to be a mediator were no longer of any interest.

Before I went I telephoned the girl. I told her I was leaving, and gave her a contacting address, and said if she wanted we could keep in touch. Then I said I loved her, and hung up.

I went to the station on my own. Nobody came to see me off. At the post office in the station I sent my girlfriend a telegram, so she'd meet me at the other end. This whole trip had turned out back to front. I thought how I'd already got used to living at home, and that going back now, I might not fit in. I used what money I had left to buy lots of things to eat and got on the train. This time there was an unfriendly looking middle-aged couple beside me, who never moved from their seats. The journey back was just as long as the journey out, and I filled the time by eating endlessly. The next day, the train was just about to pull into a small station, when we were delayed four or five hours. Someone said the road ahead had fallen in. The passengers all around me were losing patience, and even the couple beside me got up to go and ask the attendant. Throughout the process I was the only one who didn't say a word, keeping quiet on my seat. I opened the ring-pulls, tore the lid off the box of biscuits and peeled the fruit. Patiently I worked my way through most of them, and threw my rubbish out of the window. It was lucky I'd bought so much to eat, I thought. That's how it was, and that's how it stayed until the train began to move again.

NOTES ON AUTHORS AND TRANSLATORS

A CHENG (pen-name of Zhong Acheng, also spelt 'Ah Cheng') was born in Beijing in 1949. After returning the Yunnan countryside where he spent the late 1960s he established himself as a painter, storyteller and member of the 'Stars' group. His story *The King of Chess* caused a great stir on publication in 1984 and was later filmed by Chen Kaige. *Three Kings* was published by Harvill, London, 1990.

AI YAN (pen-name of Han Dong) was born in Nanjing in 1961 and graduated with a degree in philosophy from Shandong University. He now teaches in Nanjing, and has published two collections of poetry.

BAI Hua was born in Chongqing in 1956 and graduated in English from the Guangzhou Foreign Languages Institute in 1982. He studied Comparative Literature at Sichuan University and is currently working as a journalist in that province. He has published two collections of poetry.

Alison BAILEY teaches modern and pre-modern Chinese literature at the School of Oriental and African Studies (SOAS), University of London.

Steve BALOGH is a graduate of SOAS and a freelance translator who lives and works in Cumbria.

BEI DAO (pen-name of Zhao Zhenkai), born 1949, is one of the finest and best-known of contemporary Chinese poets. He was a founder editor, with Mang Ke, of the original *Today* magazine and was crucial to its revival in 1990, continuing to act as its chief editor. His collection of short stories, *Waves*, was published in English in 1987, and he has two selections of poetry in English translations currently available, *The August Sleepwalker* (1989) and *Old Snow* (1992). A third is shortly forthcoming. He is currently teaching at the University of Michigan.

John CAYLEY is a poet and literary translator as well as the founder editor of the Wellsweep Press. His most recent published work is *Under It All* (Many Press, London, 1993).

CHEN Maiping, born 1952, is co-editor, with Bei Dao, of *Today*. He left China to study in Oslo in 1986 and now lives and works in Stockholm.

DAXIAN (pen-name of Wang Jun), born in Beijing in 1959, is now a sports correspondent for *Beijing Youth News*. His poems were collected in *Zaidu Huihuang* (*Return to Glory*).

DAOZI (pen-name of Wang Min) was born in Qingdao in 1956. He worked as a farmer, carpenter, miner, secondary school teacher and editor of literary magazines before studying at the Northwest University, the Lu Xun Academy of Literature and Beijing Normal University, where he received his MA. He has published two books of poetry, translated Sylvia Plath and T S Eliot, and is now editing a photography magazine in Shenzhen.

DU MA (pen-name of Li Feng) was born in Guangxi Province in 1968. He was a graduate student at Nanjing University when he wrote the story included here. He now teaches at Guangxi University.

DUO DUO (pen-name of Li Shizheng), born 1951, is a prominent young poet and prose writer associated with Bei Dao and other members of the so-called 'Misty' (*menglong*) group of poets. Before leaving China he worked as a journalist. A collection of his poetry, *Looking Out From Death*, was published by Bloomsbury, London, 1989. He has also been widely published in Holland where he lived and worked for some time.

HAIZI (pen-name of Zha Haisheng) was born in Anhui province and studied Law at Beijing University where he started to write poetry. After graduation he taught philosophy at the Beijing Institute of Law and Political Science. In March 1989, he committed suicide by lying down on a railway line, stating in a letter that 'My death has nothing to do with anyone.' He has left behind an extensive body of unpublished work including poetry, drama and fiction.

Harriet EVANS lectures in modern Chinese studies at the University of Westminster, London and is currently writing a book on women and sexuality in the People's Republic of China.

Angela GEDDES is a graduate of the School of Languages, University of Westminster.

GU Cheng was born in Beijing, 1956. In 1969 he went with his family to Shandong where they raised pigs. In 1979 he started to publish poetry, taking part in the literary movement associated with *Today* magazine. One of the major figures of the 'Misty' (*menglong*) group of poets, he was highly productive and influential. In 1987 he went to New Zealand, and an English version of his *Selected Poems* was published in Hong Kong, 1991. After murdering his wife, the writer and artist Xie Ye, he committed suicide on Waheki Island in October 1993.

GU Xiaoyang was born in Beijing in 1956. After secondary school he was in military service for three years. In 1982 he graduated from the People's University, Beijing. For some years he worked as a journalist on *The Art of Film*. In 1988 he went to study in Japan, and in 1990 he travelled to the USA. He is now an editor of *Press Freedom Herald* in Los Angeles.

Duncan HEWITT has worked for the Research Centre for Translation, Chinese University of Hong Kong and the World Service of the BBC. He is currently freelancing as a journalist and continuing a degree in South-East Asian Area Studies in London.

David HINTON has produced some of the best recent literary translations of Chinese poetry into English, including his *Selected Poems of Tu Fu*. He is currently working on Bei Dao's forthcoming collection.

Brian HOLTON teaches at the University of Durham. His translation of Yang Lian's new collection, *Non-Personal*, is forthcoming from the Wellsweep Press.

HONG YING (pen-name of Chen Hongying) was born in Chongqing in 1962. She started to write poetry in 1981, and fiction in 1988. She has published four collections of poetry and one collection of short stories.

Gregory LEE teaches Chinese literature at the University of Chicago. He has published *Dai Wangshu: the Life and Poetry of a Chinese Modernist* (1990) and his translations of Duo Duo's poetry are also to be found in *Looking Out From Death* (1989).

LI Li, born 1961 in Shanghai, studied Swedish at Beijing Foreign Languages Institute. In 1989 he went to study in Stockholm, where he now lives. He has published several collections of poetry in Chinese and Swedish.

LI Tuo is a writer and critic. During the greater part of the 1980s he was deputy editor of *Beijing Literature*. He travelled to the USA in 1989 and has since been a visiting scholar at Duke, Berkeley, Chicago and other universities.

Dean LÜ (Lü De'an) was born in 1960. He has published two poetry collections and now makes a living from portraiture in New York State.

Bonnie S MCDOUGALL is professor of Chinese at the University of Edinburgh and a leading authority on modern Chinese literature. She recognized the importance of Bei Dao's work early on and was the translator (with Chen Maiping for the most recent) of the two collections of his poetry currently available in English.

Beth MCKILLOP works in the Chinese section of the British Library and is also in charge of its Korean collections.

MENG Lang (Meng Junliang), born in 1961 in Shanghai and graduated in engineering from the Shanghai College of Technology in 1982. In 1984 he co-founded the unofficial literary publications *Haishang (Seaside)* and *Dalu (Mainland)* and in 1988 co-edited the influential anthology, *Zhongguo Xiandaizhuyi Shiqun Daguan, 1986– 1988 (A Compendium of Modern Chinese Poetry)*.

Deborah MILLS recently completed a PhD thesis on the works of Lu Xun. She lives and works in Durham.

John MINFORD is one of the best-known translators from Chinese into English. He completed the fifth volume of David Hawkes monumental translation of the *Honglou Meng (The Story of the Stone)*, and is currently working on a new translation of the *Liaozhai Zhiyi* amongst other projects.

NAN FANG (pen-name of Zhang Liang) was born in Shanghai in 1962 and studied architecture at Tongji University. He went to France in 1992 and is currently studying for an architectural degree in Paris. He began writing poetry in 1981 but later turned to fiction and has since published one collection of short stories.

SONG Lin was born in 1959 in Xiamen (Amoy) but spent his childhood in the countryside. He was a graduate of Shanghai Normal University where he stayed on to teach Chinese Literature for eight years. He has published both poetry and prose. He was imprisoned for nine months in 1989 and left China for France in 1991. He now lives in Paris.

Jonathan D SPENCE is George Burton Adams Professor of History at Yale University and one of the foremost historians of China. His two most recent books are *The Search for Modern China* and a collection of essays, *Chinese Roundabout*.

Janet TAN (pen-name of Tan Jiadong) writes and publishes fiction, essays and poetry in both Chinese and English. She has studied at St John's University in New York and recently received her MFA from Brown University's Creative Writing Program.

Helen WANG is a graduate of SOAS and currently works in the British Museum.

Anne WEDELL-WEDELLSBORG teaches at the University of Aarhus, Copenhagen.

Frances WOOD is the head of the Chinese Section of the British Library and a well-known translator and writer about China. She recently completed the *Blue Guide* to China.

XU Bing was born in Chongqing in 1955 and is a graduate of the Central Academy of Fine Arts, where he went on to teach. In 1990 he was made an Honorary Fellow of the University of Wisconsin-Madison, Department of Art. Recognized initially as a talented printmaker working a great deal in woodcuts, he went on to produce more radical and challenging work. His 'Book from the Sky' (Tian Shu) caused a sensation when it was first exhibited in 1989. Since then his work has featured in a number of exhibitions world-wide.

YAN Li, poet and writer, was born in Beijing in 1954. In 1985 he left to study in the USA, and in May 1987 founded *Yihang* (One Line), a journal of poetry, in New York. He has published collections in both English and Chinese.

YANG Lian is another prominent name associated with the 'Misty' (*menglong*) group of poets. He has been widely published and translated and two collections of his work have appeared in Australia, *The Dead in Exile* (1990) and *Masks and Crocodile* (1989). A new collection, *Non-Personal*, is forthcoming from the Wellsweep Press.

YOU YI (pen-name of Meng Yue) studied Chinese Literature at Beijing University, went on to work as a researcher for the Chinese Academy of Social Sciences and published several books in her field. In 1991 she went to the USA and is currently studying at the University of California, Los Angeles, for her PhD.

Jane Ying ZHA (Zha Jianying) was born in 1959 and educated in China and the United States. She currently lives in Chicago and works as a project director at the Center for Psychosocial Studies. Her publications include *Chinese Whispers*, New York, 1994.

ZHANG Zao was born in 1962 in Changsha. He studied English at the Hunan Normal University and the Sichuan Foreign Languages Institute. In 1986 he went to (what was then) West Germany to study for a PhD in literature at the University of Trier. He started writing poetry in 1977, and has published two collections.

ZHANG Langlang was born in Yan'an, 1943. He studied French at the Beijing Foreign Languages Institute and went on to study the history and theory of art at the Central Academy of Fine Art. In June 1968 he was detained by the Public Security Bureau and was sentenced in 1974 to 15 years imprisonment. He was released in 1977. He contributed to, and worked on, various journals. He left Beijing in late May, 1989 and went to the USA. Since 1990 he has been a visiting scholar at Princeton University.

ZHANG Zhen was born in Shanghai in 1962 and studied Journalism at Fudan University. She went on to study in Sweden, Japan and the USA. She is currently a doctoral candidate at the University of Chicago.

Henry Y H ZHAO (Zhao Yiheng) is a critic, writer and poet. He studied for his MA at the Chinese Academy of Social Sciences and completed a PhD at the University of California at Berkeley. He is currently teaching at the School of Oriental and African Studies, University of London. He is the editor of *The Lost Boat: Avant-garde Fiction from China* (Wellsweep Press, 1993) and his *The Uneasy*

Narrator: Chinese Fiction from Traditional to Modern will be published in 1994.

ZHONG Ming was born in Chengdu, 1953 and graduated from the South-Western Normal College in 1982. After teaching for two years he began to work as a journalist. While at university he co-founded South China's first unofficial poetry magazine, *Ci Senlin*. He has published several collections of poetry in Chinese.

ZI AN (pen-name of Wang Jiaxin) was born in Hubei Province in 1957. In 1982 he graduated from Wuhan University. From 1985–90 he was an editor for the magazine *Poetry (Skikan)*. He has published a collection of poetry and a book of criticism. He studied in England from 1991–93. A selection of his work, *Stairway*, in English translation, is available as an electronic book from the Wellsweep Press.

Wellsweep

THE LOST BOAT
Avant-garde Fiction from China
edited by Henry Y H Zhao
Forget everything you know about contemporary Chinese fiction. These stories will shock and compel. You will learn something new about about life and literature, not just 'life and literature in China'.
£7.95 pbk, **£14.95** hbk.
256 pp, 198 x 130 mm. ISBNs 0 948454 13 X pbk, 0 948454 83 0 hbk.

AFTER *THE EVENT*
Human Rights and their Future in China
edited by Susan Whitfield
'... an important collection of essays on human rights in China.'
— John Gittings, *The Guardian*, London
£7.95 pbk. 128 pp, 198 x 130 mm, tables, ISBN 0 948454 18 0.

RUAN JI'S ISLAND & (TU FU) IN THE CITIES
by Graham Hartill
The fine poetic sequences in this book are based on the author's reading of two Chinese masters, the third century Ruan Ji and China's most famous poet, Du Fu.
£4.95 pbk. 64 pp, 210 x 130 mm, approx. 10 ill. ISBN 0 948454 14 8.

RITUAL & DIPLOMACY
The Macartney Mission to China (1792–1794)
Edited by Robert A Bickers
A collection of essays presented at the 1992 conference of the British Association of Chinese Studies marking the Bicentenary of the Macartney Embassy.
£7.95 pbk. 96 pp. 198 x 130 mm. Frontispiece. ISBN 0 948454 19 9.

wellsweep
The Wellsweep Press, 1 Grove End House, 150 Highgate Road, London NW5 1PD, UK
Tel / Fax: (071) 267 3525.

All titles available from good bookshop, or direct from us.

PLEASE, when ordering direct, add 10% for postage.